IN
PURSUIT
OF
SPENSER

"A close and revealing examination of Robert B. Parker—the author, the man, and the husband— brought to life by the observations and insights of fellow authors who knew him and his work. Extraordinary!"

—JOAN PARKER

IN
PURSUIT
OF
SPENSER

MYSTERY WRITERS ON
ROBERT B. PARKER
AND THE CREATION of an AMERICAN HERO

EDITED BY OTTO PENZLER

SMART
POP

An Imprint of BenBella Books, Inc. | Dallas, Texas

BenBella Books, Inc.
10300 N. Central Expressway, Suite 400
Dallas, TX 75231
www.benbellabooks.com
Send feedback to feedback@benbellabooks.com

Printed in the United States of America
10 9 8 7 6 5 4 3 2 1

Library of Congress Cataloging-in-Publication Data is available for this title.

978-1-935618-57-7

Copyediting by Erica Lovett
Proofreading by Cape Cod Compositors, Inc.
Cover design by Michael Fusco
Text design and composition by Neuwirth & Associates, Inc.
Printed by Berryville Graphics

Distributed by Perseus Distribution
(www.perseusdistribution.com)
To place orders through Perseus Distribution:
Tel: 800-343-4499
Fax: 800-351-5073
E-mail: orderentry@perseusbooks.com

Significant discounts for bulk sales are available. Please contact Glenn Yeffeth at glenn@benbellabooks.com or (214) 750-3628.

For Joan Parker and,

in affectionate memory,

Bob

CONTENTS

June 1, 1923, issue of *Black Mask*. When he wrote a second Race Williams story, "Three Thousand to the Good," for the July 15, 1923, issue, he had created the first series character in the history of the hardboiled dick. Just as there subsequently have been better airplanes than their Kitty Hawk contraption, it is Wilbur and Orville Wright who will always be remembered for getting there first, and this is Daly's place—though he is less remembered today than either the Wright brothers or the infinitely superior tough-guy writer who immediately followed him, Dashiell Hammett.

While Daly was little more than a creative hack writer, Hammett elevated the private eye story to the status of serious literature. Arguments persist about whether Hammett influenced Ernest Hemingway's work or the other way around, but publishing chronology cannot be debated, much to the disgust of those academics and critics who refuse to concede the irrefutable point that the best mystery fiction can, and should, be accepted for its significant literary contributions.

Hammett's first story about the Continental Op, the nameless detective, or operative, who worked for the Continental Detective Agency, appeared in *Black Mask* on October 1, 1923. The outstanding character appeared in many further stories, as well as in Hammett's first two novels, *Red Harvest* (1927) and *The Dain Curse* (1928). Hemingway's first book, *In Our Time*, was published in Paris in a limited edition in 1924 and in the United States in 1925 with a tiny print run of 1,335 copies, by which time Hammett was already a well-established and highly popular regular contributor to the most important pulp magazine of its era (or any era, for that matter). It is possible, of course, that two profoundly brilliant writers separately turned away from the prevalent style of the time, the orotund prose of Henry James and his Victorian predecessors, to the lean, swift, straightforward dialogue and exposition that raced a narrative to its conclusion. However, just in case someone wants to open the conversation, one need only compare the dates of first publications to reach the only possible conclusion: Hammett deserves to be in the literary pantheon with the greatest of the greats.

Possibly the greatest stylist in the history of detective fiction is Raymond Chandler, whose first novel, *The Big Sleep* (1939), was published five years after Hammett's fifth and final novel, *The Thin Man* (1934). Plot was not first among Chandler's priorities. That first novel, marking the debut of Chandler's PI, Philip Marlowe, has a plot so convoluted that a rather large hole went undetected by its editor and eventually confused the people making the motion picture version. Humphrey Bogart, who played Marlowe in the 1946 Warner Brothers film, asked director Howard Hawks who killed the chauffeur. Baffled, Hawks turned to the screenwriter who had written that sequence, William Faulkner, who acknowledged that he had no idea. Hawks wired the question to Chandler, who immediately wired back, "The butler did it." There is, of course, no butler in the book or film.

It is the unmatched use of metaphor and simile in his prose, plus the nobility of his Everyman protagonist, Marlowe, that elevates Chandler's works. An intellectual who came late to the writing life, Chandler was the first to define his detective as a savior of humanity in its battles with the forces of evil, likening him to the knights of history and legend. In his landmark essay "The Simple Art of Murder," he described the role of the private detective:

> Down these mean streets a man must go who is not himself mean, who is neither tarnished nor afraid. The detective in this kind of story must be such a man. He is the hero, he is everything. He must be a complete man and a common

man, and yet an unusual man. He must be, to use a rather tarnished phrase, a man of honor . . .

Hammett would not have defined any of his private detectives in such romantic terms, but his protagonists operate on a similar principle, which is a code of honor. It would be difficult to think of his detectives as heroes because of their many flaws, whereas Parker unabashedly regards Spenser as nothing less than heroic.

Parker analyzed the private eyes of Hammett and Chandler in his doctoral thesis, defining them as the purest form of archetypical American heroes, who have three options open to them. The hero, he wrote, "may adjust his moral vision to the practices of his society. He may make a separate peace and withdraw to a place where his moral vision may be enacted. He may actively oppose those things in his society which he finds corrupt." Parker avers that, in most American literature, the evolution of the protagonist is from the first option to the second, but that the hardboiled private eye already possesses knowledge of evil and, sometime during the course of his life, has made the decision not to accept it, but to fight it. To do less would be an act of dishonor; he would be complicit.

It is from this position, from this perspective, that Spenser was born. One of the most popular literary heroes of our time, Spenser is the love-child of his creator. Although Parker never used the words himself, he might well have paraphrased Ross Macdonald (another of Parker's literary heroes), who said of his own creation, "I'm not (Lew) Archer, exactly, but Archer is me." This is, of course, an acceptance of the reality that the detective is an idealized version of his creator, the man he would choose to be if he were a man of action rather than a solitary figure in the solitary profession of fantasizing.

For all his brilliance, both as an academic and as a creator of fiction that will endure as long as the world retains an appreciation of, and affection for, the written word, Parker was a simple man. He knew what he wanted to do with his life, which was to write detective stories. To earn a living, he taught at Northeastern University. He sought his Ph. D. and delighted in earning it because it gave him tenure and reduced his teaching load, enabling him to spend more time writing what he wanted to write.

Timeline: Doctorate, 1971. First Spenser novel, *The Godwulf Manuscript*, 1974. Full-time professor, 1976. Good-bye to academia and hello to full-time writing, 1979. Simple.

This clarity of thought extended to his love life. It has been written about often, but a rollicking dinner I had with the principals filled in extra details about the early meeting of Parker and Joan Hall. They were very young—generally stated as three years old, but a little leeway is called for as they were not exactly the same age—when they were at a birthday party. Joan threw her ice cream cone at Bob, who burst into tears. The sweet little girl's response was to shout, "Crybaby!"

They lived in the same neighborhood as children and met again in college. Joan actively disliked the man who set out to win her heart, which he eventually succeeded in doing. They were married in 1956 but later separated because of fundamental differences about how they wanted to live. His desire was mainly to be left alone to write, while she was outgoing, gregarious, and social, happy to go to dinners and parties. Of their brief estrangement, Bob said, "I learned that I could live without Joan, but I didn't want to." They soon remarried but chose an unusual living arrangement in which she lived on one floor of the house and he on another. Totally devoted to each other (Parker dedicated virtually every one of his books to Joan), their happy marriage lasted until his death on January 18, 2010. He found the woman of his dreams and devoted the rest of his life to her. Simple.

Parker's approach to writing was little different from his approach to the other aspects of his life. Once he was established as successful writer, he went to work most days and wrote. He got his style and rhythm down cold and remained consistent, with few books soaring above the others and few failing to match his usual level of excellence. Because Parker was occasionally criticized for producing slim plots, his publisher pressed him to write a bigger book, a longer one, as a way of getting him onto the bestseller list. He wrote *A Catskill Eagle*, which had many more pages and a lot more dead bodies, but seldom appears on lists of readers' favorite Spenser novels. He never did it again. "This is what I write," he said. "If you like it, you like it; if you don't, you don't. This is all I know how to do." Simple.

Okay, maybe not exactly. While he enjoyed writing his books about Spenser, the Boston private detective on which Parker's reputation will endure, he also tried several other types of books. First there was a straight adventure novel, *Wilderness* (1979), then a pure romance, *Love and Glory* (1983), his completion of a Philip Marlowe novel left uncompleted at the time of Chandler's death, *Poodle Springs* (1989), followed by another Marlowe novel, *Perchance to Dream* (1991), and a sprawling, multi-generational novel about Boston cops, *All Our Yesterdays* (1994), which was his own favorite novel, an opinion shared by few. In 1997, with *Night Passage*, he created his second series character, Jesse Stone, a former member of the Los Angeles Police Department with a rocky past who moves east to become the police chief of a small New England town. It was not exactly a breathtaking surprise to find that Stone's voice had the ring of familiarity, that his short, straightforward dialogue bore a strong resemblance to Spenser's.

And Stone is not the only one of Parker's characters who sounds like Spenser. Even Sunny Randall does, which is no bad thing. Her integrity and sense of honor are chiseled from the same block of marble as Spenser's, so it is unreasonable to think that her responses to situations and people would be markedly different, and those responses are framed in language that evokes those sensibilities. Unlike Spenser, Sunny can't cook, but that is not the point.

After she won an Oscar for *As Good As It Gets*, the actress Helen Hunt requested Parker to create a protagonist that she could play and, as soon as he learned that she wanted a novel, not a screenplay, he agreed, producing *Family Honor* for her in 1999. Sony immediately bought the rights for Hunt, who loved the book and the character. Sunny Randall had been planned as a series, because Hunt had hoped to play a single character over many years as both she and the heroine matured, but eventually the deal fell apart. Too bad, as Hunt, an actress much admired by Parker, would have had the role of a lifetime: a Boston private eye who likes to paint (as Hunt does), has a difficult relationship with a former husband with whom she is still in love, and is described by her sidekick Spike, a gay waiter and karate expert, as a "shooter, shrink, painter, and sex symbol." Even though the motion picture never came to pass, both readers and Parker's publisher liked the character so much that he continued the series anyway, producing an additional five novels.

Dickens had pretty much the same voice, whether writing about David Copperfield or Oliver Twist, and there was little to differentiate the dialogue of Athos, Porthos, Aramis, and D'Artagnan. Hammett's Sam Spade and the Continental Op could have switched roles with little discernable difference. Chandler's short stories and novellas featured a variety of private eyes, all of whom morphed into Marlowe when the short works were cannibalized for use in his novels without the need to alter their language.

Parker's voice, too, remains recognizable and consistent, whether in the Spenser opera, cases involving an official officer of the law, tales about a female private eye, or the adventures of characters in the West from a different era (Virgil Cole and Everett Hitch, introduced in *Appaloosa* in 2005). It is the sound of Parker's heroes that make them endure, but it is who they are that made them so loved in the first place. They can be counted on. When John Wayne rode into town, things were going to be fine. Superman wasn't ambivalent about what to do with violent criminals. The Lone Ranger didn't warn bandits that anything they said would be used against them in a court of law.

Spenser understands that justice doesn't always coincide with the law. The world truly *is*, in fact, black and white; if you study a situation carefully enough you will find the line of demarcation and know what is right and what is wrong. For Spenser, that line is a chasm, and he chooses, from the beginning, to be on the right side. God help you if you choose the wrong side.

That is what a moral divide is about.

That is what a hero values.

That is why Spenser is one of the great heroes of our time.

• •

This *festschrift* assembles essays by many of today's foremost authors of mystery fiction, mainly writers of private eye stories. It is a tribute to Robert B. Parker that so many have been influenced by his work and have no difficulty in acknowledging their debt to him. Each writes here of a specific element of the Parker world: the books themselves, his personal life, and the philosophical principles that guided both.

Chosen to continue the Spenser series, Ace Atkins provides a thoughtful essay about how Parker and, inevitably, Spenser, helped form his notion of what it is to be a man, especially the right kind of man.

Bestselling mystery writer Dennis Lehane shares a Boston background with Parker, even if they weren't raised in the same neighborhood, and tells of how they came to know each other, and how they both knew that the other was someone with whom they'd like to share a beer.

Mystery writers don't often rate other writers on their plotting skills. It's the style, or the voice, that matters, and Grand Master Lawrence Block makes it clear that Parker had a really good voice.

Much has been written about Spenser's code of honor, which is explored here by mystery writer Parnell Hall, who also points out that it is impossible to think about Parker's dialogue without commenting on the humor inherent to it, and that humor is examined as well.

Loren D. Estleman, whose career straddles both the mystery and Western genres (with numerous awards in each), draws parallels between Spenser and the individualism of so many men of America's old West.

A sense of place is a major element in Parker's Spenser series, and Jeremiah Healy, whose Patrick Cuddy private eye series is also set in Boston, walks those same mean streets and reminisces about his relationship with his old friend.

How a man as macho as Spenser can still be an overt and outspoken feminist is discussed by award-winning author Brendan DuBois, focusing mainly on the titular character of *Looking for Rachel Wallace*.

While several characters in the history of detective fiction have been noted for their culinary talents, including Rex Stout's Nero Wolfe and Georges Simenon's Jules Maigret, mystery novelist Lyndsay Faye maintains that Spenser was the best at building a great sandwich *and* cooking a meal as an expression of love.

Perhaps the second-most beloved character in the Spenser series is the borderline psychopath, Hawk, whose literary antecedents are examined by Los Angeles crime writer Gary Phillips.

Of all the characters about whom Parker wrote, there appears to be the greatest divergence of opinion about Susan Silverman, Spenser's faithful and independent lover, and Edgar-winner S.J. Rozan illustrates both points of view.

Spenser is simply too good a character not to have made it to the screen, and mystery writer Max Allan Collins, with his frequent collaborator Matthew Clemens, provide an overview of the *Spenser: For Hire* television series and the popular TV movies.

While Spenser quickly became an iconic figure in detective fiction, Parker also created the memorable small-town peace officer, Jesse Stone, and the cult-favorite mystery writer Reed Farrel Coleman explores the similarities, and significant differences, between those protagonists.

The American private eye is a direct literary descendant of the West's lone gunslinger, so it is no surprise that Parker had great affection for Westerns and began to write them late in his career. Ed Gorman, the author of numerous Westerns and mystery novels, offers a paean to those novels.

Literary critics, both professional and amateur, have devoted thousands of pages to examinations and analyses of Spenser, but no one could do that as well as the creator himself, so Parker's profile of the greatest detective character of his era concludes this collection. It is told in first person of course, as all the novels were.

Naturally, and inevitably, Spenser has the last word.

SONGS SPENSER TAUGHT ME

| ACE ATKINS |

MY INTRODUCTION TO Robert B. Parker came in the form of an aged paperback of *The Godwulf Manuscript*, its cover featuring a .45 automatic, a yellow rose, and bullet holes. "What a Find!" declared the *L.A. Times*. The name— as big as the title—read SPENSER. I got it for ninety-nine cents at a second-hand bookshop a few weeks after the unexpected death of my father. I was a sophomore at Auburn University, where I played football on scholarship, and I was, at the time, absolutely lost on all fronts.

Even before my dad had died, I wasn't particularly having the time of my life in college. I had coaches who'd changed their mind about my talents and quickly used my father's death to try to push me from the program and free up my scholarship. I spent a lot of time running laps and doing meaningless and demeaning drills. I was caught in that time between teenager and man and was still in need of a mentor to help me find my way out. Coaches were useless. My father was gone.

Spenser appeared in typical Spenser fashion: right when you need him most.

When someone asks me what made Spenser the character matter to me, the answer is pretty complicated. As a writer, I learned everything about hero-driven detective fiction—and just fiction in general—from Spenser and Robert B. Parker. Through Parker, I was introduced to the Big Three—Hammett, Chandler, and Macdonald, an exclusive group he's now joined. Spenser would lead me to a career as a crime reporter in Florida, where I often used what Spenser taught me to get people to open up or to dig into internal affairs investigations, con men scams, or cold case murders.

I think about Spenser every time I need motivation to go for a jog or lift weights. I think about Spenser when I travel, pick up a menu, or decide on a restaurant. Or if I'm asked if I would like another drink. *The answer is always yes.*

But as a young man just discovering Robert B. Parker, Spenser first gave me the tools to be the sort of adult I wanted to be. Through Spenser's smart-assed individualism, Parker let me know that all of those little things that made me different from my teammates and annoyed my coaches were actually okay. He taught me a great deal about tolerance and what was really good about life and how to live it well. He brought me to classic jazz and standards, taught me how to properly dress a salad and core an apple, and instructed me on what kind of beer one should order. You can stumble through life drinking Miller Lite, or you can reach for the Sam Adams Winter Lager. It's up to you.

DO WHAT YOU LIKE

Spenser has mentored plenty of lost souls on the page, most notably Paul Giacomin, who's introduced in *Early Autumn*. The novel is written much more in the style of Hemingway than Hammett and the other Spenser books, a coming-of-age story about a fifteen-year-old caught between warring parents, neither of whom could care less about him. After spending weeks protecting Paul and his mother, Spenser works out an agreement to take the boy and finish the job of raising him. He helps Paul become completely autonomous, not needing approval or direction. Spenser teaches him how to box, how to cook, and how to dress properly.

I was never as lost as Paul, a kid who couldn't button his coat and was self-medicated on soap operas and sitcoms, completely uninvolved in life. My parents were loving, capable, and had done a fine job. I knew how to dress. I knew how to fight.

But after the early death of my father, I was left with a lot of questions about being a man.

In *Early Autumn*, Spenser provided me with one of those answers when he tells Paul: "The point is not to get hung up on being what you're supposed to be. If you can, it's good to do what pleases you."

That may sound basic, but it was an absolute revelation for me, a young man who, up till that point, was always supposed to be something that other people said was important. I was not so sure. I felt some kinship with Paul, who admits halfway through the novel that he actually wanted to be a dancer. He tells Spenser this in almost embarrassment. For me, talking about wanting to be a writer was almost as tough.

Those of you who aren't from the South may have a difficult time fully understanding the importance of football there, especially in my native Alabama. Everyone—no, *everyone*—identifies themselves through their allegiance to either Auburn or the University of Alabama. Children don't get much of a say in the matter, as they are born into Auburn or Alabama families, much in the same way someone is born Jewish or Catholic. As the son of Auburn's 1957 national championship team's MVP, I was expected to bleed orange and blue. Except that I didn't.

I was expected to believe that playing Auburn football was the apex of my existence, the single greatest thing I would ever do, something I would look back on with misty tears one day while greeting friends with a heartfelt "War Eagle!" Notably, my father, although he worked for the NFL for thirty years, never got sentimental about football. But he did care about it deeply, enough to make it his life's work, and enough that one of his biggest insults for someone he didn't like was that they were a "non-athlete."

Instead, I found I just didn't care all that much. I liked challenging my body physically and working hard. I liked sacking a quarterback about as much as I loved talking about books, music, and classic movies. But all the pomp and circumstance, the team chants and cheerleading, felt stupid to me. I did not cry after a loss; I only thought of what could be fixed or done better.

You have to understand that my lack of enthusiasm for the football culture would be like an Orthodox Jew not caring about being kosher. It was heresy to some. Spenser let me know that not being a joiner or cheering on the team was more than fine. You could actually read books and enjoy them and still be a tough guy and a good athlete.

I had coaches who thought I wasn't serious enough about football because I read novels while getting my ankle taped for practice. They'd scoff at me for carrying around a paperback, as if reading for pleasure was some kind of novelty. Often, that paperback was Parker's, or Hemingway's, or Elmore Leonard's. I learned through Spenser that a man could equally enjoy plays and film and good jazz and kicking someone's ass now and then. A man was not just one thing. A man could take pleasures in all things, athletic and cultural.

IT'S GOOD TO KNOW STUFF

As a teenager, I already had a love of classic film, most notably *noirs* and Westerns. After discovering Parker, I decided to take classes at Auburn on film and screenplay writing. I learned even more about the structure and technique of writing from a professor who I'd later find out had been a star football player at the University of Mississippi.

I began to do more than just watch movies and read books, I dissected them and learned from the masters: Alfred Hitchcock, Sam Peckinpah, Billy Wilder, Howard Hawks, Fritz Lang, and John Ford. (Someday, I'd correspond with Bob Parker about our shared obsession with *Shane* and *The Magnificent Seven*.)

I did the same with music, often digging through the CD bins for music that Spenser liked: Monk and Coltrane, Miles Davis and Chet Baker. Most college students I knew were into disposable Top 40 or those too-earnest college bands. Through Spenser, I found myself drawn to all things good and classic. Spenser tells us that the quality of everyday things makes life worth living. You should also shine your dress shoes, shave carefully, and handle your liquor.

About a year into meeting Spenser, my mom stood in line for more than an hour at a bookstore in Atlanta to get me a signed copy of *Double Deuce*. Through that meeting, I found out that Bob Parker's nickname was also Ace, after a Hall of Fame football player who'd been a friend of my dad's. I could not have been more proud. The first edition Bob signed is one of my prized possessions to this day.

Yeah, I collected rare books, too.

I recently had a discussion about being an athlete who wanted to be more with a friend who'd had a similar situation. We talked about being stranded between two worlds that each wanted us to be one thing. We'd both had professors who were just as bigoted as my coaches, believing the dumb jock stereotypes. They'd either grade me harder or discount me entirely because I was a football player. They could not imagine that a guy who could bench press more than four hundred pounds might actually really dig William Faulkner and Flannery O'Connor.

It kind of upsets the rules.

Or, as Spenser says in *Early Autumn*: "Because they don't know any better. . . . Because they don't know what they are, or how to find out, or what a good person is, or how to find out. So they rely on categories."

About this same time, I'd tried to gain admittance into an undergraduate creative writing program only to be told the class was too full. I still feel—although I may be wrong—that it had something to do with me being a football player. I was pretty much ostracized on both fronts. Damned if you do . . .

Thank God for Spenser. He basically told me, "Who gives a shit." And as far as respecting authority, he taught me that you're a fool if you don't question it at every turn.

Spenser tells Paul why his father can't contemplate a more truthful way of defining oneself in *Early Autumn*:

"But he doesn't really know how to be a good man, so he goes for the simple rules that someone else told him. It's easier than thinking, and safe. The other way you have to decide for yourself. You have to come to some conclusions about your own behavior and then you might find that you couldn't live up to it."

YOUR INNER SMART ASS

As Parker tells us, Spenser had played football on scholarship at Holy Cross but wasn't much on being told what to do or much of a "rah-rah" kind of guy. He left early to join the Army and later work for the Middlesex DA's Office, or as Bob later put it, "be a cop." Spenser didn't last long working in a hierarchy and reporting to others. He wanted to handle situations himself. He liked being his own person—he thrived on it. I understood.

Being a novelist is a lot like being a private investigator. You spend a lot of time studying others. You always keep a bottle in your desk drawer. I don't think I could do anything else to make a living. Operating under someone else's rule system never appealed to me.

At Auburn, I was surrounded by a lot of zealous self-proclaimed Christian coaches. Several of them were hypocrites, unrepentant adulterers and alcoholics every day but Sunday. In situations that should have bred contempt and disenchantment, Spenser taught me to only expect more of the same and rise above it. Just because they were adults doesn't mean they were to be respected and followed blindly.

It's better to just recognize who you are dealing with and act accordingly. Spenser can share space with a vicious thug or a pompous professor without it changing him. He even finds some enjoyment in watching them work.

I had always had a distrust of authority, but Spenser really taught me how to laugh at those who try to control others, those who try to rattle and upset whomever they challenge. Nothing pisses off controlling personalities more than laughing at them.

Sometimes this would get me into trouble. Burning through all the existing Spenser books—at the time from *Godwulf* to *Paper Doll*—finely honed my natural smartass talents and increased my confidence to use them in interactions with coaches. These were grown men telling kids they'd never amount to anything and had better just quit now. They wanted to run you down as far as you could go to show who was in control. By using humor (with new confidence, thanks to Spenser), I was able to battle back and gain admiration from my teammates.

My junior year I had a run-in with my strength and conditioning coach, a portly guy who barely stood above five feet and was known for his always-present tobacco spit cup and his sanctimonious prayer meetings before weights. One day, I caught him in a long repose on a bench press, holding his head up with the flat of his hand, inadvertently posing like a centerfold model. Before I thought about it, I said, "Looking sexy today, coach."

He got off the weight bench and started to admonish me for acting like "a damn homosexual."

I assured him that if I were a homosexual, he definitely was too short and fat for my taste.

A lot of stadium stairs were run that day.

I also learned it wasn't a good idea to correct my position coach's grammar. He said the only books worth reading were either the Bible or were written by televangelist Pat Robertson and believed the past tense of the word squeeze was "squez." After the hundredth time hearing this, I raised my hand, telling him the truth.

More stadium steps were run.

The laughter from my teammates was worth every step. And the confidence I gained from making light of the men trying to run me from the program allowed me to finish what I started. I made it through my senior year, a season where a new coach led us to an undefeated year and I was fortunate enough to be featured on the cover of *Sports Illustrated*.

I think Spenser would have liked how it all turned out.

TOLERANCE

I don't think I ever considered how a man wouldn't go for a hot Jewish woman like Susan Silverman or trust his life with a tough black guy like Hawk. After all, I'd grown up with a father working in the NFL, and some of the coolest, most bad-ass dudes I met in my youth were black, as were my present teammates and buddies. But as a teenager, the idea of being around someone gay was fraught with a lot of questions, hesitations, and jokes. This was something I'd never really considered at a young age. Most men who played football or sports would use offensive gay slurs for men who didn't. There was a lot of locker room humor and dummies like that weight coach who looked at homosexuals as people afflicted by a disease—as if you could catch it.

In college, Spenser absolutely molded my views on sexual orientation. Why should a man fear or look down on a man or woman who's gay? This has been a topic of conversation for Spenser since *Looking for Rachel Wallace*, when Spenser is hired to guard an outspoken lesbian writer. Hate mongers and bigots have threatened to kill Rachel Wallace if she publishes a book on oppression. Spenser muses over why he should pass judgment on someone's sexual orientation; after all, he's sure that he and Susan "weren't all that slick in the actual doing ourselves. When you thought about it, maybe none of us were doing Swan Lake."

In *Paper Doll* we first meet Detective Lee Farrell, a hard Boston cop whose partner is dying of AIDS. The relationship between Spenser and Farrell is of two men who live by the same code of honor and believe in the same thing. Who they take to bed is completely irrelevant.

The meeting of the two starts off in rocky fashion, with Spenser telling Farrell to let go of the chip on his shoulder:

> "I don't care if you are as good as I am or not. I don't care if you're tough or not, or smart or not. I don't care if you are gay or straight or both or neither. I care about finding out who killed that broad with a framing hammer, and so far you're not helping me worth shit."

But the conversation is between two men who set out to do a job, all prejudices aside.

Later in the series, we meet Teddy Sapp, an exceptionally bad-ass Georgia bouncer who just happens to be gay. Spenser judges Sapp on his ability as a tough and someone to count on. Again, not exactly ideas I'd considered as a teenager. But if Spenser could respect a gay man for his professionalism and personal code, then I figured I would, too.

In the world of tough crime fiction, Spenser's acceptance and appreciation of the gay community was light years ahead when *Paper Doll* was published twenty years ago or when *Rachel Wallace* hit stores more than thirty years ago. Spenser talked about discrimination in the work place, the AIDS epidemic, and committed gay relationships long before these were mainstream conversations. If Spenser can influence a young man raised in a traditional home and living in a very macho-driven world to change his thinking, imagine what Spenser has done for millions of other readers.

LIVING WELL

When we think of Spenser, we all think of good food and drink. It's as much a part of his character as his love of baseball or the .357 he keeps in his right-hand desk drawer. No one is better at throwing a meal together from assorted items found in the refrigerator or pantry. Although he enjoys a steak at Grill 23 or a lobster sandwich at Locke-Ober, he also has a deep appreciation of an assorted dozen from Dunkin' Donuts. Spenser is never snobbish, but self-assured on what he likes to eat and what he likes to cook.

I know Spenser definitely led me to cooking. As a teenage boy, I had no interest in making apple fritters or baking corn muffins. But a few books into the series, I realized how much fun and how relaxing cooking can be. I started to experiment with ingredients, diving more into Creole and Cajun cooking, looking for places to find really good andouille or redfish. I have hand picked apples to be cored, dipped in a simple batter and fried in rings for fritters. Grocery shopping isn't just monotony with Spenser; it's full of possibilities and excitement.

As Spenser noted in *Pastime*,

"I've spent a lot of my time alone, and I have learned to treat myself as if I were a family. I give myself dinner at night. I give myself breakfast in the morning. I like the process of deciding what to eat and putting it together and seeing how it works, and I like to experiment, and I like to eat. There is nothing lonelier than some guy alone in the kitchen eating Chinese food out of the carton."

As a young newspaper reporter in Tampa, I lived in a small studio in a brick apartment building built in the '20s. I didn't have a lot of money, but I always stocked Sam Adams, good whiskey, and basic items that could create a quick and delicious meal. I was often on my own, even on the weekends, and I'd pour myself a cocktail, turn on some Coltrane, and have a terrific evening. Being alone and being content was a fine place to be. Self-sufficiency is being content with yourself.

HARD WORK AND SWEAT

"What you're good at is less important than being good at something. You got nothing. You care about nothing. So I'm going to have you be strong, be in shape, be able to run ten miles, and be able to lift more than you weigh and be able to box. I'm going to have you know how to build and cook and to work hard and to push yourself and control yourself. Maybe we can get to reading and looking at art and listening to something beside situation comedies later on. But right now I'm working your body because it's easier to start there."

—*Early Autumn*

Early on, I didn't really need Spenser to tell me to keep in shape. I had to keep in shape, or I could be hurt pretty badly or lose my scholarship. Training was an everyday thing. I checked into the weight room daily, ran sprints and distance. It was one part of the college athlete experience that I actually enjoyed.

But after college, I really had to find drive and motivation to keep making time for this. I was working a pretty competitive beat at the newspaper, and a few hours in the gym or jogging wasn't easily found. But as Spenser tells us, the purpose of a training regimen is developing discipline, not necessarily to lift the most weight or be the fastest. Keeping in check with your body and pushing yourself will manifest itself in other positive ways.

As a young reporter, I ended up joining a gym that stepped right out of a Parker novel. It was run by a tough, short, ex–pro wrestler named Harry Smith, who was every bit as tough and salty as Henry Cimoli. Harry is the kind of guy who gave every ethnicity grief for their known stereotypes while proudly flying all the flags of his member's ethnicities on the gym roof. The gym became like my second home when I lived in Tampa, and it was a hell of a good place to learn some one-liners.

I've just hit my forties, about the same age as Spenser when we met him in *The Godwulf Manuscript*, and the training gets harder every year. But it's become a core part of my writing routine, especially now that I'm writing two physical heroes. I work out storyline ideas as I run or battle some tough rednecks or Southie thugs as I hit the heavy bag. Spenser taught me that sometimes the toughest answers are found while you sweat.

WHEREVER YOU GO

I'd spent most of my life looking around in dark places that were often appalling. But oddly, I was never really appalled. I looked where I needed to look to do what I did. And what was there was there. I'd done it too long to speculate too much on why it was there. When I needed to, I could flatten out my emotional response until it was simply blank. I liked what I did, probably because I was good at it.

—*Painted Ladies*

I don't know if anyone could ever fully be Spenser—I've never met anyone that cool in real life. Parker always said Spenser could do five times what he could do. I don't think he just meant physically. Not only was Spenser unflappable around the assholes he met, he could find enjoyment anywhere he went. He entertained himself equally by knowing and recognizing the details of a police house, a fine restaurant, or a flophouse motel.

I think the reason readers have stayed with Spenser for nearly forty books, making him arguably the most successful private eye series of all time, is Spenser's outlook. There is something in the pages of the novels that makes readers take note of the world around them, maybe enjoy that cup of coffee as they sit at the airport or pay more attention to where they are at that very moment. And I feel this is a crucial lesson these days as people become more absorbed in the digital world without experiencing the actual world. Spenser is all in the here and now. This serves him well as an investigator, a bodyguard, and as someone who has survived numerous attempts on his life. But it's also a worldview that helps him enjoy life more than the rest of us.

There have been countless times I've returned to Spenser when I feel I've run aground, when I'm experiencing grief, or when I feel I'm overwhelmed with too much in my head. There is a rhythm and a Zen energy that Parker developed for Spenser that transfers well beyond the page, adjusting readers' outlooks even if it's just for the time they're reading the novel. You can hear the wind, the leaves in the trees, and appreciate the change of seasons.

In that, Bob Parker has left us much more than just an entertaining series and compelling hero. In the spaces between and during the action, he's taught us how to untie our minds and stand still, to watch and enjoy what's going on around us. To be here now.

As Spenser heads into his fortieth adventure, I was honored to be chosen by the Parker estate to continue this iconic series that has meant so much to me. As I started the task, I was filled with natural self-doubt and hesitation. I found it a bit ironic, knowing that Spenser chose an ex–college football player with an appreciation for bourbon as his apprentice in *Sixkill*, the last novel that Bob wrote. In that book, Susan and Spenser talk about Sixkill's transformation:

> SUSAN: If he learns what you know, and behaves as you
>   behave, then it allows him to slough off the costume.
> SPENSER: So I haven't helped him change as much as I've
>   helped him get out.

And as I write, I keep in mind what Spenser tells Sixkill when they first take on a bunch of thugs together, feeling like I'm walking with Bob as I do this:

> Four men came out of the entrance tunnel and onto the
> field.
>   "Don't think about it. You've trained enough. It should
> come as needed. Like riding a bicycle."

After two decades of friendship, I've learned a hell of a lot.

VOICE OF THE CITY

I DENNIS LEHANE I

I DIDN'T PUBLISH anything worth noting until the second chapter of my first novel. I say the second chapter, not the first, because the second chapter opens with the line, "The old neighborhood is the Edward Everett Square section of Dorchester." That's my voice. The opening line of the *first* chapter is, "The bar at the Ritz Carlton looks out on the Public Garden and requires a tie." That is not my voice; that is Robert B. Parker's voice. In fact, the whole first chapter, with its self-consciously flashy repartee and overtly smartass main character, Patrick Kenzie, cracking wise with excessive abandon, is so faux-Parker, so mimeo-Spenser, so wearing the anxiety of its influence on every inch of its sleeve, that if I could publicly disown it and still have the book make sense, I would do so.

The reason I discovered myself only in chapter two was because that's when I left downtown for the neighborhoods. My Boston is the Boston of the neighborhoods, the ring around the hub. Robert B. Parker's Boston is the city proper, The Hub itself. I write about the Victoria Diner and the Ashmont Grill in Dorchester; he wrote about the Parker House and Maison Robert on School Street by Old City Hall. He wrote about Newbury Street, Marlborough Street, and Commonwealth Avenue. I write about East 2nd, the Melnea Cass, and Dot Ave. And when I did wander into Parker's backyard, I trod lightly and with respect. Because it was his zip code; I was visiting.

We were both, from the outset of our respective careers, unshakably and unquestionably Bostonian. I got that way by birth; he came it to it by choice and certain inextricable "Bostonianisms" that defined his character and that of Spenser, his indelible PI hero.

A defining characteristic of a true Bostonian is, I sometimes feel, a lack of tolerance for rudeness. Being rude is very different from being impolite, which is good because Bostonians might be the least polite people in the Western Hemisphere. (Take that, Philadelphians.) But there's an ocean of difference between the impolite and the rude. Rude is stepping on someone's foot and not apologizing even when you realize your mistake. Impolite is someone saying, "Why'd you step on my foot and not fucking apologize, asshole?" Rude is cutting someone off in traffic, so they crash their car, and then driving off. Impolite is cutting someone off in traffic. Rude is taking two parking spaces. Impolite would be keying the car of someone who took two parking spaces. (And if you *really* want to be impolite you do what's known as a "Dorchester key" and key both sides of the car.)

Much like with pornography, you know the difference between the rude and impolite when you see it. I've often been accused of being impolite—so have most of my friends (usually when we're visiting another state or dating a Yankees fan)—but I've only been accused of being rude once, and that was by some asshole who really meant I was being impolite but didn't know how to pronounce three-syllable words.

You don't have to be from Boston to be a Bostonian. (See Damon, Matt; Affleck, Ben; and Leary, Denis.) And you can be from Boston and still not be a Bostonian. (You know who you are; or better yet, you don't. But we do.) Robert B. Parker of Maine was a Bostonian. He loved tall tales and hated bullshit; he could be impolite but never rude; his favorite facial expression was deadpan; he knew exactly the word to italicize when he spoke; he had no time for phonies, people who put on airs, or people who, in the parlance of Old Boston, outgrew their hat sizes. I'm fairly certain he never used a smiley face emoticon.

As I write this, a football game plays on a TV in the next room. It's an exhibition game between the Patriots and the Lions and mostly meaningless for everyone but the players on the bubble who may or may not make the team. But I've left it on because I love the sounds of the thuds and the ref whistles and the white noise of the crowd. Also, possibly, because Patriots games remind me of Robert B. Parker, which, on the surface, could seem weird. Bob and I knew each other only casually. We enjoyed each other's company the few times we ran into each other with enough time to have a quick drink, but we were acquaintances, not friends exactly. I knew very little about him beyond the standard biography available on his website or the back of a book jacket. I don't know if he was a fanatic about football, I don't know if he ever played it, I don't know much at all about him and his relationship, if any, to NFL entertainment. I just know that during Christmas season one year in the late '90s, he and I shared a very satisfying moment together while watching a football game on TV. It was undoubtedly politically incorrect, and arguably involved the emotional abuse of a child. But it served to bring Bob and me together on a meeting of the minds so complete that I never felt I had to know much more about the man.

I first met Bob Parker in the summer of 1984. I was eighteen and working for a bookstore in downtown Boston, and my manager had given me the responsibility of organizing a Parker book signing because she knew I was a fan of his work. The book, if memory serves, was *Valediction*, one of the great Spenser novels that fell in an amazing string of them, from *The Judas Goat* to *Looking for Rachel Wallace* to *Early Autumn*, *A Savage Place*, *Ceremony*, and *The Widening Gyre*. It's a career run, actually, comparable to the Rolling Stones four-peat of *Beggars Banquet*, *Let It Bleed*, *Sticky Fingers*, and *Exile on Main Street*; Dickens pulling off *The Pickwick Papers*, *Oliver Twist*, and *Nicholas Nickleby* back to back to back; and seasons two through four of *Seinfeld*. Yes, that level of greatness.

At the time of that signing, I had been reading the Spenser books since high school. Back in my mid-teens, I'd had to hunt them down, often in used bookstores, which is how I discovered so many backstreets in Boston and in Cambridge—hopping on and off subways to trek to yet another used bookstore in hopes of scoring a Parker or an Elmore Leonard, neither of whom enjoyed the kind of popularity that would befriend them just a few years later. And, in that relentless searching, I learned my city as much as I learned it on drives through the neighborhoods with my father or, later, as a floral delivery driver and then a chauffeur.

Another way I learned the city was through the reading of the Spenser novels themselves. It was in *Looking for Rachel Wallace*, for example, where I was first introduced to Locke-Ober, a venerable institution of Old Boston, which is not something a kid from Dorchester would have ever learned about without help. It's at Locke-Ober where Spenser meets with John Ticknor, an editor who wants Spenser to protect angry, unapologetic, lesbian feminist Rachel Wallace, who's written a book that's bringing her death threats. Ticknor warns Spenser that Rachel will hardly be an easy gig; Spenser and his testosterone-fueled code of ethics (or so Rachel presupposes) represent everything she's hoping to dismantle in society. At one point, Spenser, ever the smartass, says something smartass and "Ticknor smiled again, but not like he wanted me to marry his sister."

Looking for Rachel Wallace was the first Parker book I read. And that line about Ticknor, which shows up on the third page, was the first line I read of Bob's that made me sit up straight and laugh. I may have even flipped the book over in my hand to look at the cover again and ask, "Who *is* this guy?" There was something so immediately Bostonian about the understated sarcasm and the left field nature of the analogy. Bostonians care fairly little about your political, sexual, or religious affiliation but everything about whether you're full of shit. Full of shit or full of yourself—those are cardinal sins in The Hub. And Parker, though a transplanted Mainer (but Mainers, flinty souls that they are, are possibly less tolerant of bullshit than Bostonians), was a Bostonian from the day he took his first teaching job at Northeastern.

So I read on, and within another twenty pages, I knew something transformative was happening. It's hard to remember now how revolutionary the early Spenser books were, but they were gate chargers and wall busters. For starters, they were politically and socially astute in a way that a lot of the more ham-fisted PI novels of the time weren't. Spenser was a tough guy, a former cop and former boxer, and he was brave and nearly fearless and would sooner take two in the hat and two in the chest than betray his principles. In that way, he wasn't much different than so many heroes of the genre who preceded him or ran alongside him as contemporaries. But Spenser was also well-read, articulate, a connoisseur of good food and fine wine, and, dare I say, sensitive. At the end of *Looking for Rachel Wallace*, for example, after he kills two gun thugs, he holds the woman he's just rescued and *cries*, for God's sake.

Spenser deals with cases that challenge his preconceived notions (and maybe the preconceived notions of the genre, itself)—notions about feminism, gay rights, the educational system, parenting, religion—and often he is forced to reconsider those notions. That is the arc of each book—a journey to transformation. Spenser—no first name—so resolute in his code of ethics, is not, however, unyielding about the nuances of that code. So while his macro code never changes— always fight for those who can't fight for themselves; never take a bribe and never take a knee; break your word for no one; to thine own self be true—the micro code can and does. He is open to epiphanies, new journeys and perspectives, a challenging of his personal status quo.

That doesn't just make him interesting, it makes him human. And when a character is recognizably human, he is vulnerable. You fear for him. So even though Spenser is not only the self-professed "toughest man in Boston," and is also the "toughest man in New England" (in *Pale Kings and Princes* he goes to Maine or New Hampshire—I can't remember which—to prove it by beating a guy's ass to the ground)—he is admittedly flawed, which makes him vulnerable. And that gives his mano-a-mano confrontations something at stake. He has something to lose, and we have something to lose too, because we've befriended him.

Another pioneering aspect of the novels (particularly in the late '70s and early-to-mid '80s when they were hitting their stride) was that Spenser has a girlfriend. Not a girlfriend who stays faithful to him and is endlessly understanding as he fools around on her with exotic Russian hit-women or love-the-one-you're-with damsels in distress. And not the girlfriend who exists to get kidnapped and then rescued by the hero so she can be held in his masculine arms and forever define herself by how she can best play a supporting role in his life. Not even a girlfriend who would appreciate being called "girlfriend." No, this woman is a professional woman, far better educated than Spenser (no slouch himself when it came to referencing literature or the intricacies of food), utterly self-sufficient, a practicing psychiatrist. I'm speaking, of course, of Susan Silverman, a polarizing character in the Parker canon—hell, a polarizing figure in the crime fiction world as a whole. And while it is true that, as the series entered its later decades, Ms. Silverman becomes smug and tiring to a nearly indefensible degree, she is fresh air incarnate in the early novels.

Girlfriends in detective fiction had, up until that point, existed to be discarded. They could be killed in order to give the detective a personal vendetta upon which to embark, as often happened in, say, John D. MacDonald's brilliant Travis McGee novels, to the point where I found it hard to believe a self-respecting South Florida insurance company would underwrite a policy for any woman who bumped uglies with McGee. Or, as mentioned above, they could get kidnapped (pretty much a guarantee if our hero was facing off against a serial killer or thugs who also owned a warehouse by the docks). Or they could just sort of hang around, keeping the home fires burning, until our hero came back and needed to get himself some. No wonder women hated to read PI books back then. They couldn't find themselves in them.

Susan Silverman is her own woman all the way. She loves Spenser, has lusty, regular sex with him, and often psycho-analyzes him at convenient moments in the narrative so he can continue on his course with the assurance that he is, in fact, truly the bravest and most virtuous man in the book (or all of New England). But Susan also fights with Spenser, challenges him and his assumptions, refuses to be defined by him, and for one long stretch, breaks up with him until he stops expecting her to be anything but what she is.

Some of the reason that male readers dislike Susan is be-cause of these very attributes. (And, yes, in later books some of the reason is because an air of smug entitlement and self-regard covers her like a second skin.) But one can never discount how, through her, Robert B. Parker created a new archetype in American PI fiction—the woman-as-equal.

That would have been enough of a day's work, but Parker wasn't through. Once he'd gotten Susan up and running, he introduced Hawk, the Cristal-drinking, shaven-headed (long before shaven heads were cool; hell, it was Hawk who prob-ably made them cool), mostly heartless but endlessly loyal "dark angel" to the author's more virtuous Spenser. Hawk's descendents are legion—Walter Mosley's Mouse; James Lee Burke's Clete Purcell; Robert Crais' Joe Pike; Harlan Coben's Wynn; my own Bubba Rogowski. I'm not going to say none of those just mentioned would have existed without Hawk, just that Hawk existed first, so any question on the subject starts with him, no one else.

The dark angel can do what the good guy hero can't. He's unbound by morality—either his own or the readers'. In one novel, when Spenser and Hawk have just had a confrontation with a particularly nasty piece of work who they know will continue to come after them, they leave the guy lying on the floor, a bloody mess. But then Hawk tells Spenser he has to kill the guy or they'll never be safe. Spenser says, "I can't kill a guy lying on the floor," to which Hawk replies, "Shit, I can." And shoots the guy.

If a hero does that enough times, he's no longer a hero. But the dark angel can do it and the audience applauds. Maybe because everyone wants a dark angel, and maybe because everyone has experienced the exquisite pleasure of giving into the will of the id. A main character who consistently gives in to the will of his id grows morally reprehensible and—far worse—dramatically uninteresting. But a secondary character who occasionally gives in to his id *becomes* the main character's id. That's what the dark angel archetype is—the unrestrained id of the otherwise above-board main character.

And if Parker didn't exactly create the archetype, he certainly perfected it. Soon nothing was more disappointing to discover in a Spenser book than the news that Hawk would not be appearing in it. Luckily, after a while, Parker realized it and kept Hawk, if not front and center, certainly at the top of the cast list.

When I ran that signing for Bob in 1984, Hawk was part of every third question his creator got. The questions were variations on a theme that can be distilled to this: "Do you know a real Hawk, and how can I get one?"

I watched Bob answer a permutation of that question at least fifty times in the hour he signed. And his answer was always steady, never annoyed. That's not to say he wasn't annoyed (if you like answering the same question fifty times in an hour, I've got a group of four-year-olds I'd like to send to your house), but that the annoyance was easily tempered and even wholly overwhelmed by the gratitude he felt toward people who cared so much about his work. There was nothing about Bob that was obsequious or eager to get you to like him. He was gruff and gravel-voiced and clearly had a limited tolerance for idiots and small talk. But he was also ever the gentleman, ever gracious with his fans.

Afterward, I walked him out of the bookstore and asked him if it ever got old—the same questions, the same requests, the same signature, over and over.

He stopped. He cocked his head and looked at me with his deadpan face and walrus moustache. "How in God's name," he said, "could it ever get old, kid?"

I remember watching him cross Tremont Street and then turn down School Street and I thought, "That is one cool son of a bitch." And then I thought, "How *could* it ever get old?"

Fifteen years later, I discussed that moment with Bob. He didn't remember the signing (I hadn't expected him to), and he didn't remember the exchange. But he told me nothing had changed. We lucky, lucky few get paid to sit in a room and think shit up. We put that to paper and people read it and show up at bookstores to tell us thanks. Anyone who ever has a problem with that, in my opinion—and in Bob's—needs to try a real job on for size. One where no one applauds you or thanks you for your effort or even notices you. We have one of the best jobs in the world. And I know it not just because it's true but because he knew it and told me so when I was callow and knew nothing and needed to hear it.

Boston is, as I've acknowledged, an in-your-face town that values honesty and a lack of airs or pretension. But it's also a provincial town with an insecurity complex about its own provincialism. The local media sometimes manifests this insecurity by refusing to give its local authors, actors, artists, or directors any kind of hometown pass, even if the pass is clearly deserved. Boston talent, some have argued, are not babied by the Boston media, they're targeted by it. Even when they do give a prop or two, it helps if they can do it at the expense of another in the same line of work.

So it was that in the early stages of my career, the headlines of some reviews of my books read "Move Over, Spenser" and the like. This became an elephant in the middle of the room Bob and I never talked about when we would run into each other at the annual Christmas party thrown at Kate's Mystery Bookstore just outside of Porter Square in Cambridge. Kate Mattes, who founded and ran Kate's Mystery Bookstore, threw that Christmas party every year, and every local mystery writer showed up to drink eggnog and beer and wine and schmooze with local fans who supported our work and supported Kate and were—and continue to be—the reason I'm not greeting you through the voice box at the McDonald's drive-thru, asking if you'd like to super-size your order.

Kate's was a very small store—it comprised, essentially, the living room and dining room of the first floor of a Victorian. Where the kitchen should have been was the shipping and receiving room. Where you'd put a mud room and washer and dryer, however, Kate had fashioned a small study at the back of the store. I have no idea what went on there during regular business hours, but during those annual Christmas parties, that room was a place to sign stock or step out of the dense crush of the crowd for a moment. And, if the gods aligned, it was the room in which to catch a Patriots game if they were playing that day.

The Christmas party in question, they were. It was 1998 and the game had potential playoff implications. I was (and remain) a serious Patriots fan. I don't name my sons Bruschi or Ben-Jarvis Brady Lehane or anything, but I've missed only one game in fifteen years and only because I was out of the country.

So this is a game that has a bearing on whether we enter the post-season or go home. And this is pre-Tom Brady. This is the Bledsoe years. The Pete Carroll years. The never-won-a-Super-Bowl years. So I'm keeping in mind how lucky I am to be at the party, to have fans, to be rubbing elbows with the likes of Linda Barnes and Jeremiah Healy and William Martin and, of course, Bob Parker. Except Bob and I have sort of been avoiding each other of late because of those headlines and the pissing contest the local press seems determined to start between us.

There's a child at the party. Well, actually there are several of them, but one is hard to miss because, while he's only nine or ten years old, he's kind of a prick. Actually, that's not fair—strike "kind of." He pushes through the crowd without ever saying "Excuse me," and pushes his way back again the same way. He whines constantly to his parents—*When are we going home? I don't like it here. This place smells. The food sucks. These people are boring. Books suck. I don't like you.*

This is not impolite behavior. This is rude behavior.

To which his parents, well-meaning Cantabrigians that they are and thus choking on politically correct language to an Orwellian degree, mention that his behavior is verging on the "inappropriate" and ask him to "please respect the rights of others," etc. But mostly they beg and bargain with him and tell him they "understand his feelings" and he's being such a "trooper" putting up with boring adult things and they'll be sure to buy him an ice cream on the way home.

No one else seems aware of how repulsive this is (we are in Cambridge, after all, where political correctness didn't just find a home, it built a castle). I shouldn't say "no one."

I'm repulsed. And Bob, judging by the glances we keep shooting one another, is pretty mortified himself. As we go on about our business that snowy afternoon, there are lulls in the signings and the chitchat and during those lulls, I sneak into the back room and watch the game until the next commercial break. And I begin to run into Bob doing the same thing.

As the party winds down and we are relieved of our official duties, we both find ourselves back there, sitting on the couch, each with a Sam Adams in hand, watching a very tense game. And we are clearly in our element. And all the strange not-quite-tension-but-close that had managed to find its way between us begins to evaporate. Not because we "talked about our feelings." We're two Micks from working class backgrounds; talking about our feelings isn't really on the dance card. But every time one of us gets up to get a beer, we ask if the other would like one, and a simple camaraderie begins to flavor the air in the room. So this is where we're living, late in the fourth quarter, with the Pats clinging to a three-point lead when the Rude Kid walks in the room with his mother. The mother says, "He's going to watch football with the manly men because he loves football." And she leaves.

I say to Bob, "Did she say manly?"

Bob says, "She did."

"Manly men?"

"Unfortunately," Bob says, "I believe this too occurred."

The kid says, "I hate football."

Bob and I drink our beers and say nothing.

"Just a bunch of stupid guys throwing a ball."

Bob and I drink our beers.

"Why would you even watch something like that? Must mean you're stupid."

Bob and I glance at one another and then back at the game.

The kid walks in front of the TV. "I mean, look at how stupid they all are. Look at it. I'm going to watch something else."

And he reaches out to turn the channel.

"Kid," I remember somebody who sounded a lot like me saying, "if you touch that button, I'll break your friggin' wrist."

There must have been something in the tone of the guy who sounded a lot like me, because the kid visibly paled and looked back at me and then at Bob.

I nodded.

Bob said, "Oh, he's serious."

The kid dropped his hand. He scurried over to the couch by us. He asked if he could sit on the couch, and we both shrugged. He climbed up beside me.

Bob looked at me with a face so deadpan an F-16 couldn't have shaken its cheeks. He said, "We should hang out more," and clinked his beer bottle against mine.

For the rest of the game, the kid sat on the couch, attentive and well-behaved. During commercials, he'd ask mostly intelligent questions. The only time he became a nuisance again was when his mother came to take him away and he kicked up a fuss because he didn't want to go.

At some point, though, as we all watched the game, Bob and I exchanged a glance, similar to the ones we'd exchanged when the kid was making a pain of himself during the party and his parents were wheedling and sniveling before him. It was a look that said something like, *Where we come from, there are rules to how a boy and then a man behaves. There aren't too many rules and they're not written down anywhere, but they're inviolate.*

Spenser embodies those rules. I'd hope Patrick Kenzie does as well. And in that moment, their creators recognized kindred spirits.

Bob and I did hang out a few times between that moment and the last time I saw him, also at Kate's Christmas party, in the final weeks of 2008, and they were always fine times.

I miss him because I liked him but also because I'm not sure what Boston fiction is without him. We have many outstanding writers working in the region, don't get me wrong, but Bob embodied the flat, deadpan, self-contained sarcasm of our regional voice better than any writer I can think of. When he wrote, "I smiled. Time was, they [women] would have started to undress when I did that, but I guess the smile had lost a step," or, "Hard to warm up to someone who didn't like beer" (*Early Autumn*), he nailed a voice as distinctive as that of Elmore Leonard's Detroit or Richard Price's New Jersey. It was the voice of a city and maybe even a bit more than that; it was the voice of a time. And with his passing, that time has gone with him.

THEY LIKE THE WAY
IT SOUNDS

| LAWRENCE BLOCK |·

INTERVIEWER: Why do you think your work is so
popular?
ROBERT B. PARKER: I dunno. I think people just
like the way it sounds.

THAT'S A WONDERFULLY quotable exchange,
and I wish I could be sure I was quoting it correctly. I wasn't
there when these words were spoken. It was passed on to me
second- or third-hand, but what I heard rang a bell, and I can
still hear the echo.

Because I believe he got it right. Why is everything Bob
Parker wrote so popular? I think we just like the way it sounds.

• •

Ruth Cavin was a great mystery editor who left us too soon,
although not before she'd lived ninety-two years. She stressed
the great importance of the writer's voice. It was, Ruth said,
as unique as a thumbprint, and the chief factor in the success
or failure of a piece of writing. And it was inherent in the

writer. You couldn't learn it. You couldn't do a hell of a lot to develop it or refine it. What you had to do was find it, which was task enough.

And what you found might or might not be worth the effort.

. .

We think of voice more in connection with the performing arts. An actor has a voice, and it amounts to something rather more than pitch and register and tone; it's what makes us listen intently or puts us to sleep.

"I could listen to him read the phone book," we say with admiration.

A musician has a voice. The touch of a particular set of fingers on the keys of a piano, the notes that come out of the bell of a horn—they are individual, and sometimes unmistakably so. You might, if you practice enough, and if you're talented to begin with, play the same sounds Louis Armstrong played. But they won't sound the same.

A singer has a voice. One can almost say that a singer *is* a voice, that anything learned—phrasing, breath control— merely allow the true voice to be heard.

A story, if I may. An aspiring singer went to audition for a great vocal coach. While the last notes died out, the coach sat for a few moments in silence. Then he strode to the window and threw it open, motioning to the singer to join him.

"Listen," he said. "Do you hear the crow?"

"Yes."

"*Caw, caw, caw.* You hear him?"

"I do."

"The crow," the old man said, "thinks his song is beautiful."

. .

But writing is silent, isn't it? It's an act performed in silence, and its creations are appreciated in a similar silence. (The medium of the audiobook is an exception, in that one reads it not with one's eyes but with one's ears, and there are accordingly two voices involved, those of the writer and the narrator.)

"As idle as a painted ship/Upon a painted ocean," wrote Coleridge, in his own unmistakable voice. We do, in fact, hear the voice of the writer, all the silence notwithstanding. It falls upon the inner ear. We hear it.

• •

Voice. Isn't it just another word for style?

No.

Different people will define style differently. But I'm writing this, so I get to use my definition. Which goes like this:

Style is that façade a writer erects to conceal his voice.

• •

If Bob Parker wrote a phone book, people would read it.

Well, perhaps I exaggerate. But his voice did have magical properties. On two separate occasions I picked a book of his off a library shelf, just intending to read a few pages and get an idea of what he was up to in this latest effort.

Fat chance. A few pages? A couple of paragraphs and he had me, and both times I read the book all the way through to the end.

(This would have been less likely had the books had more heft to them, but they were short. There wasn't all that much in the way of incident, nor were all that many words used to tell the tale. In an effort to keep the novels from looking as short as they were, Parker's publishers typically used larger type and wider margins. And they leaded out the text, so that there was often enough space between the lines of a Spenser novel to contain another whole book. The net effect of this typographic enhancement was to make the books even easier to read—as if that were necessary.)

From the opening lines of *The Godwulf Manuscript*, Spenser's first-person voice is a delight to that inner ear. Spenser would become more his own man over time, and less a Back Bay Philip Marlowe, but that's to be expected in a series of any length; the character undergoes a process of self-realization. But when it came to voice, Spenser was Spenser from the jump.

And what makes us want to hear it? What makes us listen, even when that mellifluous voice is telling us things we aren't all that eager to hear, even when the story's too thin and the premise too frail and Spenser's task insufficiently challenging?

One ought to be able to take that auctorial voice apart and explain why it does what it does. And maybe someone can do this, but not I. All I can do is say that I think the man got it right:

We like the way it sounds.

.   .

I've had occasion to think about Bob Parker's irresistible voice lately, upon the announcement that two writers have been approved by Parker's estate to continue his two most popular series. Ace Atkins will write new books about Spenser, while Michael Brandman already has written the next Jesse Stone novel, called *Killing the Blues*.

I was surprised when I learned this, but decided upon reflection that I had no reason to be. Writers have been taking up the lance of a fallen colleague for a century or

more. In today's publishing climate, beset by its own equiv-
alent of global warming, death means never having to say
you're done writing. The market dominance of brand name
authors, the glut of books by living authors with acknowledged or unacknowledged "collaborators" or out-and-out
ghostwriters, and the pastiche/homage of writers producing
prequels and sequels to classic works all combine to make a
continuation of Parker's work an appealing proposition to
all concerned.

Though perhaps not quite all. I'm not sure it's such a great
deal for the reader.

• •

First, though, there's the question of what Parker himself
would think of it. Is he likely to be spinning in his grave at
the very idea?

I didn't know the man anywhere near well enough to ven-
ture a guess. Ego could tug a writer in either direction; he
might be reluctant to see his characters follow him to the
grave, or he might be loathe to see others putting words into
their mouths.

But any objection from this particular writer would seem
to stand on shaky ground. Parker completed *Poodle Springs*, a
Philip Marlowe novel that Raymond Chandler left unfinished
at his death; later, he wrote a sequel to Chandler's *The Big Sleep*,
with the felicitous title *Perchance to Dream*. The man's motives
could not have been higher, as he admired Chandler hugely,
wrote his doctoral dissertation about him, and quite clearly
drew Spenser more from Marlowe than any other source.

And I suppose the books are all right, although one is never
in doubt for a moment that another hand than Chandler's is
at work there. (In *Perchance*, Parker includes flashback passages

from *The Big Sleep,* set off typographically so you'll know they're Chandler's. This was remarkably daring on his part, I always thought, and not necessarily the best idea he ever had.)

Spinning in his grave? No, probably not.

• •

There are, we should note, some reasons to engage a new author to take over a series. And not just the most obvious one ("We can sell some books! We can make some money!").

I remember questioning the decision to bring out new Nero Wolfe titles after Rex Stout's death. Some years previously, I'd written two mysteries in which the narrator, one Chip Harrison, plays Archie to a road company Nero Wolfe named Leo Haig. John McAleer, Rex Stout's biographer, told me that Stout had indeed been aware of the books, and, like Queen Victoria, was not amused. If Stout bristled at pastiche, how would he feel about downright usurpation of his characters? I figured he could only hate the idea, and I wondered at his family's acquiescence to the proposition.

Then a publisher friend pointed out that it takes a supply of new books to keep the old titles in print. Sales of the Wolfe books had dwindled since their author's death; without new works by a fresh hand, the publisher was inclined to let them go out of print. But if another writer in the person of Robert Goldsborough were to step in, the original books would not only remain in print but would be completely repackaged, with various outside writers commissioned to provide introductions.

All of this sounds itself like a repackaging of *We can sell some books! We can make some money!* and there may well be a self-serving element here. But isn't it safe to presume the author would prefer his own books to remain in print? Wouldn't he want to increase their sales?

Sometimes posthumous sequels work. Sometimes they don't.

And opinions differ. One online reviewer gives high marks to Parker's *Poodle Springs*; a comment follows, decrying the book as a tragedy and saying the publisher should have issued Chandler's four chapters and let it go at that.

I must have read half a dozen of the Oz books when I was a boy, and would have read more if I'd had the chance. While I didn't notice the difference, I remember my mother thought the later books by Ruth Plumly Thompson weren't up to the standard set by L. Frank Baum. (Baum published *The Wonderful Wizard of Oz* in 1900, and the series continues to this day; the most recent entry, licensed by the Baum family, is *Trouble in Oz*, by Sherwood Smith.)

Series continue after the original author's death for the same reason that they become popular in the first place; a reader, having had a pleasant experience, wants to repeat it, wants to renew his acquaintance with a character or characters whose company he's enjoyed. If the author who provided that initial experience is on hand, so much the better. If not, well, too bad; as long as the characters are present, doing what they do, does it really matter who's telling us about it?

It doesn't seem to have mattered much to the young readers who wanted to go back to Oz. Because that's indeed what they wanted, to re-enter that magical realm, and they didn't much care—or notice—who it was that unlocked the door for them. L. Frank Baum may have created that world, but other writers seemed capable of accessing it, or some acceptable variant thereof. And that's what the books were about, not Baum's perceptions, not his voice.

On the other hand, without departing from the world of juvenile fantasy fiction, try to imagine a later writer taking up the mantle of Lewis Carroll and turning out a third Alice book. It wouldn't astonish me to learn that the attempt has been made, because there's nothing that someone somewhere is not fool enough to try, but aren't you happy you don't have to read it?

· ·

I was an impassioned fan of Rex Stout's Nero Wolfe books and read them all more than once. I read the first of Robert Goldsborough's sequels and found it troubling. Stout's auctorial voice, and the voice he gave to narrator Archie Goodwin, was more than distinctive; it was to my mind unique, and it had everything to do with the books' success. One wanted to hear that voice, even as one wanted to spend more time in the rooms of that magical brownstone house and in the presence of those perfectly realized characters.

Goldsborough came to his task more as a fan than an author. He wrote the first book, *Murder in E Minor*, for the private pleasure of his mother, who longed to read more about her favorite characters; it was his own first novel, and wasn't published until 1986, eight years after he'd written it. By 1994 he'd published six more, and that was that. A decade later he began writing books of his own.

As I said, I found *Murder in E Minor* unsettling. It almost felt as though Stout had written it, and the narrator almost sounded like Archie. There was one stunning glitch, in that Archie smoked a cigarette or two in the book's course, and that was about as startling as if Lilian Jackson Braun's Qwilleran were to whip out his pen knife and geld a cat. A few thousand readers called this to the author's attention and in the books that followed we heard no more of Archie and tobacco.

But the rest, as I said, was almost right. And, naturally enough, Goldsborough improved as he went on. He became a better writer, as one is apt to do with practice, and he also became better at sounding like Stout and at putting Wolfean words into the mouths of his characters.

It's my impression that members of the Wolfe Pack, that enduring sodality of ardent West 35th Street Irregulars, have varying degrees of enthusiasm for the post-mortem Wolfe books. They did bestow the Nero award on the first book and surely read the others. The consensus seems to be that they're glad to have these seven further adventures but do not for a moment confuse them with the genuine article.

I read the first, as I've said, and one or two others. For all I know, they may have been more suspenseful and more strongly plotted than the originals, but I'd never read Rex Stout for plot or suspense. I read, like everybody else, for the pleasure of the writing and the charm of the characters, and Robert Goldsborough was not entirely lacking in those areas. He worked very hard at sounding like Rex Stout and at letting his narrator sound and act like Archie Goodwin.

Rex Stout, of course, never worked at it. He didn't have to.

• •

And there, I submit, is the problem. Ace Atkins is a fine writer, and at least as gifted in plot construction as Parker himself. (Here's a Spenser plot: 1. A client brings Spenser a problem. 2. Spenser studies the situation and figures it out. 3. Spenser addresses the problem and brings it to a successful conclusion. There's a lot of snappy dialogue and some of the best physical action anyone ever wrote, but those three sentences pretty much cover it in terms of plot.)

I don't know what Ace Atkins has going for him in the way of mimetic ability, but I'm willing to believe he'll do a fine job of sounding like Parker. I gather he's a Parker fan even as Parker was a Chandler fan, and Goldsborough a

Rex Stout fan. We can assume he understands Spenser and Hawk and Susan, and will know what words to put in their mouths, and how they'll react to the situations in which he places them.

I can't make all of the same assumptions about Michael Brandman, with whose writing I'm not familiar. As I understand it, his background is TV, and he worked closely with Parker on the adaptations of the Jesse Stone stories for that medium. One might infer that his strengths lie in plot and story construction, but there's no reason he might not be able to provide a reasonable facsimile of the Parker voice.

Here's the thing: No matter how good a job either of these fellows does, no matter how much skill and sensitivity they bring to the table, and no matter how much thought and effort they apply, all they can attempt to provide is an imitation of a genuine original.

I guess there's a place for that sort of thing. Look at all the Elvis impersonators, all the tribute bands.

•   •

I alluded to this a few paragraphs back, but it can stand elaboration: Nobody ever wrote a better fight scene than Robert B. Parker. Whether the violence is hand-to-hand or includes weapons, whether it's one-on-one or there's a whole crowd on hand, whether it happened the day before yesterday or back in the Old West, the man always got it down brilliantly. He did so with great economy, and spared us the gore and the sadism, but you were right there while it went down, and you could see just what happened and how it happened and, well, it was breathtaking. I'd read through one of his scenes a couple of times before going on, not because I was going to school (although I probably was) but because I didn't want to let go of the experience.

• •

There's another observation Parker made about his work that has stayed with me ever since I first came upon it. He pointed out that he was not writing realism, that he was in fact writing romance.

Let me capitalize that. He was writing Romance. Not, God help us, in the Harlequin/Solitaire sense, but in the Malory *Morte d'Arthur* sense. And that's why it's perfectly acceptable that Spenser remain the same age forever, that his shining armor remains untarnished, and that, in his affair with Susan, forever wilt he love and she be fair.

It was Parker's special province to write Romance in a realistic style. And that works quite wonderfully, because it tricks us into suspending disbelief to a remarkable extent. We don't strain at gnats, but neither do we refrain from swallowing camels.

Consider the sequence in *Early Autumn* when Spenser takes Paul Giacomin off to make a man out of him. The physical routine he puts the kid through would flat-out kill him, and Spenser doesn't even give him days off to recover. Parker would have to know as much; he was a weightlifter, if perhaps a less diligent one than his hero.

But he writes it this way anyway, because this is Romance, and he makes it work. A realist would teach the kid a couple of basic exercises and start him off with two or three light sets a day of each, and progress would be a gradual thing. That might make just as good reading, but it would be a different sort of book from the one Parker wanted to write.

And one thing he knew was that everything worked out for the best if he wrote the book he wanted to write.

• •

I had my troubles with *Early Autumn*. I'd spent enough time lifting heavy metal objects, and enough days afterward with sore muscles, to find the departure from plausibility hard to take. I've had my problems with Spenser and Stone and Virgil Cole, all of whom may be described as true-blue, uxorious, or pussy-whipped, as you prefer. (The three terms are hardly mutually exclusive.)

So? I was never the Ideal Reader for Parker's work, and God knows he got along fine without me. But I did read almost all of the books, and not because of the stories he chose to tell or the characters who peopled them.

I just kind of liked the way they sounded.

. .

And I liked and respected the man. Let's not leave that out.

I don't think Parker and my paths crossed more than six or eight times, and we never came close to sitting down for a heart-to-heart. There were a couple of dinners where we were both on the dais, a couple of book biz events that threw us together.

Once, I think at a Left Coast Crime conference in Scottsdale, Bob was doing a one-man act in a large room that was predictably packed. He said he wasn't comfortable preparing talks, but would do a Q&A—and, not surprisingly, turned out to be very good at it.

Somebody asked him which of his own books was his favorite. "Gee, I don't know," he said. "Once they're done I never look at them." I was all the way in the rear, but I guess he'd spotted me. "How about you, Larry?" he called out. "Do you ever read your own work?"

"I read nothing else," I said.

Lord, that was satisfying. You have to love a guy who floats one belt-high across the plate like that, and does so on the one day in twenty when you're quick enough to get your bat on it.

• •

I was a bad choice to write this piece, and would have passed if I felt I could. But if my feelings for the work are mixed, those for the man are not. I was in fact honored to be invited to this particular clambake, and simply could not say no. Both Bob and the singular voice we know as Spenser will be missed.

SPENSER'S CODE
OF HUMOR

I PARNELL HALL I

THERE'S NOTHING UNIQUE about a wise-cracking private investigator. Smart-mouthed PIs are a dime a dozen. Every private eye writer in the last thirty years has one—and for good reason. They've all read the Spenser novels, and they've molded their private eyes after him. I know I did. When I started my first Stanley Hastings novel, back in the mid-80s, I wanted a private eye that talked like Spenser. Never mind that my private eye was an ordinary family man who never had fist fights or car chases, and didn't even carry a gun. (I was working as a PI at the time, chasing ambulances for a negligence lawyer, and I modeled the character after myself.) If my PI could talk like Spenser, I was convinced he'd be fun to read.

Other writers felt the same. And so a whole generation of clever PIs was born. Many were closer to Spenser than mine, being tough and athletic and jogging and having dangerous sidekicks like Hawk. But all, to the best of their authors' abilities, talked like Spenser.

And yet Spenser stands out.

It is not just that he is better at it, though he is. His remarks are rooted in his personality. Spenser is a knight in shining armor, a do-gooder, a man who lives by a code of honor, with values and standards and principles. His jests humanize him, mask his heroism, diffuse the macho image that is rightfully his. Without humor, he would appear a self-righteous prig, adhering to a strict moral code. With it, he is a jaunty, cocky son of a bitch, constantly ridiculing himself while he ridicules others.

And he is just so damn good at it.

Whatever the situation, Spenser is as quick with a quip as he is with his fists. He hits the ground running in *The Godwulf Manuscript* with his description of a blond co-ed: "She was wearing something in purple suede that was too short for a skirt and too long for a belt."

And he doesn't let up, asking Lieutenant Martin Quirk, who tries to intimidate him, "Can I feel your muscle?"

Or asking mob boss Joe Broz, "Do you always dress in blue and white . . . or do you have your office redone to match your clothes every day?"

And he tackles everything from sex to politics to religion, always with the same irreverent attitude.

In *The Widening Gyre*, he is asked to bodyguard a senatorial candidate who has been getting death threats. The candidate questions his religious beliefs: "Do you believe in almighty God?"

Spenser answers, "Why? Does he want to hire me?" As the candidate reacts in shock, Spenser, always the feminist, adds: "Or she."

It's not only the attitude and circumstances that characterize Spenser's wit. It's also his ability to convey volumes with just a few words. When Spenser meets the radical feminist with whom he clashes in *Looking for Rachel Wallace*, her editor, desperately trying to placate her, says Spenser has read her book. Rachel asks him what he thought of it.

He answers, "I think you are rehashing Simone de Beauvoir."

Notice the delicious triple-thrust of the remark. First, he fails to pay her a compliment, which is clearly what she expected. Second, he demonstrates a knowledge of feminism that Rachel, in her prejudice, assumed he would not have, plus the fact he was aware of that assumption. And, third, he offers the opinion that she is merely a second-rate imitation of other, genuinely important feminists.

That's a hell of a lot to pack into one short sentence. But Spenser does it with ease.

Rachel, fighting back, proceeds to grill him on his knowledge of Simone de Beauvoir, perhaps to make sure he is not quoting something he read in the press release. Spenser passes the test while labeling it for what it is.

Rachel asks, "What did you feel was her most persuasive insight?" To which Spenser answers, "Her suggestion that women occupied the position of *other*. Are we having a quiz later?"

Rachel has no sense of humor and tells him so. Instead of reassuring her it will be no problem, he says, "Okay if now and then I enjoy a wry, inward smile if struck by one of life's vagaries?"

Perhaps he is trying too hard to impress her with his erudition; still, the remark is priceless.

Spenser's intelligence is on display in every quip. In *Early Autumn*, Spenser has to rescue Paul Giacomin, a teenaged boy, from his dysfunctional family. This is not, of course, the job for which he was hired. In this case, the divorced wife is the client, and the initial task is to retrieve the boy from the father, who won't return him.

Spenser quickly realizes the boy is nothing more than a trophy the two are fighting over in order to hurt each other. Not one to pull his punches, he sums up the situation for the wife: "Capture the flag."

Short, punchy, insulting, and rude, but dead-on accurate.

To find Paul, Spenser tails the father's girlfriend to his house, breaks in, and surprises the two of them. The father immediately threatens to call the cops.

Spenser's response? "I enjoy meeting policemen. Sometimes if you're good they let you play with their handcuffs."

Spenser has the father and girlfriend buffaloed. As he describes the situation: "He looked at me. Elaine Brooks looked at me. If there'd been a mirror, I would have looked at me. But there wasn't, so I looked at them."

Humor permeates the scene. Even the description has a playful nature.

Spenser often takes delight in playing with words. In his first adventure, *The Godwulf Manuscript*, he is hired by a university to recover a rare stolen manuscript. The head of campus security takes exception to some of Spenser's questions:

> "Who the hell is employing who? I want to know your results, and you start asking me questions about professors."
> "Whom," I said.

"Huh?"

"It's whom, who's employing whom. Or is it? Maybe it's a predicate nominative, in which case . . ."

He also has fun with words in *Hugger Mugger*:

"Okay," I said. "Let me just expostulate for a while. You can nod or not as you wish."

"Expostulate?"

"I'm sleeping with a Harvard grad," I said.

And Spenser is even more playful in *Small Vices*. He narrates:

Since my name was anathema at Pemberton, I had to employ guile. I called the alumni office and said my name was Anathema and I was with the IRS . . .

"What did you say you name was?"

"Anathema. Pervis Anathema, refund enactment agent."

He claims to have a tax refund for a former student and asks for her address. And, yes, he gets it.

He also deals with the president of Pemberton College, who is surprised to find him well educated. When she tells him he speaks rather well, he replies, "You too."

She is initially taken aback by the remark, then smiles and acknowledges that she was indeed being patronizing, which he has managed to convey brilliantly with two simple words.

This is something Spenser uses humor for frequently: to highlight the foolishness of other people's assumptions. In particular, their assumptions that he isn't very intelligent.

In *Promised Land,* when he and Susan Silverman bring a runaway wife he has tracked down to his apartment, she is impressed by the extent of his book collection.

"Look at all the books. Have you read all these books?"

Spenser counters in his usual way, with self-deprecating sarcasm that mocks her prejudiced assessment of him: "Most of them. My lips get awfully tired, though."

Spenser is also not above using humor to highlight his own foolishness. While Spenser is driving Rachel in his car in *Looking for Rachel Wallace,* she pontificates on the idea that women are always named after their fathers not their mothers.

Two cars try to box him in on the highway. Spenser pushes her down on the floor, goes up on the curb to pass the car in front of him, scraping his bumper down its side, and gets away.

Spenser blames himself for letting them nearly box him in, feeling he should have noticed them sooner: "I was too busy arguing patristic nomenclature with you."

Not bad for a man who just eluded two cars that tried to force him off the road in order to kill the woman he was protecting. The remark is clever, belittling and dignifying the subject at the same time, while demonstrating Spenser's facility with language and the concept and mocking the discussion, him, and her by the use of the literate prose. Moreover, he does this with a short, descriptive sentence that is spot on. A trial attorney's long-winded argument, citing precedent after precedent, could not convey more than his simple statement does.

Later, in the bar, Rachel describes the incident to her friend, Julie, suggesting that Spenser may have made up the whole thing: "Well, I was on the floor, and he swerved around a lot, and then the car behind us was gone. I can't speak for sure myself. And if I were convinced no one were after me, Spenser would be out of work."

Spenser retorts: "Aw, you'd want me around anyway. All you chicks want a guy to look after you."

The comment is short, punchy, and effective, neatly dismissing Rachel's insinuation by ignoring it, and using an outrageous barb particularly offensive to a feminist. The fact that Julie is Rachel's lover adds yet another dimension to the wisecrack.

Spenser's quips are often deceptively simple. "I'm going to beat your man," Spenser tells Kevin Bartlett in *God Save the Child*, "so you'll know it can be done." Spenser needs to kill a fourteen-year-old boy's admiration of the steroidal body builder. The only way to do it is by beating the guy senseless. Which he proceeds to do. But that simple declarative statement of intent, confident, assured, matter-of-fact, is probably as impressive as the actual act. And this is usually the way Spenser behaves: forthrightly, with little guile.

On the other hand, his humorous quips often have layers of meaning. When Rachel's editor expresses surprise that Spenser has read the feminist book *The Second Sex*, Spenser says: "Don't tell the guys down the gym. They'll think I'm a fairy."

He is joking, yet the remark is absolutely true. The guys at the gym would find his choice of reading matter effeminate and subject for ridicule. And yet the remark is still facetious, because, while this might be true, it would not bother Spenser one bit. The opinion of ignorant louts who know no better does not concern him. He would think nothing of reading a book in the aforementioned locker room, and if some steroidal blockhead took it as a sign of weakness and decided to pick on him, he would be confident he could put the jerk in his place. Though he wouldn't feel it necessary to demonstrate his physical superiority, he would be quite content in issuing a verbal slap-down, whether his taunter could understand it or not. In either case, he would be calm, controlled, and comfortable in his own skin.

Through comments like these, too, we begin to see who Spenser is. His remarks embody a whole philosophy, a whole lifestyle, an attitude toward the world. We see here, for instance, that he doesn't care what (most) people think of him. The same is true in a strip club in *Ceremony*, where Spenser is looking for a teenage prostitute named April Kyle and is menaced by three toughs: "Come on, smart ass . . . We going someplace and see how tough you are."

Spenser replies, "You can find that out right now. I'm tough enough not to go."

It doesn't matter whether these toughs believe Spenser can take them. He knows he can hold his own. And that's all he needs.

That Spenser can sit calmly and wisecrack while being threatened just emphasizes how tough he is. Even in danger, Spenser's wit never leaves him. If anything, the worse the odds against him, the more he quips—and the more brazenly insulting those quips become. In *Early Autumn*, when he beards crime boss Harry Cotton and three goons in the man's office, Harry says, "I don't want you sticking your nose into my business, you unnerstand?"

Spenser replies, "Understand, Harry. With a *D*. Un-der-stand. Watch my lips."

Harry's voice gets shriller: "Shut your fucking mouth. And keep your fucking nose out of my fucking business or I'll fucking bury you right here, right out front here in the fucking yard I'll bury you."

Spenser, to the boy, who he brought with him: "Five. Five *fucks* in one sentence, Paul. That's colorful. You don't see color like that much anymore."

It's actually two sentences, but the gangster doesn't notice. He's too busy failing miserably at intimidating Spenser.

Spenser frequently uses humor to deflect his own vulnerability—not just physically, but emotionally, too.

In *The Judas Goat*, Susan gets misty because Spenser is leaving for London on a dangerous case.

> "I'll come back," I said. "I won't die away from you."
>
> "Oh, Jesus," she said, and her voice filled.
>
> My throat was very tight and my eyes burned. "I know the feeling," I said. "If I weren't such a manly bastard, I might come very close to sniffling myself."

He won't, but he feels that way. And he's not afraid to express it, even if it does come veiled in a wisecrack. Humor is an important part of how Spenser expresses intimacy.

For instance, in a restaurant where he takes Rachel, Spenser encounters Susan sitting at the bar next to a young man who is trying to pick her up.

> "This is Tom," she said. And then with the laughing touch of evil in her eyes she said, "Tom was nice enough to buy me a glass of Chablis."
>
> I said to Tom, "That's *one*."

Susan gets it, but Tom is confused. Spenser tells him it's the tag line to an old joke, but he doesn't tell him the joke, which could practically be a parable from *The Taming of the Shrew*: A man and his new bride are riding home on a donkey. The donkey stumbles, the man says, "That's one." The donkey stumbles again, the man says, "That's two." The donkey stumbles a third time, and the man takes out a gun and shoots him dead. The wife, horrified, berates her husband for his cruelty. He waits until she's finished, then points at her and says, "That's one."

This is typical Spenser, not sharing the joke with Tom but enjoying it as an in-joke with Susan. In two words, their relationship is succinctly defined. They have a companionable intimacy that allows each of them to understand what the other is thinking. Spenser would not have taken the guy out and shot him, and they both know it. Still, he is Susan's protector, and she is comfortable with that and loves him for it, in spite of the violence within him and the violent lifestyle that being with him exposes her to. She's also comfortable and conversant with his sense of humor.

When Susan Silverman catches him watching a girl in a white T-shirt and no bra walking away, she says, "That a suspect?"

Despite the implication that he is a sexist pig, his response is not the least defensive. He quips: "Remember I'm a licensed law officer. I was checking whether those cut-off jeans were of legal length."

And Susan is not offended by the remark, because she knows for all his macho joking, he is actually a feminist at heart.

Humor is also a key part of Spenser's relationship with the other most important person in his life: Hawk.

Hawk wasn't always Spenser's friend, of course. They started out as respected adversaries, back in the days when Hawk was an enforcer for mob boss King Powers. In *Promised Land*, Spenser warns Hawk of a police setup. Later, Hawk refuses his boss's order to kill Spenser.

After it all goes down, Susan asks him, "Why not, Hawk? I knew you wouldn't but I don't know why."

Hawk shrugs: "Me and your old man there are a lot alike.

I told you that already. There ain't too many of us left, guys like old Spenser and me. He was gone there'd be one less. I'd have missed him. And I owed him one from this morning."

The wry end of his explanation only underscores their similarity.

Once Hawk becomes Spenser's best friend, his former mob connections sometimes prove humorous; it is a joke shared between them. In *Early Autumn*, when they are working out on the speed bags at the Harbor Health club, Hawk gets a phone call from Harry Cotton, the mob boss Spenser taunted, who has just put out a contract on Spenser's life. Hawk comes back rather amused. Spenser asks:

> "That him on the phone?"
>
> "Yeah. He want me to whack you." Hawk's smile got wider. "He ask me if I know who you are. I say, yeah, I think so."
>
> I did a left jab and an overhead right.
>
> "How much he offering," I said.
>
> "Five Gs."
>
> "That's insulting," I said.
>
> "You'd have been proud of me," Hawk said. "I told him that. I said I wouldn't do it for less than ten."

That isn't the only subject that should be sensitive between them but isn't. Hawk often falls into parodies of racial stereotypes when talking to Spenser, who gives it right back. In *The Judas Goat*, Spenser picks up Hawk in the airport:

> I saw him leaning back in a chair with his feet on a suitcase and a white straw hat with a lavender band and a broad brim tipped forward over his face. He had on a dark blue three-piece suit, with a fine pinstripe of light gray, and a

white shirt with a collar pin underneath the small tight four-in-hand knot of a lavender silk tie. The points of a lavender handkerchief showed in his breast pocket. His black over-the-ankle boots gleamed with wax. The suitcase on which they rested must have cost half a grand. Hawk was stylish.

I said, "Excuse me, Mr. Fetchit, I've seen all your movies and was wondering if you'd care to join me for a bite of watermelon."

Hawk didn't move. His voice came from under the hat. "Y'all can call me Stepin, bawse."

But where Spenser and Hawk often kid like that, Spenser is sensitive to racial slurs from other people, and even before he and Hawk are friends, he is ready rush to his defense. In *Promised Land,* he tells Susan,

> "I got no special interest in playing Russian roulette with Hawk. Shepard called him a nigger."
>
> Susan shrugged. "What's that got to do?"
>
> "I don't know," I said. "But I wish he hadn't done that. It's insulting."
>
> "My God, Spenser, Hawk has threatened this man's life, beaten him up, abused his children, and you're worried about a racial slur?"

Spenser has his own code of honor—even though others don't always understand it, and even though he frequently sounds as if he doesn't take it seriously. At one point in *Early Autumn,* Spenser beats up the thugs trying to kidnap Paul. As they slink away, one taunts Spenser for not killing them, as if it is a fault: "You never were a shooter . . . It's what's wrong with you."

The boy asks Spenser why he doesn't kill people. Spenser says, "Something to do with the sanctity of life. That kind of stuff."

Except Spenser actually believes what he's saying. He's expressing a moral code he actually agrees with, while at the same time scoffing at it as a silly idea. Which, of course, is actually ridiculing the notion that the sanctity of life *is* a silly idea.

Spenser is always complicated. In *Pastime,* he finds himself confronted with Jerry Broz, a small-time mobster determined to kill him. Ordinarily, this would be no problem, because Jerry isn't good enough to do it. Spenser could easily take him out. But Jerry is the only son of Joe Broz, a crime boss who in the past has ordered Spenser killed himself. Joe feels Jerry is honor bound to kill Spenser and will not let his son back down, even though he knows Jerry isn't tough enough. Spenser doesn't want to kill Jerry, not because he's afraid of what Joe might do, but because he feels sorry for him and doesn't want to have to kill his son.

Susan says,

> "You are the oddest combination."
>
> "Physical beauty matched with deep humility?"
>
> "Aside from that," said Susan. "Except maybe for Hawk, you look at the world with fewer illusions than anyone I've ever known. And yet you are as sentimental as you would be if the world were pretty-pretty."

Spenser sees himself as a protector, a knight errant. As Susan explains to Rachel in *Looking for Rachel Wallace*:

> "What he [Spenser] won't say, and what he may not even admit to himself, is that he'd like to be Sir Gawain. He was

born five hundred years too late. If you understand that, you understand most of what you are asking."

"Six hundred years," I said.

Spenser makes a joke, but tellingly, he doesn't disagree with her.

Despite his often contentious relationship with Rachel, once hired, Spenser considers himself to be responsible for her. He never backs down defending her person and her honor against all comers, often against her will, until, finally fed up (with his actions, not his words), she fires him. Needless to say, he does not take firing personally, or at all, really, and when Rachel is kidnapped because she has no bodyguard, he still feels morally obliged to find her.

Spenser's role as the knight errant takes an unusual turn in *Promised Land*, in which Spenser is hired by Harvey Shepard to find his wife, Pam, who has run away. He finds her, talks to her, ascertains that she is healthy, happy, and not being held against her will, and then refuses to tell Harvey where she is. Spenser has decided Pam is better off where she is and the husband will only make her life miserable. On the other hand, he is willing to defend Harvey from the mob's chief enforcer, Hawk, who is, at the time, if not a personal friend, at least a respected adversary. This is not the action of the ordinary PI, but Spenser has his own code of ethics that he will not violate.

In not betraying Pam to her husband, Spenser is confident he made the right choice but he isn't happy about it. He feels he's failed them both. As he tells Susan, "I've been with two people whose lives are screwed up to hell and I just can't seem to get them out of it at all."

Susan, who understands him perfectly, has no problem putting it in perspective, with a humorous edge: "Of course you can't . . . You also can't do a great deal about famine, war, pestilence, and death."

Spenser immediately counters with a quip: "A great backfield."

Why does he care? It's not his problem. Is it because he took the job for the husband and failed to do it? Because his duty is to his client, but he can't bring himself to betray his client's wife?

He's hard on others who don't share his same sense of honor. Later in *Promised Land*, Spenser meets up with Pam, who has gotten involved with militant feminists who robbed a bank and shot and killed the guard. She is wearing large sunglasses, which she also wore for the robbery. Spenser tells her to ditch them, because they are no longer a disguise, they are a means of identification. The woman, feeling stupid about not having realized that, says, "I never thought—"

Spenser isn't about to let her off the hook.

"No, probably you don't have all that much experience at robbery and murder. You'll get better as you go along."

His scathing irony is doubtless due to the fact that she deserves it, but probably also out of the frustration he feels from realizing if he had told the husband where she was, he would have come and gotten her and she wouldn't have been involved in the robbery.

Susan tries to defend Pam: "She feels bad enough."

Which only frustrates Spenser more: "No, she doesn't. She doesn't feel anywhere near bad enough. Neither do you. You're so goddamned empathetic you've jumped into her frame. 'And you thought you felt you had to stand by them. Anyone would.' Balls. Anyone wouldn't. You wouldn't."

In tracking down evidence in *Mortal Stakes*, Spenser encounters a pimp named Violet, who refers him to Patricia Utley, the madam of a high-priced call girl service, who owns a four-story townhouse on the East Side of Manhattan. She talks of taking an eighteen-year-old hooker under her wing and teaching her how to talk to people, how to use makeup, how to dress.

"You and Rex Harrison," Spenser says. He doesn't mention *My Fair Lady*, but later in the same context calls her "Pygmalion," making his meaning clear. The literary allusions have an edge, ironically equating a sex-peddler with a professor of phonetics. And he doesn't let up, even though the woman is cooperating and giving him the information he needs. He sticks it to her for exploiting the girl: "You keep telling yourself you're a businesswoman and that's the code you live by. So you don't have to deal with the fact that you are also a pimp. Like Violet."

Spenser is so rude to the woman she has her goon throw him out. And yet he will turn to her years later, when faced with another moral dilemma: what to do with another teenage prostitute, April Kyle.

Spenser is often faced with moral dilemmas. He does not let them thwart him. As much as he may moralize them intellectually, he deals with them pragmatically. In *Ceremony*, he introduces April to Patricia Utley, the madam he denounced so eloquently for employing a teenage prostitute in *Mortal Stakes*. We have Spenser the panderer, enabling a teenage hooker—in effect, pimping for her. Has he changed his moral position? Not in the least. The one girl had a chance at a better life. The other did not. April would be turning tricks regardless. In Spenser's estimation, it would be better for her to be turning fewer tricks for a high-society madam, who would look after her health, than be a crack whore for some sleazeball who would beat her. Realizing this, Spenser doesn't hesitate to endorse a life of prostitution for the girl that he has worked so hard to save. As Susan points out during Spenser's struggle with Jerry and Joe Broz, Spenser's code is idealized; his view of the world is not.

In *Mortal Stakes,* Spenser empathizes with the baseball pitcher who is hopelessly conflicted because gamblers are threatening to reveal secrets about his wife's past unless he throws games. The man is torn between wanting to protect his family and not wanting to hurt his team.

As Spenser tells Susan,

"I know what's killing him. It's killing me too. The code didn't work."

"The code," Susan said.

"Yeah. Jock ethic, honor, code, whatever. It didn't cover this situation."

"Can't it be adjusted?"

"Then it's not a code anymore."

Yet that code is not inflexible. Though he believes in the sanctity of life, Spenser admits to Paul in *Early Autumn* that he has sometimes killed people: "I had to. I don't if I don't have to. Nothing's absolute."

"What do you mean?" Paul asks.

Spenser answers, "I mean you make rules for yourself and you know that you'll have to break them because they won't always work."

This is Spenser, plain and simple, the pragmatist, the knight in shining armor, the man with principles and ethics and a code of behavior who would readily toss it all out the window if the situation required. Unapologetically, and without making excuses. As he tells Paul, "Man's gotta do what he's gotta do, boy."

Spenser says it ironically, self-deprecatingly, mocking his bravado, and yet for him it is true. It is inherent in his code that a man has to do what he believes is right, no matter how difficult that may be. At the same time he sees the humor in that code, sees himself as a parody of a heroic figure, a lone knight championing a just cause, who won't back down, even from impossible odds. Despite his self-awareness, he is that which he mocks, a noble PI, armed and humorous, fighting valiantly to uphold his code of honor.

said, on a tradition that began in 1920. Within a handful of years, Spenser would sell in the millions and drag dozens of new private eye writers into print on the broad tails of his trenchcoat.

When a juggernaut like the Western cedes much of its share of the market to competitors, the talking heads take notice and write its obituary. They overlook the fact that no other genre has ever commanded so much attention. It stood to reason, given the spread of technology, from primitive video games to Twitter, that the Western would surrender its dominance. What it has done—as opposed to the fat historical melodramas of the 1950s and nearly all of so-called mainstream fiction—is survive. In theaters, it has outlasted the comedy short, the travelogue, and the cartoon. In 100 years, not a twelvemonth has passed that has not included a major Western motion-picture release.

The outlook was not so encouraging in bookstores, where the Western racks would have been crowded out the door long before by updated bodice-rippers, grunge-punk science fiction, and flashy techno-thrillers had not Louis L'Amour's books stood fast against the pressure, dozens at a time. Similarly, the long, quixotic, bantering, pugilistic history of the American private eye saga might have gone to the scrapheap but for the unavoidable sight of every title in the Spenser series lined up in a box display at the front of the shop.

Intellectuals—pale, dyspeptic creatures—wrung their hands at the public's poor taste. They'd rather we slogged our way through James Joyce or snarled our brains in the ropy dependent clauses of William Faulkner. Even that vulgarian Ernest Hemingway was preferable to a lug like Parker. Mickey Spillane dealt this kind of snobbery a devastating blow when some sourpuss pundit challenged him to defend the fact that seven of the ten then-bestselling novels of all time featured

Spillane's Mike Hammer: "You should be happy I didn't write three more."

While our melting-pot society was distractedly searching for its place in the cultural firmament, that spot was already being filled. Just as jazz and rock-and-roll built a national art form from material dismissed as junk, the Western and then the hardboiled detective story assumed its critical place alongside Shakespeare, Dickens, and Tolstoy, and they did it by way of dime novels and pulp magazines that were cheap enough to read and throw away—but not to forget.

How appropriate, then, that the publishing concern of Street & Smith gave us both Ned Buntline's many Buffalo Bill adventures in the Wild West and Carroll John Daly's Race Williams, private detective, thrillers in the era of Prohibition and Depression, as the rip-roaring Cody who appeared in print and the two-gun-packing Williams are one and the same: American originals, acting while others sit and make plans. A society born in the Caesarean throes of rebellion places its faith in heroes who operate outside established authority. Never mind that the hard-working, little-esteemed cowboy of frontier reality and the professional nine-to-five independent investigator of modern times bear small resemblance to their idealized counterparts in fiction. These men (and, increasingly, women) are heroes for hire, unique to a culture that lists individual initiative at the top of its virtues.

Now, the concept of the oak-hewn, native-born demigod is an impossible ideal. Inevitably, constant scrutiny and salacious revelation will break it to bits. But, as has been said, what we are and what we like to *think* we are say the same thing about us as a people. It's better to overreach than not reach at all, and to expect more than we get. Life must disappoint us in this. Good fiction never does.

Spenser is an icon straddling two centuries. Those who aren't familiar with his image in print know him through his characterizations on TV as presented by the late Robert Urich and the ubiquitous Joe Montegna. (At the time I interviewed Urich, while I was covering the taping of *Lonesome Dove* for *TV Guide*, I could not resist asking how he felt about the cancellation of *Spenser: For Hire* on ABC. He said that the network had made the decision to clear room for a new Aaron Spelling show, and that he was inconsolable over the loss of what he considered the role of a lifetime.) Spenser has even managed an enthusiastic endorsement in comic strips by way of Jimmy Johnson's Boomer-friendly *Arlo and Janis*, and has provided the clue to many a crossword-puzzle answer. Pop-culture immortality is the most enduring of all.

Women admire Spenser for his rugged good looks, his love of and respect for Susan Silverman—his brilliant and capable girlfriend—and his compassion. Men like him for his courage, strength, and determined self-sufficiency: *autonomy* is a favorite word in his vocabulary. He's a hit with cops, and that isn't an obvious slam-dunk in a genre that hasn't always paid strict attention to such trifles as standard police procedure and due process. A sergeant I rode along with years ago with the local county sheriff's department was such a fan that he carried extra copies of Parker's books in his patrol car to give out to people he encountered during the 4 p.m.-to-midnight shift—some of them suspects under arrest. He routinely sacrificed his meal break to raid the dumpsters behind bookstores for discarded paperbacks whose covers had been torn off to return to publishers when they failed to sell. His personal library of books without covers was one of the largest in Southeastern Michigan—although as Parker's popularity increased and his returns diminished, Spenser became scarce on his shelves.

Parker's cast of supporting characters is equally well-drawn as his lead. Susan Silverman, a licensed psychologist, is a devoted companion and a worthy adversary in the philosophical discussions that add a layer of dimension to Spenser's actions: Even a disastrous experiment in cohabitation, in *Double Deuce*, could not destroy their relationship. (Personally, I was surprised when it didn't work out: a man who shares beer from the same bottle with his Labrador retriever and a woman who calmly replaces the lid on a cooking stewpot after dropping it on the floor without pausing to rinse it off would suggest to me the ideal domestic arrangement. But who am I to judge? My wife washes fruit.)

Martin Quirk and Frank Belson, the Boston City police detectives who are always crossing Spenser's path, are tough *and* smart, which is not commonly the case when an outsider protagonist matches wits with them in this type of story. And the sinister Hawk—the psychopathic, atavistic Hawk, heir to the position once held by Injun Joe, Israel Hand, and the Golem—whom Parker once described as the kind of man Spenser might have become under other circumstances, is one of the standout characters in popular fiction. "Gonna get you killed someday, babe," Hawk says in *The Judas Goat* when Spenser tells him what he will and won't do. This unregenerate, cold-blooded killer has only one point of redemption: a loyalty to Spenser that parallels Doc Holliday's to Wyatt Earp. (Small wonder that *Gunman's Rhapsody*, Parker's take on the O.K. Corral gunfight, rings so familiarly.)

• •

I first became aware of Parker's series when my first novel, *Motor City Blue*, appeared and a number of reviewers compared my private detective, Amos Walker, to Spenser. The characters are demonstrably different, but they share the same sense of justice as well as the same profession. I tracked down and read the first three Spenser books and was hooked. In those days, before the rest of the world caught up, Parker was difficult to find in bookstores and libraries. Ironically, just about the time he broke through—it was around the time *A Savage Place* was published—I began to lose interest. It seemed to me that the detective had formed split personalities—a Duke Wayne larger-than-life avenger in one scene, an overly sensitive Alan Alda in another; Susan was usually present in the latter. Also, Hawk appeared to assume the convenient role of the vigilante extracting justice against the enemy, enabling Spenser to remain unsullied. It's only fair to add that at this point I'd been surviving on a steady diet of Robert B. Parker. One never does justice to a writer by reading a number of his books in close succession. The little repetitive mannerisms of style and characterization became painfully apparent.

So I navigated my own course—like Parker, in Westerns and modern-day suspense stories—sans Parker, until 1992, when the editors of the *New York Times Books Review* asked me to review *Double Deuce* for publication. I was delighted to find myself rekindling my romance with Spenser. The dialogue, which had always been razor-sharp and widely praised, was better than ever, and the descriptions of places and people were superior, contrary to Parker's own observation that "no writer likes to write description." Parker might not have liked it, but he had become one of the best at it. Perhaps he always was, and I had just forgotten during the long hiatus. In any case I bought his next and the next on my own and found again the old pleasure. It was like catching up with an old friend after many years and picking up exactly where we had left off.

Part of this renaissance may have had to do with the fact that Parker had found other things to write about in the interim. The Jesse Stone series, and later his authentic historical

Westerns, had provided a chance to rest and recuperate from the day-to-day ordeal of finding a new adventure worthy of his most famous creation. My own writing remains fresh, at least in my eyes, because I write different kinds of books. My daily shift is most diverting when I can go straight from Amos Walker to a Western, and from a Western to historical crime novels. I refer to this phenomenon as literary crop rotation, allowing one field to lie fallow and recoup its nutrients while working another. It's a sad business when someone recommends a writer, adding, "Read his early work. It's his best." In a perfect world, an artist should get better with each project, but even a Rembrandt can lose his appeal when he produces one self-portrait after another instead of trying something new.

Insofar as I can glean a colleague's theories on life based on his writings—always a dangerous assumption—I suspect Parker and I maintain the identical view that the world truly is good and evil, black and white. This is an unpopular conviction in these murky times; but I've found that if you study a situation long enough, you'll see the dividing line. While the conclusions you draw may be the precise opposite of another's having applied the same process, each is clearly separate. It's the people who insist that gray areas exist that you need to watch out for. The concept itself is evil. Spenser certainly knows the difference. So, in his way, does Hawk, although the approach he takes frequently places him on the side of the damned. The end never justifies the means. If the means don't justify themselves regardless of the result, good has not been served.

Spenser first appeared in 1973. The timing is significant. When the private eye of fiction made his debut, Prohibition was the law of the land. A major war had been fought to preserve a way of life that was destroyed by the war itself.

The great engines of destruction had for the first time been turned wholesale upon civilians. Newspaper readers learned of foreign slaughter in the telegraph columns and of civil war in their own cities on the front page. An ordinary citizen was fined or jailed for having a bottle of liquor in his pocket by a judge who was having lunch that day with a bootlegger. The police, our last lines of defense against crime, accepted bribes to look the other way while the laws of the republic were shattered. The president of the United States accepted alcohol deliveries through the back door of the White House. A crook who ought to be breaking into houses at night and hiding out when the sun was up rode in an armor-plated Cadillac in broad daylight, wearing a two-hundred-dollar suit. As the drunken 1920s awakened to the hangover of the Great Depression, the American Dream vanished, along with the jobs of millions, to reappear in the private holdings of greedy bankers and corrupt politicians. Readers, moviegoers, and radio audiences turned for distraction not to the symbols of official law enforcement, but to some small-time crusader as poor and as fed up as they were, determined to hurl a monkey wrench into the infernal machine.

In the second year of Watergate, with the bloodbath of Vietnam subsiding to expose a humiliating defeat for America, the country was once again ready for just such a hero. Enter Spenser in *The Godwulf Manuscript*: "I went to college once. I don't wear my hat indoors. And if a clue comes along and bites me on the ankle I grab it. I am not, however, an Oxford don. Now, is there something you'd like me to detect . . . ?"

No posturing there. No political doublespeak, no patience for lecturing and persiflage. And the very name, two simple syllables, no messing around with even a given name, rings with the epic poetry of the era of knighthood and holy quests. The man's business cards show a pair of crossed swords, for

Pete's sake! Rarely since a youthful John Wayne strode from the Sonoran Desert into the center frame of *Stagecoach* had America seen a man who so emphatically announced himself as a hero at first sight.

Well, that may be laying it on a bit thick, but there is more of Wayne in the character than of Humphrey Bogart, the private eye icon on film. Spenser is a big man who works out with weights, dishes up his own grub (albeit gourmet style), and wastes little time putting belligerent living obstacles in their place—usually the floor. He has battered his way out of impossible situations with nothing more than his fists and on one occasion nothing larger than a .25-caliber semiautomatic pistol, which can be mistaken for a novelty cigarette lighter. Nearly as often, however, he fails and is injured severely. But Superman without Kryptonite would be a one-note character. Admire him as one likes, and wish to be him as one prefers, the reader never identifies with him as thoroughly as when he's taking a beating.

Despite its crusty exterior, the private eye story is pure romance. The investigators who advertise online and in the yellow pages spend most of their time interviewing witnesses to traffic accidents, turning over dusty pages in libraries and county records offices, and calculating billable hours before presenting statements to their clients. (The notorious day rate plus expenses, like the fast-draw at high noon, is a literary invention.) Their clients are usually lawyers. They avoid such sleuthing staples as climbing fire escapes and picking locks and, should their efforts uncover official business like murder, they report it to the police and then get out of their way, thus sparing themselves that lecture about losing their license. Although every detective who's practiced for a number of years has encountered adventures enough to fill a book, it takes a hero to satisfy the requirements of a series.

Dashiell Hammett, a former Pinkerton operative, and Joe Gores, also once a licensed private detective, knew all this, and gave the Continental Op and the DKA Agency a solid foundation of day-to-day routine investigative work for their characters to step off from into uncharted territory. Similarly, Spenser's treks begin with a simple missing-person case, an item of stolen property, bodyguard duty—then turn into something far less prosaic. But the fate of the human animal is always the first concern. (Hammett's Maltese Falcon, we must remember, was nothing more than an elaborate red herring to divert the reader from Miles Archer's murder.)

• •

Parker based his doctoral thesis on the works of Hammett, Chandler, and Macdonald, drawing a straight line between the frontier novels of James Fenimore Cooper and the seedy world of Philip Marlowe. Yet, as his own series progressed, the differences between Marlowe and Spenser piled up until there was no confusing the two. Following tradition, Marlowe is a loner. After a brief dalliance with Brenda Loring (no relation to Chandler's Linda Loring; but my suspicion is that his decision to drop her had not a little to do with the uncomfortable parallel. Our narrow area of endeavor often opens itself to charges of undue influence), Spenser formed a lasting romantic attachment with Susan Silverman. Marlowe keeps his emotions to himself, lest he appear vulnerable to the enemy; Spenser doesn't hesitate to open up to Susan and Hawk, lest the pressures of his work crack him apart. Marlowe distrusts women; Spenser respects them. (For a time, feminism provided a major theme for the series.) Marlowe's acerbic sense of humor is the only thing that prevents him from succumbing to depression; Spenser's wisecracks expose him as a smart-aleck. Not everything is to everyone's taste.

Some readers think Susan Silverman is a shrew. But no one gets any of these characters mixed up.

The point of the above is that Parker staked out his own territory, paying homage to the pioneers who had preceded him but announcing his independence of them. My own favorite guilty pleasure is *Early Autumn*, in which Spenser revolts against a bitterly divorcing couple's desertion of their child by taking the boy in hand and teaching him self-reliance. As the youth develops into an estimable young man exclusive of his parents' neglect, the story echoes Louis L'Amour's *Hondo* far more than any influence in the specialized world of conventional urban milieu of Parker's predecessors; it encroaches upon the turf of J.D. Salinger and other masters of American literature. Ross Macdonald, too, aspired to this connection with the American mainstream. One finishes *Early Autumn* with the same sense of satiation found at the end of Macdonald's *The Galton Case*: that one has digested a substantial work of literature and been transcended by it.

This expansion on the part of genre fiction beyond the bounds of category—the nerve to annex social commentary to the business of fighting injustice—rang the death knell for the mainstream novel. Once its walls were breached, it had no course but retreat. Popular entertainment (that condescending label assigned to everything outside mainstream) already had numbers on its side. Once social commentary came into the mix, the sky was the limit.

Parker's sense of place rivals that of the great literary masters. Boston is at least as important to the Spenser series as Spenser is. For me, whenever the trail leads him out of town, the story becomes generic. It's clear that Parker is intimate with his setting, as Chandler was with Los Angeles and Ross Macdonald was with all of California. The West Coast plays a prominent role in so much detective fiction (a calculated one, in some cases; old-time Hollywood preferred to buy properties that could be filmed at home) that when cities like Boston, Chicago, Cleveland, and Detroit began to show up in the second great wave of private eye tales that started in the 1970s, critics coined the phrase "regional mysteries" to define the phenomenon, as if Los Angeles and San Francisco were any less provincial than Springfield, U.S.A.

Parker's is not the city of Beacon Hill, Fenway Park, and baked beans—although with the exception of beans he would not overlook these threads in the local fabric. It's a gritty, aging powderkeg, a place of private estates and public housing projects where the privileged and underprivileged classes cloister behind high walls, a place where speeding cars bent on dark errands thunder over streets stained with the blood of patriots, home of sinister family secrets and the Tenderloin. In his hands alone it has risen to a level in suspense lore beside Sax Rohmer's Limehouse and Arthur Conan Doyle's Baker Street. He paved the way for the careers of fellow Bostonians Dennis Lehane, Matt Damon, Ben Affleck, and Mark Wahlberg.

Not that he spends much time on physical details, of his city or anything else. He's a lean writer—gaunt would not be overselling the case—and in a publishing climate that encourages 500-page tomes on the theory of marketing by the pound, a typical Spenser weighs in at less than two hundred. For a while (it was during that bleak period when I suspect Parker had lost his taste for Spenser through overfamiliarity), the production team at his publishing house introduced wide margins and a typeface nearly large enough for you to put your fist through the Os to keep the books from being lost among the travel pamphlets in bookstores. Later, when the Parker-Spenser love affair had begun all over again, the novels acquired more meat and a new energy level, but they never lost muscle or gained fat. In this area, Parker's writing more closely resembles the rendered-down prose of Hammett, whose spare use of San Francisco landmarks could place his setting in 2012 as easily as 1925, than Chandler's evocative descriptions of wooden oil derricks and flourishing orange groves in his period's San Fernando Valley.

Despite a Best Mystery Novel Edgar and a Grand Master Award from the Mystery Writers of America, as well as his towering stature in the community, Parker's books rarely involve mysteries in the traditional sense, i.e., raising a compelling question (most often "whodunit?") that is answered in the closing pages. They're more suspenseful than puzzling, and belong more to the action genre than to the conventional detective story. Spenser acquires the information necessary to complete his assignment less by assembling physical clues and comparing timetables than by cornering those who have the information and pressuring them to divulge it, usually by dint of his formidable physical presence. To this end, the amount of time he spends in the gym and doing roadwork, his healthy eating, his moderation in drinking, and his long-ago success in quitting smoking are tools crucial to his vocation rather than just tropes to define character. (One wonders, a la the old Batman-versus-Superman debate, how the chain-smoking, whiskey-swilling Marlowe would fare in a toe-to-toe slugfest with Spenser. Certainly, Hammett's suety Continental Op would be forced to rely more on his world-weary wits than on his brawn.)

• •

Spenser has been a part of the landscape so long it's difficult to imagine a time when he was unknown. It's like watching Wyatt Earp introducing himself in the first reel of a Western and getting no reaction from the rest of the cast. But I doubt Parker's editors at Houghton Mifflin heard a choir when his first typescript arrived in the slush pile. Quite likely they greeted it with the same jaundiced eye they brought to my *Motor City Blue* six years later, as a nice neat potboiler worth gambling a token advance on but no commitment beyond that. A tombstone advertisement in the *New York Times* and advance reading copies sent to the usual suspects for comment and review would probably have been the extent of the promotion, possibly with some signings at Boston-area bookstores. Full-page screamers, multiple-city tours, and guest spots on national TV talk shows are for established performers who hardly need the push.

Yet the reviews were excellent—quotes from the earliest still appear on his dust jacket flaps—and sales were sufficient to justify bringing out a second entry, *Mortal Stakes*. I worked with some of the same staff at Houghton Mifflin later, and I'm happy to report they were patient and willing to let a writer who showed promise find his audience. This was the last generation in publishing that bought bestsellers in order to subsidize books they *wanted* to publish, which was a good working premise for more than a century. When it was abandoned, and each title was expected to pull its own weight, the first tiny fissures appeared in the foundation of an industry that is still tottering.

This willingness to take a chance in the publishing world was vital to Parker's success, since I think the series didn't really take off commercially until *Looking for Rachel Wallace* in 1980. The gender-equality issues had hardened into a solid theme, and Spenser's desperate obsession with finding and rescuing the eponymous heroine swept critics and the public along on a wild ride at a pace usually confined to globe-trotting thrillers in which the fate of the world is at stake. Word-of-mouth had caught up with Spenser. From then on, he was an institution.

For which I'm grateful. By this time, the series had moved to Delacorte, and probably some at Houghton Mifflin were regretting having let it go. It was in this mood that my *Motor City Blue* came in over their transom, with a brand-new private eye starting his career in the even more outlandish city of Detroit.

Meanwhile, private eye fiction's fortunes had changed. A tide of new readers had carried in a boatload of new titles from as far away as Australia, and an organization was founded to promote the interests of writers of private detective stories, who only a few years earlier could have held their convention in a telephone booth. From out of this new wave came Sara Paretsky and Sue Grafton. They weren't the first to showcase female private eyes—Marcia Muller had beaten them to it, and there were a few even in the heyday of the pulps, usually created by male writers—but they were a far cry from the slinky *femmes fatales* and helpless ingénues of the testosterone-fueled Golden Age, when an inordinate number of scantily clad women appeared bound and gagged on lurid magazine covers. Surely Parker's strong female characters, and Spenser's willingness to acknowledge their strength, helped prepare the readership for this new direction in literary evolution.

Sadly, it's uncertain whether today's bottom-line publishing requirements would have given the Parker-Spenser collaboration the time it needed to develop. Many houses—forgetting that few of the longest-running franchises stayed at one place—won't take on a series dropped by a competitor, believing that where one enterprise failed another cannot succeed. There's no telling how many promising properties have been left adrift by this notion, abandoned by their creators or stranded in the ghetto of self-publishing, which rarely leads to success or respect.

Some years ago, Sara Paretsky protested an insider's decision that a first novel had to sell 15,000 copies or the writer's contract would be dropped. She reminded the party that the first several titles in her smashingly successful V.I. Warshawski series didn't sell nearly that many. The unspoken question was, where did publishers think the next Paretsky was coming from? Or the next Robert B. Parker?

I'm an optimist, however. I prefer to think that talent will find a way. It wasn't long ago that Ace Atkins, who continues the Spenser tradition, broke into print through the auspices of an editor with vision and influence. We're fortunate to have him in this position: Spenser needs a writer of skill and determination to uphold his standard, and we aren't ready to let him go. The times are ripe. An unnecessary recession caused by greedy bankers and weak-willed politicians must result in a fresh and eager audience for a modern knight-errant bent on justice. And I've a strong feeling that Parker, a dedicated artist of passion who passed away while at work at his desk, would agree with the choice of Atkins to continue the series.

Spenser is just too big for one career to encompass.

BOB, BOSTON, AND ME

A REMEMBRANCE

| JEREMIAH HEALY |

WRITERS OF CRIME fiction tend to be cooperative—even collaborative—as opposed to competitive. When I broke into the mystery field during the mid-'80s, however, this "we all live in the same village" ethos within a profession was, quite frankly, surprising to me. An illustration: If Author A was contacted by a library to give a talk, A—as part of the village protocol—would suggest the inclusion of Authors B and C as well, usually with diversity of gender and sub-genre, so that all three authors could appeal diagonally to members of the audience who might have attended to see only one of them.

By then, I'd already experienced mini-careers as a sheriff's officer and military police lieutenant, trial attorney and law professor. Each of those vocations stressed team-first, yes, but given the fields involved, daily life became a confrontational, us-versus-them dynamic (including, even, the law professor/student one, which uses confrontation in order to meld the latter into the best advocate he or she can be). Over time, though, my reaction to our crime-writers' village evolved from surprised to reassured, especially when a marquee author was not just willing, but actually enthusiastic, about sharing the ephemeral spotlight.

Looking back, of all my colleagues, the one who did the most for my own career was Bob Parker. And, for the record, it was always either Bob or Mr. Parker, never Robert. In addition, although many of us think of him as the iconic Robert B. Parker, I never heard the man say or saw him write his middle name, which was Brown.

● ●

The first decade of our twenty-first century proved tragic in terms of losing American giants of crime fiction: Ed McBain (formally, Evan Hunter, though, by birth, Salvatore Lombino) and Dennis Lynds (a.k.a. Michael Collins), Tony Hillerman and Donald E. Westlake (a.k.a. Richard Stark), James Crumley and Mickey Spillane, William G. Tapply and Stuart M. Kaminsky.

And, so suddenly on January 18, 2010, the giant I knew best: Robert B. Parker, who set most of his many Spenser novels in and around our shared city of Boston.

Appropriately, there have been numerous obituaries published and posted since Bob's death. And by age seventy-seven, he'd certainly excelled in many spheres: Army service in Korea; marriage to the love of his life, Joan; the fathering of two sons, David and Daniel; and, lastly, becoming—and even more difficult, remaining—a bestselling crime author.

I first discovered his novels in the winter of 1978 while frantically shopping at the Walden's Books in Boston's Center Plaza for paperbacks to read on the planes (four of them, each way) that would take my then-to-be-bride and me to and from the then-remote island of Bonaire, off the coast of Venezuela, for our honeymoon. Prior to that day in the Walden's, I'd certainly enjoyed the occasional mystery, but I'd never heard of Mr. Parker. The book that I picked up off the shelf and opened was his first Spenser from five years earlier, *The Godwulf Manuscript.* I remember laughing—loud and long—after reading just the first sentence:

> The office of the university president looked like the front parlor of a successful Victorian whorehouse.

Thankfully, I was still a trial attorney then, wearing a three-piece suit, and therefore avoided arrest or civil commitment because of my outburst.

I could not, as they say, put Bob's debut down. In fact, I re-read it twice during that stay on Bonaire, trying to figure out, in a lawyerly fashion, how he'd managed to pull off the most entertaining story I'd experienced over the prior twenty years. Six months later, I began teaching at the New England School of Law (now renamed "New England Law: Boston") but continued to be a fan of Spenser. When assured I was going to receive tenure (the dream of every Irish-American male: lifetime employment, inside work, no heavy-lifting), I said to myself, "Okay, you've always wanted to write a novel, and you've been reading and enjoying private-investigator fiction (Marcia Muller, Bob Parker, and, stretching the category a little, John D. MacDonald). Maybe you'll enjoy writing such a book and, even if you don't succeed in getting it published, you'll have had fun trying."

Incorporating aspects of my law—and law enforcement—backgrounds, the writing of my first novel, *Blunt Darts*, was truly a blast. The selling, however? Eh, not so much.

I'd arrogantly concluded that any New York publishing house in its collective right mind would jump at the chance to provide its customers with a(nother) tough but sensitive male private eye operating out of Boston. I even naively submitted to the New England publishing house that was then bringing out Bob's books about Spenser, an established main character who shared a lot of traits with my own embryonic private eye, John Francis Cuddy.

Twenty-eight rejections later, I was humbled but unbowed (as a trial attorney, you learn to put losses behind you and continue plowing forward). Then the late lamented doyenne of mystery editors, Ruth Cavin, offered me a contract for *Blunt Darts*. When the paperback edition was released, I timidly introduced myself to Kate Mattes (of the also late and lamented Murder Under Cover bookstore in Cambridge, Massachusetts). Kate was happy to schedule a future signing for my second, accepted (but not yet published) novel, *The Staked Goat*. However, she also encouraged me to speak during the interim with her friend, Mr. Parker, about how the mystery-writing industry really worked.

Bob graciously agreed to meet me at Grille 23, an upscale restaurant in a Boston neighborhood called the Back Bay. Coincidentally (or maybe not), the grill was on Berkeley Street directly opposite the then–Boston police headquarters building (now itself a fancy hotel with a downstairs bar, called Jury's, perversely positioned right about where the recently collared would while away time awaiting arraignment in court). A reporter from a national magazine was later to interview Bob over dinner at the grill, and since I both lived and worked just blocks away, a drink with me beforehand seemed logistically sensible.

Not surprisingly, the prospect of meeting my writing idol made me a little jittery. Therefore, I arrived at the restaurant early, taking an empty barstool with a twin adjacent to it.

Funny, the trivial details that lodge in your data bank. As though it were yesterday, I clearly recall ordering a screw-driver (for the viceless: vodka and orange juice), though light on the alcohol, because I wanted to make a good first impression on Mr. Parker.

I'd brought a legal pad to jot down expected pearls of wisdom, but nothing to read, so I doodled a pretty elaborate floor plan and description of the bar and the restaurant behind it. Oddly, though, while I often try to capture as research settings that I'm visiting for the first time, I've never used Grille 23 in either a novel or a short story. In fact, I don't think I've even previously alluded to the place.

As soon as Bob came through the grill's front door, I recognized him—sort of—from his small, grainy book-cover portrait(s).

I'll confess: While I don't think I knew then that Robert Urich (since, tragically, deceased as well) was to be the first actor portraying Spenser (and more about this casting decision later), I suppose I did expect Bob Parker, life-sized, to fit my internal vision of his private eye character: Around six-foot-two, a raw-boned one-ninety-plus, with a nose broken and fixed so many times that, at different stages of his prior career as a prizefighter, its tip probably inclined toward each point of the compass.

Ah . . . no.

Envision instead a former college professor, about five-foot-eight and stocky, with close-cropped dark hair and a matching mustache framing and accenting the ruddy, moon-like face of a mischievous Buddha. If you, like me, were then a boxing fan, Bob could have been the older, shorter brother of George Chuvalo (Canada's best-ever heavyweight, and one of the few athletes in all of pugilistic history to have fought over ninety bouts without once being knocked off his feet and onto the canvas).

Grille 23's bar (and adjoining restaurant) being virtually empty, Bob homed in on me as well, perhaps helped a little by my hopping down off the stool and extending my right hand toward a manly shake.

His first words to me were, "Glad you're already here, be-cause you're covering our bar tab."

As Bob ordered an Amstel draught, I knew I'd just met not only my idol, but also my mentor for this new career of crime-writing, especially when he told me to call him Bob.

I remember pretty much our entire conversation that eve-ning. After a brief and awkward exchange of small talk, Bob asked, "So, Jerry, what can I tell you?"

I got right to the point and said, "What's your best advice about making a living from writing mystery fiction?"

A sip of his beer. "That's easy. You know much about real estate?"

Well, before that night, I'd bought one condominium, sold it myself, then bought another, also on my own, and as an attorney I'd represented a number of unit-buyers and -sellers. So, I said, "Some."

"Okay, then." Another swig of the Amstel, and Bob began warming to his subject. "You've probably heard about the three priorities in real estate."

I nodded. "Location, location, location."

Bob's turn to nod. "Well, there's a cousin to that priority system for the writer in the publishing game today."

"Being . . . ?"

Bob smiled so intensely that his eyes actually squinched shut from below. "Get an agent, get an agent, get an agent."

Back in the day, an aspiring writer who didn't yet have a literary agent could still—as I had—submit an entire manuscript directly to pretty much any editor at the thirty-seven (now, arguably only six) well-regarded publishing houses in New York City and beyond. (Another factoid: The expression "sent in over the transom" for an unsolicited manuscript came from the century-old practice of frustrated first-time novelists, whom an editor would not deign to see personally, literally hurling their manuscripts through the opened casement window at the top of the editor's otherwise closed/locked door. For my money, though, at least that desperate practice was slightly nobler than the breach of etiquette a female literary agent shared with me maybe ten years ago. Attending a writers' conference, she was sitting on a ladies' room toilet only to first hear, and then look down to see, a manuscript being slid under her stall's door.)

I fiddled some with my glass. "But, Bob, I'm an attorney who's represented writers against their publishers, and as a professor I've even written a scholarly article about authors' rights in book contracts. Why should I give a literary agent ten [soon to be fifteen] percent of my next advance?"

Now Bob shook his head. "You negotiated your own first deal yourself, right?"

"Right."

"Did you think to retain your subsidiary rights?"

"Like for movie or television adaptations? Sure."

Bob's eyebrows went up. "Good. How about paperback reprint rights?"

Already happened. "The hardcover publisher and I split those."

"Unfair to the writer, but typical of a publisher. Foreign rights?"

Embarrassingly, I hadn't read my own publishing contract for nearly two years. "I think we split translation rights, too."

Another shake of the head. "On those, you should get a hundred percent. How much did you get as an advance for the hardcover?"

I told him.

Bob asked, "And how much did your paperback reprint rights go for?"

There'd been an auction on those, so I answered, proudly, "My share was within a thousand dollars of my annual salary a decade ago as a first-year associate at a prestigious Boston law firm."

A third sip of his beer. "Jerry, how *much?*"

I told him that, too.

Bob whistled. Softly, but still . . . "All right, now double your half share of the reprint auction and ask for an advance in that range, because your track record—granted, so far a pretty short one—proves your worth to a publisher worried about the bottom-line of profitability."

I expect my expression was akin to a cow's as the sledge-hammer descends toward its forehead.

Benignly, Bob waved a hand. "Not to worry, but that's what literary agents are for." He took a full three swallows of the Amstel, as if pre-hydrating toward a long speech. "As a lawyer—and 'scholar'—you probably do know more about how to interpret a specific paragraph in a publishing contract and then also how to convince a court you're right. However, what you don't know—and maybe even can't know—is whether that paragraph is an iron-clad dealbreaker or whether it's negotiable. You also don't know what other provisions, helpful to you, aren't in the house's offer, and two minutes ago you obviously didn't have a sense of what you'd be worth to a publisher. Agents do have a grip on all three issues, because they're in the New York market every day. Hell, they gather together for lunch probably once a month, minimum, to compare notes. And therefore agents also know which editors are leaving their current houses to work for a competitor but can't take all of their valuable stable of authors with them. Or, maybe word's leaked that an established writer is leaving his or her current publisher, and the bereft editor there now has an unexpected slot to fill in the next season's schedule." Another sip, nearly finishing the Amstel, and Bob glanced at his watch, cuing me to subtly signal our bartender for "my" check.

Then Bob sighed. "Another thing. Your literary agents will also have corresponding agents on the West Coast for those movie/TV rights you were smart to keep. And similar agents overseas for selling those foreign rights on future books you shouldn't have shared on the first."

A guy—early thirties, scribe-like—came through the grill's front door, flicking his gaze around the place. Bob turned his head before turning back to me. "With any luck, that's the reporter whose rag is treating me to dinner."

Bob and I both left our perches and shook hands again.

I said, "Truly, thank you for all this. You've really broadened my whole approach to the industry."

A twinkle in the eyes and the broad smile, once again seeming to close his lids from below. "Happy to help, but just don't eclipse me, okay? I'm too old to find a real job now."

As Bob walked toward the presumed reporter and I settled our tab, I stayed stuck on the "eclipse me" part, thinking, *Eclipse you? Please, Bob, just let this recovering lawyer ride lightly on your coattails.*

• •

Oddly enough, I don't recall us talking that first evening about the actual process of writing or any secrets of craft. Those I had to learn, sometimes the hard way, by reading the Spenser novels and then trying to replicate—though never managing to duplicate—Bob's kind of magic on my own pages.

Bob's first novel, *The Godwulf Manuscript*, is set almost entirely in geo-political Boston, including a great confrontation scene in the opulent Copley Plaza Hotel (opened in 1907 by transplanted San Franciscans fearing another earthquake, the dowager is now called the Fairmount Copley Plaza Hotel but still lies kitty-corner to the original wing of the Boston Public Library, itself the first such governmentally supported library in the United States). In his debut, however, Spenser is a bit of a hound with the ladies, including having sex with both a mother and her daughter (though not, in the interests of discretion, simultaneously). That inspired me to turn the Cuddy character 180 degrees: he remains faithful to the memory of his dead wife, including visiting her gravesite and creating conversations over the headstone, until he finds another woman who might replace her in his life.

In Bob's second novel, *God Save the Child* (set mostly on the suburban North Shore of Boston, where Joan and Bob lived while raising their sons), Spenser meets Susan Silverman. This is one path where I should not have followed behind Bob in lock-step. In my second novel, *The Staked Goat*, I gave Cuddy a new love interest, only to later realize I'd have had more creative freedom by keeping Cuddy a pure widower longer. That way, a reader coming upon any eligible, female character in a succeeding book could have been kept guessing whether or not she'd prove to be Ms. Right.

Mortal Stakes, the third Spenser novel, is again set almost entirely in Boston. The private eye takes on probably the most sacrosanct of the city's sports franchises, the Red Sox. To my knowledge, this is the first time Bob as author identifies the real-life institution he exposes. And a bold uncovering it is: Spenser investigates the possibility that a star Boston hurler is throwing games rather than just pitches to opposing teams. The novel begins with Spenser watching some innings from the stands at the Sox home field, Fenway Park (opened April 20, 1912, or two years before the Chicago Cubs' Wrigley Field). The story moves quickly to the team's broadcast booth, and Bob captures that rarified enclosure perfectly.

But how, you might ask, could I know that?

Well, a fan of mine, the late and much admired major-league pitcher Ken Brett, once invited me to sit, necessarily silently, in the visitor's broadcast booth during a road game for his Anaheim Angels (mercifully, this was a decade before some geographically challenged, front-office twit decided to re-name the team the Los Angeles Angels of Anaheim). Before the national anthem, Ken and his broadcast partner showed me how everything—and everyone—functioned. Then I got to absorb the calm, measured atmosphere during their live calling of the game followed by the absolute bedlam during commercial breaks, when people are demanding—or misplacing, or just plain guesstimating—statistics, public-service announcements, etc.

In *Mortal Stakes*, Bob doesn't hit a false note in describing the parallel scenario in the Red Sox booth, and the vigilante confrontation scene near the end of the novel taught me the crime-literature version of forcing the protagonist to face a dilemma of the "frying pan or the fire" variety, where there is no clean way to resolve the problem.

Bob's fourth novel, *Promised Land*, is set mostly in the vacation/retirement nirvana of Cape Cod and the gritty under-belly of the city of New Bedford, both about seventy miles south of Boston. This book introduces the Hawk character as an enforcer for the bad guys. Released in 1975, it was another brave decision by Bob to include a rough—indeed, homicidal—African-American male into a fictional Boston crime series during the city's real-life public school racial-integration crisis. For those not familiar with that era, white parents in various neighborhoods literally threw rocks at the windows of yellow—and unmistakable—school buses carrying black children into traditionally white educational districts. Several of my military police officer basic classmates were in the Massachusetts National Guard, and they were both mobilized from their civilian jobs and deployed in uniform on our streets for nearly two years, keeping the peace by commanding platoons of forty armed MPs.

But Bob—bless him—by writing exciting fiction involving Spenser and Hawk, eventually as grudging allies, then as the closest of friends, was able to inject some rationality and tolerance into a real-world situation sorely lacking in both. And that authorial risk-taking led me to foster a wary relationship between Cuddy the private eye and "Lieutenant Detective" Robert Murphy (more on this designation later). The fictional Murphy is an African-American on Boston's homicide unit who got elevated only because a bigoted but lackadaisical city councilor mistook the Irish surname on a departmental promotion list for the actual race of the officer involved.

As the above examples illustrate, Bob Parker had a great impact on yours truly. However, he had a much wider and deeper impact on Boston itself, establishing what might be America's most insular, aristocratic bastion as a credible city of mean streets, where even the rich and famous could find a corpse on their doorsteps. Bob proved through each succeeding novel that you could set a private investigator series realistically in metro areas outside of Raymond Chandler/

Philip Marlowe's Los Angeles, Dashiell Hammett/Sam Spade's San Francisco, or Mickey Spillane/Mike Hammer's New York City. Bob's/Spenser's groundbreaking in Boston's fertile earth planted the seeds that grew to produce an entire crop of so-called "regional" mysteries in other cities as well. Think Sara Paretsky/V.I. Warshawski's Chicago, Loren Estleman/Amos Walker's Detroit, and Benjamin M. Schutz/ Leo Haggerty's Washington, D.C. Not to mention Linda Barnes/Carlotta Carlyle, William G. Tapply/Brady Coyne, and my own Cuddy eagerly following the Bob/Spenser lead in Boston itself.

I can't speak for those other writers or their creative influences, but Bob taught me how to use Boston. Since neither of us had ever been a private investigator, we followed the mantra of fictional ones from the past (although when I once asked Bob what he had learned while researching, writing, and defending his doctoral thesis on Hammett, Chandler, and Ross Macdonald, Bob replied, "Absolutely nothing"). Accordingly we both put our Boston knights of yore in situations that no sane, real-life private eye would even consider, including performing vigilante acts of violence where, legally speaking, self-defense would not have been available as a shield from criminal or civil justice-system jeopardy. In fact, one of my favorite exchanges in Bob's books was a scene where a bloodied and bruised Spenser shows up at the Back Bay front door of a wimpy neo-Nazi who lives with his mother on Commonwealth Avenue, Boston's second toniest address (after Louisburg Square on Beacon Hill, where reside the fictional *Banacek*, played on television by the late George Peppard, the real-life medical-thriller author Robin Cook, and the almost-real-life U.S. Senator John Kerry). The vigilante exchange went something like this:

WIMP (cracking open the front door): I didn't have
    nothin' to do with your gettin' beat up.
SPENSER (barging across the threshold): Pity I won't be
    able to say the same about you.

• •

Another shared characteristic that I think informed—and
perhaps even formed—Bob and me: Neither of us was a
Boston native. He was born in Springfield, Massachusetts,
about ninety miles west of the city, and attended Colby
College in Waterville, Maine, about 215 miles north of
Boston. I was born in Teaneck, New Jersey, and attended
Rutgers University in the same state, respectively about 220
and 270 miles southwest of Boston. Alas, as a result, each of
us committed some ghastly authenticity gaffes related to our
adopted city.

Let me 'fess up first. I've found that the real subverter of authenticity is when you know you know something and therefore don't bother to confirm it by independent research. For
example, I had Cuddy credit the wrong architect for Boston's
(hideous) new city hall because, while once walking past it,
a law firm client—himself an architect—gave me the wrong
information. Another: I had Cuddy offhandedly allude to
Salem, Massachusetts, twenty miles north of Boston, as the
city where witches were burned at the stake. During an im-
pressionable stage of my youth, I must have seen the movie
Joan of Arc, because, as many readers later corrected me, that
barbaric custom had not been imported via our European
forebears. In the American colonies, women so accused suffered either hanging or trial by ordeal (the latter a lose-lose
proposition for the defendant that involved drowning).

As to Bob, I recall two Bostonian errors he'd habitually
make. First example: Spenser would be walking in the Back

Bay neighborhood, the only part of the city that follows a grid-pattern (like midtown Manhattan) in its lay-out. The Back Bay's real-life cross-streets are named (like midtown Manhattan's streets are numbered) in a strict, alphabetical order from A (Arlington) to H (Hereford). Yet, despite Bob's choosing the Back Bay for both his private eye's apartment (on Marlborough Street) and his office (on Boylston Street), Spenser would routinely skip over a cross-street, moving from say the C (Clarendon) to the E (Exeter), as though the D (Dartmouth) didn't exist in between.

Okay, as errors go, the "street names" might be off-putting to a Boston local but not rise to the level of ghastly. However, Bob also had Spenser repeatedly meeting with (the fictional) Lieutenant Marty Quirk and his partner, Sergeant Frank Belson, in their homicide unit offices at the then–police headquarters (which, as indicated earlier, coincidentally was across the street from Bob's and my initial rendezvous site, Grille 23).

There are four pretty substantive authenticity problems with that last sentence:

1. Boston's police department, when identifying a plain clothes officer, always designates both duty and rank, but also always places rank before duty. I know of no other major city that does so, but, as a result, Bob should himself have been using Lieutenant [rank] Detective [duty] Marty Quirk and Sergeant Detective Frank Belson.
2. Bob always treated Quirk and Belson as partners. However, the real-life homicide unit doesn't (and didn't) work its cases through a two-detective team. Instead, Boston investigators work in squads of three detectives.

3. During most of the Spenser series' timeline, the city's actual homicide unit was shoe-horned into the second floor of an evidence-processing garage in rough-and-tumble South Boston, about four miles from headquarters in the chichi Back Bay.

4. Finally, in the mid-90s, the new Boston police headquarters opened on the corner of Tremont and Ruggles Streets in the mini-neighborhood of Roxbury Crossing. Named 1 Schroeder Plaza in honor of two police officers from the same family killed in the line of duty, the concept was to bring all the force's major units, including homicide, together in one recently constructed building toward greater efficiency and synergy, both of which goals were actually attained. However, I don't recall Bob, in any Spenser novel thereafter, having his private eye visiting Quirk or Belson in their modern, expansive suite on 2-N (meaning second floor, north wing).

• •

Notwithstanding our respective authenticity issues, I think Bob and I both realized that, in some ways, we were at an advantage in coming to Boston after growing up somewhere else. *Con*structing private investigator fiction is a bit like *de*constructing an onion, peeling off the layers one at a time, and often it helps the character and the reader for the author to have a different take on how the best onions are grown and, in this case, how the best stories unfold.

Occasionally, though, we Boston carpetbagger mystery writers would need a genuine city native to be sure an historical event would accurately come alive for our readers. Put simply, while most people don't know many details about the homicide unit's location or functioning, quite a few will remember what occurred in their city during their lifetimes, and an author cannot afford to turn knowledgeable, devoted readers into reverse-apostles spreading the word that a given storyteller did not do his or her homework.

Case in point: It took me many years before I felt comfortable setting any important scenes in the Boston neighborhood of Charlestown (called—except for gentrifying realtors—simply, The Town). The reason for my reticence? I'd heard vague allusions to the code of silence in The Town. This code apparently mandated that a resident never reported a heinous crime (such as rape or murder) to the police, nor did any resident help the official investigation of that crime. Instead, you and some of your "people" (family, friends, etc.) would simply settle the score directly with the culprit in an eye-for-an-eye sort of way. A newcomer writer couldn't possibly pick up the nuances of this unspoken rule overnight, but not knowing could temporarily destroy that author's credibility with a reader.

I think this need for thorough research applies whether the event involved was devastating, mundane, or merely bizarre. The devastating: driving on a cold, late November Sunday morning in the early 1940s past the Boston City Morgue and seeing surviving family members of the half-thousand (not a typo) victims killed during the Cocoanut Grove nightclub fire, the survivors standing—and praying and crying—in blocks-long lines as they waited to identify the bodies of their relatives. The mundane: the assigned route number of the Boston bus that ran during the 1950s between Andrews Square in South Boston and Copley Square in the Back Bay. And the bizarre: a blue-collar tavern where, during the 1960s, well-intentioned (if misguided) construction workers would buy junior-high boys a "dimey" (one six-ounce draft beer costing a dime) to teach them how to hold their alcohol early and thereby avoid the consequences of getting drunk later on in life.

And, speaking of history, Boston's goes back nearly to the Mayflower pilgrims stubbing their toes on Plymouth Rock. Such a long span creates incredible diversity for the crime author to work into novels and even short stories.

We can begin with the architecture along those mean streets Bob Parker and his Spenser character made famous (okay, and infamous as well). Federalist Period homes (red brick and wooden shutters) on Beacon Hill, originally begun in the late 1600s and restored after the so-called Great Fires of the next two centuries. Victorian Age townhouses and mansions (granite with bay windows) in the Back Bay, constructed over fifty years beginning in the 1850s, as, bit by bit, the original Back Bay (Boston's former sewage lagoon) was dredged and filled, soon providing five decades of architectural variety viewable by an easy twenty-minute walk westward from the Public (think, Botanical) Garden. Eighteenth century wharves that were built to last, with their customs houses and warehouses, an entire such wharf available in the 1970s for $10,000 to pay off tax liens, then refurbished into honeycombs of multi-million-dollar, harbor-view condos. Three-deckers (read, fragile wooden fire-traps) built for the waves of immigration that followed the pilgrims, sometimes by hundreds of years. The Irish and Lithuanians in Southie, the Italians in the North End, and the Portuguese in East Cambridge (technically outside geo-political Boston). Not to mention African Americans in Roxbury, with their stately mansions tracing back to the pre-Civil War Underground Railroad for escaping slaves, and a generation of Cubans who fled Castro's communism to settle in the bow-front townhouses of the South End.

Bob's and Spenser's Boston also brought to readers the many languages matching this diversity: Irish (which we Americans tend to call Gaelic), Italian, Spanish, and French (a sure-thing bar bet: Can you name the largest identifiable ethnic heritage in Massachusetts? Answer: the Quebecois, who during World War I came down from their province to work in our commonwealth's armaments factories). And novels also brought the reader the despicable, knee-jerk discrimination many of these immigrants suffered, like help-wanted ads in the classified sections of the city's newspapers which too often ended with NINA (always in all caps, and standing for No Irish Need Apply; when the waves of Italian men and women began arriving in the first quarter of the twentieth century, the biased employers didn't even have to change the acronym they hid behind).

Now combine these peoples and their cultures with the food, music, and sports they brought to Boston and then hybridized with pre-existing forms of American entertainment. Provide universities (eighty-five institutions of higher learning within a ten-mile radius of Boston's Statehouse, despite the fact that nearly a hemisphere of said circle is comprised of the vast waters and tiny islands within Boston Harbor). Inject radically different modes of transportation (train and plane, subway and trolley, commuter ferries and water taxis), and it's easy to see how and why Boston's diversity in all aspects of life provides terrific fodder for any crime writer.

But Bob wasn't just any crime writer. Well before his passing he'd become part of Boston's more modern urban lore. In the early 1980s, a bookstore called Spenser & Marlowe opened on the Back Bay's Newbury Street. The shop carried only titles of poetry and mystery, sagely promoting itself by borrowing the proper spellings of two actual poets' names

(Edmund Spenser and Christopher Marlowe, both popular in 16th century England) and the (matching) proper spellings of two twentieth-century fictional private investigators. Talk about your four-cornered matrix of puns. The poetry side of the store didn't last terribly long, but proprietor Andy Thurnauer kept the mystery spirit alive in the city proper for nearly twenty years more.

It was also Andy who first explained to me yet another aspect of Boston as crime-novel setting. Informally surveying independent mystery bookstores around the country (probably 125 in number during their heyday, but fewer than forty as we entered the second decade of the twenty-first century), Andy uncovered an interesting trend: Books set in a particular region sold best in that region's cities (say, Rocky Mountain novels offered in Denver's and Boulder's shops); however, the second bestselling setting in almost every region was . . . Boston. In the end, Andy and I thought we'd figured out the reason for this quirk: So many people nationwide had come to Boston for some level of higher education—or even just an enlightening, walkable vacation—that they wanted to revisit those good memories via the classic landmarks, current events, and just plain buzz emanating from the pages of crime novels set in the city they'd come to love.

●　●

During the 1990s through the mid-2000s, Bob and I, as Boston-based private eye writers, would appear together fairly regularly. I remember congratulating him after a vaguely worded press release announced the Spenser character would be made into a television series.

Bob shook his head. "Jerry, you don't know the half of it," he said, "I'm at home in Massachusetts and I get a call from my literary agent in New York, asking me to come down and meet the star projected to play the Spenser role." For clarity's sake, your essayist will morph into theatrical-play mode to paraphrase, as accurately as I can remember, Bob's recounting of what happened next.

PARKER (still telephonically, but also a little confused):
   Well, who is it?

AGENT (measured): I don't want to tell you over the phone. I think a spontaneous, face-to-face talk would be better.

[A somewhat uneasy Parker travels by plane, arrives at Agent's office, and is nudged by same into a conference room as Agent closes the door behind him.]

PARKER (seeing only one other person, seated at the table):
   Well . . .

ROBERT URICH (standing up and beaming a smile):
   How are you? I understand from your agent that we're supposed to talk about my appearing in the pilot for our television series.

PARKER (stage whisper to audience): *Our* series? I mean, I could get killed here, folks. Robert Urich? One of the kiddie-cops from *S.W.A.T.?* "Dan Tanna," the slick dick of *VEGA$?* Not my image of Spenser, whom I've always pictured as a younger Karl Malden, not classically handsome, but rugged, with obvious scars from his prize-fighting days.

[Here yours truly harkened back to my own, off-the-mark, assumptions about Bob Parker's appearance at our initial Grille 23 meeting.]

PARKER (Having ended his audience aside and again addressing the actor): Excuse me a second?

URICH: No problem.

[Parker leaves the conference room and closes the door behind him, thereby entering Agent's office.]

AGENT: Something wrong?

PARKER: My contract with the television production company gives me a veto on the leading man, right?

AGENT: It does.

PARKER: Okay, so if I ding Urich as Spenser, do you know who the producer has in the on-deck circle?

AGENT: I do. Erik Estrada, late of the motorcycle-police show *CHiPS*.

PARKER (swallowing hard and forcing a smile): I think Robert Urich is a great choice.

Bob Parker was like that. He could be self-deprecatingly funny ("If I hadn't been in Korea to qualify for the G.I. Bill, I never could've become an English professor or a crime novelist; hell, I'd be driving a bakery truck").

• •

More seriously, though, the fact that Bob died just across the river from Boston, at his desk in the Cambridge home he shared with his wife, Joan, and while writing, would, I think, have given him at least some solace during what we can only hope was a mercifully quick passing.

Bob. Rest in peace. You earned it ten times over, and we will never forget you.

A MAN FOR ALL SEASONINGS

| BRENDAN DUBOIS |

DURING THE BENIGHTED years of the early 1970s, a time of gas lines, a constitutional crisis, disco, and polyester leisure suits, most enthusiasts and observers of the mystery field generally accepted that the private eye novel, if not dead, was at least on life support, fading as fast as a snowflake on a hot stove. The idea of an armed man seeking justice on his own, using his fists and his intelligence, seemed out of time and place during an era when America was in decline and in retreat, when the presidency itself was under siege.

By its very nature, the private eye novel depended on a main character of honor, skills, and fortitude to carry the narrative. But in the troubled times of the 1970s, when the country seemed impotent, where questions of competence and truthfulness were directed to the very foundations of

American society and government, was there really a literary PI hero out there who readers could possibly identify with?

The answer was yes, and what an answer it turned out to be.

It came from a relatively unknown college professor from Northeastern University, who published his first novel in 1973 featuring a one-named private investigator: Spenser. The first few paragraphs of that novel seemed to indicate that a new version of the smart, wisecracking private eye was making its debut.

From page one, chapter one, of *The Godwulf Manuscript*:

> The office of the university president looked like the front parlor of a successful Victorian whorehouse. It was paneled in big squares of dark walnut, with ornately figured maroon drapes at the long windows. There was maroon carpeting and the furniture was black leather with brass studs. The office was much nicer than the classrooms; maybe I should have worn a tie.

From these few sentences, it seemed a worthy successor had been found to a noble lineage that included such usual suspects as Sam Spade, Lew Archer, Philip Marlowe, Mike Hammer, and Travis McGee. Quiet, hard, determined men who not only walked down mean streets, but owned them and didn't flinch from violence. Firearms and cheap drinks, diner and restaurant food defended and sustained them, while the women in their lives, for the most part, were babes, dames, or broads. Their bleak lives were filled with yearnings and past desires, tainted with dark cynicism about the world about them.

Increasingly enthusiastic readers and reviewers learned Spenser was as quick with his fists as with a quip as he worked the streets and alleyways of Boston. Standing just an inch over six feet, he weighed about two hundred pounds, was a

Korean combat vet, a boxer, and then a Massachusetts state police officer. He worked out at a gym and usually ran five miles a day. His nose had been broken a few times. He often carried a firearm and, when things got out of hand and his life and those of others were in danger, he didn't hesitate to use deadly force. While the bodies didn't pile up in heaps as in many other detective novels, the use of deadly force was always an option for Spenser.

Spenser sounded cool. He sounded mean. He sounded sharp.

In the second book of what would later prove to be a forty-book series, *God Save the Child*, Spenser starts a monogamous relationship with psychologist Susan Silverman. He always flirted with women, but he always went back to Susan. No one-night stands for Spenser, no babes or hook-ups like his famous predecessors.

Okay, then. Maybe Spenser was just a bit different from that noble lineage.

Like many private detectives, he'd conduct surveillances from his car. For lunch during these surveillances, he'd pick up fresh Syrian bread, feta cheese, and a pound of kalamata olives.

Sure, why not. Other private investigators lived on sandwiches while doing stakeouts. What's a little feta cheese among friends?

He loved to cook fine food, making meals such as pork medallions with rice and a pineapple-based cream sauce, or pasta with spiced oil and broccoli.

Um, hold on.

He drank beers such as Utica Club Cream Ale, Labatt 50, and Pilsner Urquell.

Huh?

He was proud that his name was identical to that of

Edmund Spenser, the sixteenth-century English author of *The Faerie Queene*.

What. The. Hell?

Who was this guy, anyway?

It might have been easy to dismiss Spenser as a nut or a wimp, except a close reading of the novels show that he is anything but. He never backs down from outside pressure, is incredibly loyal to friends and associates, and is willing to expose himself to great danger to do what's right.

But in addition to that traditional two-fisted, hardboiled private detective, there's also the Spenser who not only tosses off literary references, but also enjoys gourmet cooking and has a healthy respect and admiration for women.

Good food and gourmet cooking is an integral part of Spenser's life. In every Spenser novel, there's either a cooking or a shopping lesson. In *Playmates*, after a dreary day of reviewing basketball game tapes with a friend who's a sports expert to see if a star player is shaving points, Spenser returns home and thinks of his evening meal. Most private detectives, hell, most people, when driving home after a particularly rough day, head for the nearest drive-through, a frozen dinner, or their collection of Chinese take-out menus.

But not Spenser.

This is what he's thinking:

> I was playing a Matt Dennis tape in my car and planning supper. Fresh crabmeat, maybe, sautéed in olive oil and white wine with red and yellow and green peppers, and mushrooms, and served over rice. Or I could pound out some chicken thigh cutlets and marinate them in lemon juice and tarragon and a drop of virgin olive oil and cook them on my new Jenn-Air indoor grill. I could have a

couple more beers while I waited for them to marinate, and
I could eat them with some broccoli and maybe boiled red
potatoes. I'd put a honey mustard dressing on the broccoli.
Or maybe tortellini . . .

Leaving aside the fact of who the heck Matt Dennis is
(okay, I know, I know, he was a famous jazz singer and writer
and arranger; thank you, Google), can you imagine any kind
of private detective thinking like that, besides Spenser?

Probably not. But Parker got away with it with Spenser. Because right from the very first books, it was clear that Spenser
lived by his own rules and codes, and if he enjoyed cooking
and fine food, by God, so what? Who would dare criticize or
tease him? (Except for Hawk, of course, but Hawk inhab-
ited a universe all his own.) But don't get me wrong. Spenser
wasn't a snob. He just enjoyed fine food and good restaurants
and interesting recipes.

In all of the Spenser novels, all the restaurants that Our
Hero visited and enjoyed were described with such detail and
affection that you knew that Bob Parker had tested them . . .
performing what some would call literary research.

Nice work if you can get it, eh?

In fact, just a few miles from where I'm writing this, there's
a well-known restaurant in downtown North Conway, New
Hampshire, called Horsefeathers. In *Early Autumn*, Spenser
is driving from Massachusetts to Maine, bringing along a
teenage boy, Paul Giacomin, who is caught in the middle of
a custody fight between his parents. But even when on the
road with a sullen teenager, Spenser still has time to eat:

We got to North Conway, New Hampshire, about one thirty
in the afternoon. I stopped at a restaurant called Horsefeathers opposite the green in the center of town. There was

a softball diamond on the green and some kids were playing a game without umpires.

I said, "Let's eat."

He said nothing, but got out of the car and went into the restaurant with me. We'd been in rural New England. Now we were in rural chic. North Conway is a major ski resort in winter, and summer homes abound around it in New Hampshire and across the border in Maine. Horsefeathers had brass and hanging plants and looked just like restaurants in San Francisco.

The food was good and at two twenty we were in the car again heading for Fryeburg.

What's wonderful about this scene is that in a place of honor over the Horsefeathers' bar to this day is an autographed copy of *Early Autumn*, a printed copy of the above excerpt, and a handwritten note from Bob Parker to the then-owner of the restaurant stating that he always had a good meal at Horsefeathers.

But why gourmet food? Why the recipes? Why the fascination with getting fresh ingredients for complicated meals? Why not—like so many of us, including other PIs—rely on frozen food, meals in a box, or take-out food?

My theory, as strange sounding as barbecued ice cream, I admit, is that Spenser's love of fine food and cooking reflects on his professional life as a private investigator. Think clues, and then think ingredients. For what does an investigator do but look at, evaluate, and review the key ingredients to a solution, not unlike what a chef does when looking at possible ingredients for a fine meal? The ingredients are pondered, combined with other factors, and are pondered and tested yet again, all while looking to the ultimate pay-off of a grand solution to a crime—or an award-winning recipe for a special gourmet meal.

So consider again Spenser's interest in fine food. Look again at that earlier scene in *Playmates*, where he's going through the list of options of what he might have for dinner. Perhaps that's also the template Spenser uses when he's considering what he's learned about a crime, juggling different aspects of a case, looking for that perfect solution versus that perfect meal.

Then there is Spenser's unorthodox approach toward the women in his life, or, more accurately, the woman. Spenser also has a healthy interest in fine women, especially one fine woman, Susan Silverman. Save for the first novel in the forty-book series, Spenser and Susan are together, one way or another, in every one.

Why is that?

Why Susan Silverman?

Or to be a bit more general, why a steady and monogamous relationship? What does it gain a private investigator and a loner like Spenser? Most other PIs we've known and loved other the years did quite well without the proverbial "ball and chain." Women came and went depending on the character and depending on the story. They played a supporting role, serving the needs of the plot and the more, ahem, basic needs of the male private investigator.

When it's Spenser and women, it's time for another theory.

Remember that what brings all private investigators together is that code of honor and the need to walk down those mean streets to seek justice, to seek a solution. Those streets can be dark, they can be forbidding, but they can also be enticing, seductive, and romantic in a twisted way. Recall Joseph Conrad and his *Heart of Darkness*, which portrays with great skill the pure seductiveness of an evil place with no limits. Shadowy places that are not only acknowledged but explored by the strangers who come there to seek money and fame, among other things. There are literally no rules, and anything is permissible.

From *Heart of Darkness*: "He declared he would shoot me unless I gave him the ivory and then cleared out of the country, because he could do so, and had a fancy for it, and there was nothing on earth to prevent him killing whom he jolly well pleased."

Ah, yes, "the horror! the horror!"

So what can bring a man (or woman) back from those evil, seductive mean streets, that heart of darkness, to a place of safety and what passes for normal life?

An anchor, a soul mate, someone to whom you can return and confess all, without being judged, without being criticized. After you've seen men fall and die because of you, when you have the stench of spilled blood and burnt gunpowder on your hands, it's a wise and wonderful thing to have an understanding woman at your side.

Spenser loves women, appreciates women, and admires women. But never does he see them as objects or things or lesser than himself.

So. Cooking and feminism. Not the usual attributes that pop into mind when one thinks of private investigators. How did this all happen?

The blame, of course, should be assigned to the author. Take a look at the book jacket photos for Parker and his Spenser series, especially the early ones. You see a dark-haired man, with a moustache and piercing eyes, giving out a fierce "don't bleep with me" look. Bob had a lot of similarities with Spenser: Korean veterans, weightlifters, runners, and lovers of special women: in Bob's case, his wife Joan. But still, he looked like someone you didn't want to approach suddenly, or in a dark alley.

After I started my career in writing mystery fiction, I did eventually meet Parker, at Kate Mattes' famous mystery bookstore in Cambridge (where he had helped build the bookshelves), and I found him in a corner with a group of fans and fellow authors. He was built like a fireplug, looked strong and confident, but one other thing was quite apparent.

He was a big teddy bear!

Those dark, piercing eyes . . . when he was laughing and joking (a very common occurrence), those eyes would narrow as his elfin-cheeks rolled up and his moustache would twitch with delight. He was self-deprecating, poking fun at himself and his career, and he would gladly sign autographs for anyone who approached him. To someone who was just starting out in the field, Bob was gracious, treating me like a fellow professional. He had the bulk of a weightlifter, but he also had the bulk of a man who enjoyed fine food and fine beers.

There's an old saying about an attractive male, "that all men want be like him, and all women want to be with him."

That was Bob Parker. And that is also Spenser.

And the women . . . they do find Spenser so very attractive. But though Spenser is flirtatious and enjoys their attention, Susan is always, always nearby, either in his mind or in his apartment. There's a funny bit that's played and replayed in *Playmates*, where Spenser makes it a point to leave his office door open so he can see the beautiful paralegal from a nearby office walk by in the hallway. Sometimes he's lucky, but other times he has visitors and the door is closed, meaning all he hears is the *click-click* of her heels as she walks by. During those moments, he sighs at the apparent injustice of it all. One afternoon Hawk comes by and Spenser finds himself irritated to see Hawk in the lawyer's office, flirting with the paralegal. He even tries phoning the paralegal to warn her off from Hawk, to no effect.

This goes on for most of *Playmates* and then is gently and neatly wrapped up when he meets up with Susan for dinner and a lovemaking session. Afterward, this is what happens:

We lay like that for a bit, quietly. Then Susan rolled away from me and sat up without using her hands and got out of bed and walked across to the bedroom closet, where she kept a robe. *Eat your heart out, Paralegal.*

Romantic, yes, and incredibly corny. But that is Spenser. He is dedicated to one woman, a keystone throughout the entire series, even during that brief time when Spenser and Susan are separated.

But there is one woman early in Spenser's career who definitely isn't impressed with him, or attracted to him, or who initially wants anything to do with him. That woman is Rachel Wallace, from Parker's sixth novel, *Looking for Rachel Wallace*. She's a feminist lesbian author with a new book coming out who's been subject to a number of death threats.

It is quite the pairing. I can't quite imagine how Mike Hammer would react to protecting a feminist lesbian, and there is certainly a lot of opportunity for Spenser and his soon-to-be client to be at odds.

(An aside: Re-reading *Looking for Rachel Wallace*, just over thirty years after its publication, is an amazing lesson on how much has changed over the years. The key plot point in the book is the homophobic and ignorant reactions Rachel Wallace gets from characters throughout the novel, just because she's a public figure who proudly informs the world she is a lesbian. Now, Massachusetts, the home turf of Spenser, has an openly gay congressman, a gay Supreme Judicial Court justice and, along with New York State and my own conservative state of New Hampshire, has gay marriage. I think Spenser would be pleased.)

When Spenser and Rachel Wallace meet, sparks fly, but not in the traditional romantic sense. Rachel grills Spenser as to his suitability of being her hired protector, especially when she learns that he has read an earlier book of hers. The discussion then turns to the French author and feminist Simone de Beauvoir, and Spenser begins to lose patience with his new client, asking her if there's going to be a quiz later.

Rachel says, "I wish to get some insight into your attitude toward women and women's issues."

To which Spenser retorts, "That's dumb. You ought to be getting insight into how well I can shoot and how hard I can hit and how quick I can dodge. That's what somebody is giving me two hundred a day for. My attitude toward women is irrelevant. So are my insights into *The Second Sex*."

Rachel Wallace finally agrees to let Spenser serve as her bodyguard, with strict instructions on how he should act and dress. As the book gets underway, there are a couple of cringe-worthy scenes for fellow authors as Rachel does bookstore and library appearances for her book, where she meets up with readers who either don't know or don't care about her and her work. Spenser watches her in action and, as Spenser does so very well, observes everything that's going on. We also sense that Rachel is watching him back. It's like two prizefighters of a sort, circling around, eyeing and evaluating each other.

At one point, Spenser brings Rachel along for a dinner date with Susan Silverman. While it's no clash of the titans, there's an interesting dynamic in seeing a radical feminist and a feminist who loves a certain man check each other out. During this process, Spenser being Spenser, tosses off various quips and one-liners as Rachel and Susan comment about Spenser, about radical feminism, about his penchant for violence. Hilarity definitely does not ensue, as Rachel takes offense. But Susan being Susan, she provides Rachel with an explanation for the way Spenser thinks and operates.

Speaking of Susan, Spenser says:

"Maybe I shouldn't cart her around everyplace" . . .

"Machismo," Rachel said. "The machismo code. He's locked into it, and he can't explain himself, or apologize, or cry probably, or show emotion."

"I throw up good, though. And I will in a minute."

Wallace's head snapped around at me. Her face was harsh and tight. Susan patted her arm. "Give him time," she said. "He grows on you. He's hard to classify. But he'll look out for you. And he'll care what happens to you. And he'll keep you out of harm's way." Susan sipped her wine. "He really will," she said to Rachel Wallace.

"And you?" Rachel said, "does he look out for you?"

"We look out for each other," Susan said. "I'm doing it now."

Rachel Wallace smiled, her face loosened. "Yes," she said. "You are, aren't you?"

Confrontation avoided, or explained, but note what else is going on during this exchange. Rachel relaxes upon seeing Spenser and Susan dealing with each other as equals. Despite Rachel's bluff talk of machismo, she recognizes the deep affection and bond that Susan and Spenser have for each other. Rachel's clichés of how brutish Spenser is—he can't explain himself, apologize, cry, or show emotion—crumble under the complex reality of who Spenser is, a reality indicated by his strong female companion.

The learning process for Rachel continues soon after this dinner. A Boston-based morning television show invites her to talk about her book, and the well-dressed, well-coiffed, and brainless woman interviewer doesn't ask her any questions about her work. Instead, there are questions about lesbian marriage, whether lesbians should be allowed to teach children, and whether lesbians can be good role models for children.

When the interview is over—and in one last insult, a producer calls out, "Thanks a lot, Mrs. Wallace"—Spenser escorts her out of the television studio and drives away. Within a few minutes, the hard, tough, feminist, lesbian author begins sobbing.

When faced with something like this, a tough woman who starts crying after a rotten encounter with what passes for the news media, I'm not sure how some traditional PIs would react, but Spenser doesn't hesitate:

> I said, "Feel like a freak?"
> She nodded.
> "Don't let them do that to you," I said.
> "A freak," she said. Her voice was a little thick and a little unsteady, but if you didn't see the tears, you wouldn't be sure she was crying. "Or a monster. That's how everyone seems to us. Do you seduce little girls? Do you carry them off for strange lesbian rites? Do you use a dildo? God. God damn. Bastards." Her shoulders began to shake harder.
> I put my right hand out toward her with palm up. We passed the business school that way—me with my hand out, her with her body shaking. Then she put her left hand in my right. I held it hard.
> "Don't let them do that to you," I said.
> She squeezed back at me and we drove the rest of the way along the Charles like that—our hands quite rigidly clamped together, her body slowly quieting down.

What a wonderful scene that is. You have two characters, a macho male PI and a radical lesbian feminist, a recipe for conflict, for confrontation, for misunderstandings. But after Rachel's disastrous interview focusing on her sexuality and nothing else, at a time when she is vulnerable in front of the rugged PI, the two characters are just two human beings. Period. Spenser does what he can to comfort her, and Rachel accepts the gesture.

Some macho, huh?

But it doesn't get better for Spenser and Rachel Wallace. In fact, it gets worse. A third of the way through the novel, there is an incident where Rachel is attending a meeting of some women employees at an insurance firm in downtown Boston where, before the session even begins, the head of security for the firm arrives to prevent Rachel from talking to the employees. Spenser tells the company officials that if they touch Rachel or attempt to physically remove her, there will be consequences. But Rachel is insistent: "Spenser," Rachel said. "I don't want any of that. We will resist, but we will resist passively."

By now, the astute reader knows that peaceful resistance is not part of Spenser's vocabulary. The situation escalates. Two company officials grab Rachel and try to drag her from her chair. She goes limp, passively resisting, but Spenser cannot stand by as a passive onlooker. Threats are exchanged, punches are thrown, and the two men end up sprawled over a cafeteria counter.

Rachel looks to Spenser, says, "You stupid bastard," and slaps him across the face. A few moments later, she says, "Back there you embodied everything I hate. Everything I have tried to prevent. Everything I have denounced—machismo, violence, that preening male arrogance that compels a man to defend any woman he's with, regardless of her wishes and regardless of her need."

Spenser is then fired, and when he later meets up with Susan Silverman, she listens carefully to what has gone on and quietly asks, "So why didn't you keep out of it?"

Spenser replies by saying, "And stand there and let them drag her out?" to which Susan says, "Yes."

Spenser's response?

"No," I said. "I couldn't do that. Maybe I could have stood by, or maybe if there were a next time I could. But I couldn't lie down and let them drag me out."

To which Susan replies:

"No, You couldn't. But you didn't have to deprive Rachel of a chance for a triumph."

This causes Spenser to pause, to reflect, and to realize that, in her own way, Rachel has her own sense of honor, her own sense of rules, as worthy as his own.

And what, exactly, drives Spenser? What are his rules? We learn it cleanly and clearly in *Promised Land*, where Spenser explains, "I try to be honorable. I know that's embarrassing to hear. It's embarrassing to say. But I believe most of the nonsense that Thoreau was preaching. And I have spent a long time working on getting myself to where I could do it. Where I could live life largely on my own terms."

Following the incident in the company cafeteria is the point in the novel where Spenser realizes that, like him, Rachel Wallace is living life largely on her terms, and he respects that, even though she has slapped him and dismissed him as her bodyguard. They are both honorable people, though from vastly different backgrounds and with different definitions of honor.

When Rachel is kidnapped, even though he is no longer officially responsible for her, even though he is no longer her bodyguard, as a man of honor Spenser is compelled to search for her. Like the old knights of yore seeking to rescue a maiden in distress, once Spenser has a good idea of her location, he goes to find her.

Oh, by the way, he goes alone.

With no backup.

On foot, after a blizzard has crippled traffic and trains in

Massachusetts, with the whole commonwealth under a state of emergency.

That's Spenser.

Rachel Wallace is successfully located and Spenser kills two men during the rescue and, even then, Rachel will remain true to her own sense of honor.

From the conclusion of *Looking for Rachel Wallace*, there's a brief exchange between Spenser and Rachel, after he has rescued her from the kidnappers:

> Rachel drank some more bourbon. "What I am trying to do," she said, "is to thank you. And to say it as genuinely as I can. And I do thank you. I will remember as long as I live when you came into the room and got me, and I will always remember when you killed them, and I was glad, and you came and we put our arms around each other. And I will always remember that you cried."
>
> "What'll you charge not to tell?" I said. "Makes a mess of my image."
>
> She went on without pausing. "And I shall in a way always love you for those moments." Her glass was empty. I filled it. "But I am a lesbian and a feminist. You still embody much that I must continue to disparage." She had trouble with disparage. "I still disapprove of you."
>
> "Rachel," I said, "how could I respect anyone who didn't disapprove of me?"

A pretty open-minded and thoughtful response.

So where did Spenser get his enlightened attitude toward women? One would think that he grew up in an urban household with lots of women, or a strong mom, or a strong aunt. And one would be wrong. Spenser was born in Laramie, Wyoming, and his mom died in childbirth. He was raised by his dad and his two uncles—all carpenters—and then moved with his family to Boston at a young age, where he got a football scholarship at Holy Cross.

The womanly influence, then . . . where did it come from? From his creator, of course.

My wife, Mona, an avid reader of mysteries herself, likes to think that Parker grew to appreciate strong, independent women when he attended Colby College in Maine, my wife's alma mater and a known incubator of strong, smart women, like the historian Doris Kearns Goodwin. Maybe so. But here's Parker himself, talking about his (and no doubt Spenser's) view of women:

> I have known an interesting, sexy, independent woman for some 50 years and have had many opportunities to observe her in many different situations. And one of the many things I have learned during the course of our relationship is that ultimately the things that separate women from men are less significant than the things that we have in common with each other.

What a great yet simple explanation of why Spenser was Spenser. Seeing women as equals, as partners to enjoy and cherish along life's bumpy path.

And along the way, if you drank some Pilsner Urquell along with fresh crabmeat, sautéed in olive oil and white wine with red and yellow and green peppers, with mushrooms, and served over rice, well, that just makes it much more memorable.

Just like Spenser.

SPENSER AND THE ART
OF THE FAMILY TABLE

| LYNDSAY FAYE |

"Scotch and soda," I said, "lemon chicken, and thou."
—Spenser to Susan, *Hundred-Dollar Baby*

ROBERT B. PARKER'S iconic Boston private detective Spenser is a true gourmet not only in that he creates and appreciates fine food, but in that he understands the fundamental principle of eating: food is about love. Having worked in restaurants from suburban chains to Park Avenue flagships, immersed in the culture that accompanies food enthusiasm, it has become clear to me that gastronomes exist in many incarnations, and some of them fail to follow this precept.

The chef de cuisine of BLT Steak (a talented fellow who was selected by Laurent Tourondel and remains the creator of the best Chinese five-spice rubbed duck breast I've ever eaten) once remarked to me that there is a difference between people who collect experiences at trendy restaurants for trophies, consuming delicacies like sea urchin and bone marrow simply for bragging rights, and people who instead want the shared communion of a memorable meal (at which sea urchin and bone marrow could certainly appear). "Foodies" are frequently charged with pretension and elitism, and often rightfully so, but in my opinion exclusivity is the exact antithesis of truly fine dining. When food is about love, then food matters, and loving food is elevated from a hobby some might call absurdly self-indulgent to a lifestyle that celebrates our time on the planet and with each other. Without doubt, Spenser falls into the latter category, and his attitude toward food thus becomes one of his most endearing character traits.

Previous to Spenser, food could not have been pegged as any sort of defining interest in the life of many private detectives (Nero Wolfe being a notable exception), in part because private detectives were such lone wolves as to be positively anti-domestic. To name but a few examples, Sherlock Holmes' attitude towards food is to avoid it entirely—though admittedly he is capable of appreciating a brace of woodcock or a good Scots breakfast on those rare occasions when he is neither the victim of ennui nor of near-manic brainwork, and once planned so far ahead as to shove a sandwich in his trouser pocket. God forbid, however, that any Victorian gentleman be called upon to cook his own meal.

Philip Marlowe will deign to eat food, but the allure of repast offers only a pale shadow of the comfort that he finds in occasional swigs of neat liquor and, more importantly, in his ever-present cigarettes. Although Sam Spade is perfectly willing to consume lunch and dinner, in such establishments as Herbert's Grill on Powell Street or the Palace Hotel on Geary, he is seldom interested enough in the fare to report what he actually ordered, whether it was any good, or why.

Pickled pigs' feet make an appearance to represent bar fare, as do scrambled eggs with bacon, toast, and marmalade in a more domestic setting, but they are incidental items and in no way does eating them affect Spade. All three detectives eat for utility and remain entirely disengaged from the act of dining itself.

By contrast, Spenser's entire outlook can be shifted by means of a perfectly rendered snack. In *Hugger Mugger,* for instance, he remarks, "The donuts were everything donuts should be, and the bright beginning of the day contained the prospect of unlimited possibility." It is difficult to imagine Spade evincing the same emotional reaction to a pig's foot. But it is equally difficult to imagine Sam Spade as blissfully contented in love, or to conceive of Philip Marlowe finding an untroubled domestic arrangement, or to imagine Sherlock Holmes going within ten feet of any female whosoever. Spenser's relationship with food differs from Holmes', Marlowe's, and Spade's because he is a different man than they are: a man possessed of warm and, at times, even uncomplicated domestic ties.

The warmth so evident in Spenser's makeup is of course primarily devoted to Susan Silverman. As Spenser's longtime friend Hawk remarks in *Now and Then,* "You love her . . . More than I ever seen anybody love anything." The mere fact of Spenser's commitment to a passionate and monogamous affair with an intelligent, wry, capable female forever altered the landscape of hardboiled detective fiction. Whether the romantic interludes are to the tastes of the more cynical readers of dark crime fiction is debatable, but surely no one doubts that Spenser's love life adds a great many human facets to the ex-boxer and ex–state trooper tough guy.

Spenser's own opinion of his relationship with Susan is that their differences wholly complement one another despite the fact that they are not alike. In *Painted Ladies,* he muses, "What we had in common was that we loved each other. What was different was everything else. She could feel deeply and think deeply, but she tended to rely more on the thinking. I was probably inclined somewhat the other way." In *Crimson Joy,* he goes so far as to say to Susan, "It's not only that I love you. You complete my every shortfall." It is impossible to imagine words of this tenor emerging from the mouths of Holmes, Marlowe, or Spade, and I would equally argue that it is this quality of completion that defines Spenser as a food-lover. He is no aloof iconoclast, divorced from humanity's softer emotions save for a friendship with an army doctor and occasional violin rhapsodies. Neither is he a hard-drinking PI roaming the mean streets without so much as a secretary as ally, nor a "hard and shifty fellow" destined to break the hearts of femme fatales. Rather, Spenser is a spiritually open man deeply invested in family life, and from the moment of falling in love with Susan, he gains the perfect audience for his forays into the heights of culinary exertion. The meals he creates for her are, in the truest sense, a series of love letters. When Spenser is most engaged emotionally, it is with Susan, and when he engages most deeply with food, it is in the context of their relationship.

Food for Spenser is an art, but it is a refreshingly unpretentious art, and he prefers to practice his hobby at home, hands-on, than to indulge himself at chic establishments. In *Painted Ladies*, Spenser says, "We sat at the bar. The Harvest was a bit elegant for the likes of me. I was probably the only guy in the place wearing a gun. I asked for a beer." While pork tenderloin en croute (featured in *God Save the Child*) is a Spenser effort so delicate, tricky, and time-consuming that I would never dream of serving it save for a dinner party of my closest friends and relations, he also makes johnnycakes (in *Ceremony*), a cornmeal and water pancake concoction that is so old-timey and simple that Civil War soldiers would have eaten it within camp when they could get their hands on the flour.

Spenser also has a sense of humor about food, an ironic perspective less smug than the wit he wields against antagonists; more good-natured. In *Chance*, he reports, "I ordered something called a Roman salad. I didn't know what it was, but Vegas was very taken with ancient Rome, and I wanted to be with it." The aforementioned salad turns out to be a normal green dinner salad with the improbable elements of green olives and artichoke hearts added in, as Spenser informs us in a dryly distant fashion. And thus we are made aware that food is not about hat tricks for him, posh ingredients dressed up to look like special effects. Spenser is not a "foodie" in the trophy-hunting sense; Spenser is, instead, a lover of food. The distinction is an important one.

The food Spenser makes himself, often for Susan, has soul. The venison chops marinated in red wine and rosemary he creates for her at the end of *Chance* are served alongside yellow-eye beans baked in an "old-fashioned brown and tan" pot, as well as classic cornbread and bread pudding with whiskey sauce. That the food is for Susan matters, but that the beans are cooked in an old-fashioned pot matters, too. Kitchen equipment, in particular non-electronic items like casserole dishes, cast iron skillets, and pots, acquire profound character by means of their past achievements, imparting flavor and an indefinable spirit of legacy to otherwise humble dishes. When a cooking vessel has a history, it will produce superior food. I have no doubt that Spenser's recipe for yellow-eye beans elevated the humble bean to the level of a gorgeous venison accompaniment, and I hope that bacon was involved somehow, but I also appreciate the fact that he understands that beans baked in an old pot are better. Cornbread baked in my grandmother's cast iron skillet is also better, and though Spenser's cornbread technique is unrecorded other than with the note that a "pan" is used, my hope is that it was a venerable pan, and worthy of association with the old-fashioned brown and tan pot. Were I making yellow-eye beans for dinner tonight, I would employ the much-used purple Le Creuset casserole pot that one of my closest friends left at my house after a recent barbecue for which she made dirty rice, and I'd ask her over to eat them. I would do this because food is about relationships, and I think that Spenser, if I chatted with him about it, would agree with me.

When I've cooked at home, I have made everything from Thai curry staples to garlic scape risotto with poached egg to rabbit carnitas over carrot mint puree, but these concoctions must inevitably be *for* someone. Alone, when my husband is working and I am writing, my most often repeated dinners include: tinned sardines with crackers; corn tortillas warmed in a pan with grated cheddar and slices of pickled jalapeno; that timelessly delectable classic, Top Ramen, with the addition of fresh pepper and a liberal dash of sesame oil; and leftovers, always eaten straight from the plastic container.

Spenser likewise cooks, when he does cook, for an audience. When Spenser first cooks pork tenderloin en croute for Susan in *God Save the Child*, he watches her avidly during the meal. He observes, "She ate with pleasure and impeccable style," and one wonders, had Susan been picky or critical or faddish or apathetic or whiny about food, whether their relationship would ever have gone anywhere. One has doubts.

Susan, meanwhile, finds Spenser's proficiency in the kitchen amazing, possibly because she owns no such technical skill herself. Her function as domestic partner in the Spenser series inevitably grows to mean Primary Eater of Spenser's Home Cooking. Of her own prowess in the kitchen, Spenser says in *Hundred-Dollar Baby*, "She was halfway into the preparation for some sort of chicken in a pot. As she spoke she chopped carrots on a cutting board. It was slow going and I feared for her fingers, but I was smart enough to make no comment."

Not only is Spenser's love of food tied up in his love of Susan, but he himself is well aware of the fact. Perhaps it is true that his appreciation of fine cuisine predates *God Save the Child*, in which Susan is introduced. But as is so often the case with significant others, Susan grows to be the axis of Spenser's food hobby. In *Hundred-Dollar Baby*, during a stint of investigating out of town, he says, "We had been five days in New York. I was sick of room service, sick of eating out, sick of not being at home. I missed Susan." Room service (impersonal food) and eating out (impersonal food) equals not being at home (personal food) equals missing Susan (who eats the personal food with Spenser). I have never seen a passage better illustrating the point that shared food is the best food, that when food is not domestic it is less satisfying, that the depth of emotion that the act of eating can grow to be entangled in is profound.

I don't personally mind dining alone in New York restaurants, but I always do so at the bar, and I would never go anywhere in which my husband had expressed the smallest interest because I want the experience to be shared. Food is about family. The fact that Spenser makes this point in *New York City*, of all places, only drives the argument home. New York features arguably the most sophisticated food culture in the United States, and Spenser the gourmand is having none of it (despite relishing a tongue sandwich on light rye) because Susan is not there. Dining out in New York for me means finding a restaurant where my loved ones and I have never eaten, then going together and each ordering something different off the menu so that we can spend the night wildly switching plates around like the maddest of gourmet tea parties. Dining there alone is not the same. I once ate an absolutely lovely pumpkin and sage ravioli dish with amaretto biscotti crumbled all over it, in solitude and while jotting down writerly notes for a project, and found myself highly irked that the dish was so good and *no one was there to taste it with me.* Small wonder that Spenser wanted only to return home again.

In *Rough Weather*, eating at a favorite restaurant, Spenser reports, "I was having pasta with Bolognese sauce, which is what I always had. Traditions matter." Well said, Spenser. They do indeed, and it is a significant character trait for Spenser to be untempted by a veal chop when he knows the Bolognese to be superior at that particular location, that a classic trumps a show-offy entrée, and that ritual matters at the dinner table. At the end of the day, a tried and true favorite will beat out novelty each and every time, and perhaps Spenser's complete adherence to this principle can be paralleled with his effortless monogamy. There is no other woman save Susan for Spenser, just as there is no other entrée at Davio's than pasta a la Bolognese. This constancy is an admirable trait in an already admirable man, a man greatly resembling his creator, and Robert B. Parker's interweaving of personal honor into the world of food is a masterly effect.

When Parker speaks of food, it is never superfluous and seldom simply atmospheric. Rather, every aspect of Spenser's attitude toward food laterally informs us about his attitude toward the world at large, which is of course why the author speaks of the food in the first place. The best writing is the ability to echo character within seemingly unrelated details and specifics, reflecting personality through thousands of tiny mirrors. Spenser orders Bolognese at Davio's because he is loyal; he takes the time to squeeze fresh orange juice in *Painted Ladies* because he is meticulous; he orders Sterling sauvignon blanc with his paillard of chicken in *Chance* because he is discerning; he finds Roman salad funny in the same novel because he owns a keen wit; and he feeds Susan pork tenderloin en croute in *God Save the Child* because he is falling in love.

All this affection for domesticity, of course, has everything to do with Robert B. Parker himself. In a 2005 interview with Dean James and Elizabeth Foxwell, co-authors of *The Robert B. Parker Companion*, Parker was asked about the genesis of his departure from the typical private gumshoe as a cynical loner into a happily paired family man. Parker answered, "I am a happier man than Chandler was, and the center of my being is Joan and my sons. They are not only context. They are life. It was inevitable, I think, that I would evolve Spenser into a man with a similar center."

Like Parker with regard to his wife, Spenser sees no possible world outside of Susan. What is rewarding about Parker's re-orientation of the private detective's center of gravity is that it makes Spenser no less of a relentless protagonist just because some of his discussions of cases now take place at the kitchen counter with Susan as he slices green apples into a bowl for fritters (*Painted Ladies*)—as opposed to, say, in the back corner of a sordid and smoky bar, in conversation with a sociopathic informant, or in a dark alley with a decaying lady of the evening. Parker understands that a man who remembers to slice his prettily crisp and tart green apples into lemon juice to prevent the browning process caused by oxidation is not feminized by the act, but rather is all the more capable for it. If you are going to make your protagonist a chef, a loving chef, a good chef, then that chef would be appalled by a brownish-colored green apple fritter. And because Spenser is respectful of the classics, he would also put nutmeg in the dredging flour, and Parker makes no apology for reporting such. He is not worried about what we will think of Spenser's manhood, because it is never in doubt.

Spenser, when ruminating in *Back Story* over having killed several antagonists and pondering the moral weight of his chosen profession, concludes, "Was it worth a lot of dead guys? I did this work because I could. And maybe because I couldn't do any other. I'd never been good at working for someone. At least this work let me live life on my terms." Spoken as matter-of-factly as any deadly private vigilante, and better expressed than many. As an unabashed hardboiled detective, Spenser is appropriately forceful, sarcastic, and, according to Susan in *Chance,* one of the "hardest people I've ever known . . . And most of the time, you enjoy it, except when you have one of these little sentimental spasms."

In the arena of palate, however, Spenser owns another key difference from detectives of his ilk like Marlowe and Spade, and that is his attitude toward alcohol. When Marlowe drinks highballs and takes pulls from his bottle of rye, it is far more likely to be the result of impossible situations, corrupted women, and acid thoughts than it is for simple enjoyment, and the same goes for Spade. Drinking is a part of the culture of the hardboiled detective, which is a culture with a hard and glittering edge to it, a world of dangerous men making sad and ruthless choices.

Spenser, on the other hand, drinks because he likes the taste and enjoys the sensation and wants something appropriate to pair with dinner. When he drinks, he drinks methodically and with pleasure, but never to excess. Alcohol is a gustatory diversion for him, and not a crutch to allow him to limp through the world with a recent emotional flesh wound a little more effectively. He is also highly eclectic in his choices; everything from Laphroaig to champagne to Calvados to Burgundy to beer to Bailey's on the rocks are all considered fair game, depending on his whim and what he happens to be eating. The alcohol is a pleasant and welcome divertissement and though, like Marlowe, he keeps a bottle of liquor in his desk drawer (Irish whiskey, a fine choice), one never worries that he might put it to ill use. His steady domestic life hardly warrants the melancholy swigs from a flask so typical of the genre's more spiritually corrosive protagonists.

The single meal that I think best characterizes Spenser's love of food appears in *Paper Doll* and naturally is created for Susan. He prepares grilled buffalo tenderloin marinated in red wine and garlic with fiddlehead ferns, corn pudding, and red potatoes cooked with bay leaves.

Where to begin when discussing this hugely ambitious dinner plan? First, buffalo meat, also known as bison, resembles beef closely but cannot be cooked in the same manner and exhibits a leaner, gamier, darker flavor profile. Spenser, of course, would have known this. The white marbling of fat that one sees in cuts of ordinary beef are largely absent from buffalo, which means that cooking buffalo with a beef technique would produce dry, unpalatable meat because there are too few striations of fat to melt into the flesh while it heats.

Classically, if grilling is the desired cooking medium (which really would produce a lovely, smoky char on the bison tenderloin), it is necessary to first marinate the buffalo (as Spenser did, and aptly, too, because wine is a tenderizing agent), and then to cook it just off flame over a very low heat—either on an indoor gas grill or else on a barbecue with coals that have died down somewhat—basting frequently to retain the moisture. This would produce a gorgeous cut of meat, but it is an operation requiring meticulous care, not to mention technical knowhow and the desire to make life hard for yourself in anticipation of future reward. First Spenser must have created a marinade and soaked the meat in the fridge, probably for several hours, and then he chose to grill it, which would have required him hovering over the grill for the entire cooking time. This is not an endeavor for the faint of heart. To those who suppose he wouldn't have bothered doing all that, my answer is that no way in hell did Spenser cook bad bison for Susan.

Let's take the corn pudding next; a bad corn pudding is a terrible, terrible thing. A good corn pudding, however, is a fit subject to write home about. Retaining our hypothesis that Spenser would have produced a fantastic specimen, the best corn pudding is neither too heavy nor too light, tastes like the very embodied essence of sweet July corn kernels, is a gorgeous pale yellow color, is soft without being at all insipid, and includes no creative elements jarring enough to distract from the whole, though additions like jalapeno and bell pepper are often used.

Most corn pudding recipes involve one can of creamed corn, one can of corn kernels, one eight-ounce package of corn muffin mix, a beaten egg, a dollop of sour cream, etc., and can be made in about fifteen minutes. I make corn pudding every Thanksgiving, however, and have experimented with the help of a truly good recipe, and here is what Spenser might have done instead, as the man is nothing if not particular. First he would have taken three or four ears of fresh corn and grated the milk and kernels off into a bowl with a box grater (this step alone takes me about half an hour every year, as I'm doing twelve ears). Next he would have heated butter in a skillet and cooked up some celery, onion, and garlic and set that aside. He'd have separated the yolks from the whites of two eggs, whisked the yolks until frothy, stirred that in with the corn and the mirepoix and some crème fraiche, and then beat the whites into nearly a meringue and gently stirred the soft wet peaks into the rest. If he were me, he would have added a dash of cayenne and some fresh parsley and English thyme along with the seasoning, but I leave that to Spenser. He'd then have baked the pudding in the oven in a cast iron skillet, and I think he would have been very happy with the results, though they would have taken him about forty minutes longer than necessary.

Red potatoes with bay leaves are delicious, but let that pass and instead we can address the subject of fiddlehead ferns. They are among the most prized and most difficult to obtain vegetable ever to lend grace as a side dish, and the fact that Spenser wanted to cook them reveals something about the quality of grocers the man frequents. Not only are fiddleheads only available in the Northeastern part of the country, and then only in specialty grocery stores and farmer's markets, but they are only in season for three short weeks during the month of May, which is when Spenser would have been shopping for them.

Actually ostrich fern fronds, they are picked up by professional foragers during the very brief springtime window when they are small and tender enough to eat, and then the pickers will take only three fronds per plant so as not to damage the fern population, which accounts for the greens' rather high price tag. Their flavor is akin to a toastier, more bitter-almond version of a very young asparagus tip, and they are absolutely exquisite. After being picked, they expire all too quickly, which means that Spenser did his shopping on the same day he cooked them. Then he would have removed any of the light chaff that remained by hand, cleaned them carefully to eliminate any microbes hidden in the tight furl, and prepared them, either in a classic Bostonian style (steamed with Hollandaise) or otherwise. Personally, I sauté them in butter with hen of the woods mushrooms, shallots, and a little garlic, and have never been disappointed by them. But regardless of his preferred fern method, think of the sheer amount of time involved when Spenser planned this meal: presumably, he did the shopping, made the marinade and trimmed the bison, assembled the corn pudding for baking, cleaned and prepped the fiddleheads, and still had the audacity to make potatoes. My hat is off to him, and doubtless Susan made this epicurean feast well worth his while, as it was all for her.

True food lovers find inspiration everywhere, and nothing tempts us like the allure of attempting a hitherto unknown dish. We crave the challenges of new landscapes no less keenly than golfers and mountain climbers, though our setting is a gastronomic one. In *The Godwulf Manuscript*, Spenser cooks a classic French recipe called Coquilles St. Jacques. From the instant I read this, I was hopelessly intrigued. I have never attempted this particular little number before, which is more than reason enough for me to try it, and thus I took the steps I like to imagine Spenser also takes when trying something new: I looked up several versions and then wrote my own. Spenser seems almost never to be working from a recipe, which is much to both my style and liking, but I did first want to grasp the principle of the thing. Spenser would never dream of cooking a dish improperly, despite his kitchen being so remarkably free of cookbooks and jotted down instructions. So here follows the way I would reproduce the St. Jacques sea scallops that Spenser served, though admittedly his flourishes would surely have differed from my own.

◆ COQUILLES ST. JACQUES A LA SPENSER ◆

(serves 4)

1 pound of bay scallops	2 Tbsp. all purpose flour
4 Tbsp. unsalted butter, divided	½ cup milk
1 small leek, chopped fine	½ cup heavy cream
4 cloves garlic, chopped fine	½ cup shredded Gruyere
2 Tbsp. Spanish brandy	A pinch of nutmeg
1 cup of clam juice	A pinch of cayenne
½ tsp. lemon zest	2 Tbsp. fresh tarragon, minced
8 ounces shitake mushrooms,	½ cup bread crumbs
sliced	Salt and pepper to taste

1. Take four large oven-safe ramekins and line them with butter.

2. Heat a large sauté pan with one tablespoon of butter and sweat the leeks and the garlic until soft and fragrant, about 8 minutes.

3. Add the scallops, brandy, clam juice, and lemon zest to the pan and poach the scallops, about 2–3 minutes until barely firm. Season to taste. Strain the contents over a bowl and reserve both the solids and cooking liquid.

4. Melt another tablespoon of butter in your empty pan and sauté the mushrooms, seasoning as you go, for 4 minutes or until tender. Add the mushrooms to the scallops and leeks.

5. Melt your remaining two tablespoons butter in your empty pan and cook the flour, stirring constantly, for 2 minutes, forming a roux. Whisking rapidly, add your poaching liquid and simmer until thickened, 3 minutes.

6. Stir in the milk, cream, Gruyere, nutmeg, cayenne, and tarragon, and season your sauce to taste. Continue cooking 1–2 minutes, until the sauce is fully incorporated.

7. Fold the sauce into the scallops, leeks, and mushrooms, and then divide in four ramekins, topping with bread crumbs. Crisp under the broiler for 2 minutes, until tops are golden brown.

This sounded, when I'd completed it, like a fantastic dish to me, and I was naturally eager to try it. However, I was regretfully forced to put that plan off, because my husband was working that night, and I was writing, and thus alone. Coquilles St. Jacques requires company and, like Spenser, I am much more inclined to cook for others than for only myself. I am happy to say that, when the proper day arrived and the dish was at last tested, it was entirely lovely. I can thus thank Spenser and, of course, the unforgettable Robert B. Parker for a meal that included fine fare, paired wine, and a loved one to share it with—the final essential ingredient.

LOOKING FOR HAWK

| GARY PHILLIPS |

Hawk appeared to be listening to the faintly audible
ball game. And he was. If asked, he could give you the
score and recap the last inning. He would also be able
to tell you everything I said or Nevins said and how
we looked when we said it.

—Hush Money

IN DASHIELL HAMMETT'S first Continental Op
novel *Red Harvest*, the no name Op is summoned to Person-
ville, a cesspool of a town called Poisonville by its inhabitants.
Two factions, the capitalists and the gangsters, are competing
to rule the place. The Op, charged with cleaning up the city,
decides to set these factions against one another. He understands that tough choices have got to be made. "I've got hard
skin all over what's left of my soul," he laments toward the
end of the novel, after the violence he's unleashed has taken
its toll.

On first glance, Hammett's Continental Operative is an
unassuming-looking, pudgy, balding, middle-aged fellow
who you might mistake for a shoe salesman. But if you went
up against him, you found out this bastard was a cold-eyed

son of a bitch with anthracite for a heart, an individual who, by his own admission, engaged in "necessary brutality." Over more than seventy short stories and two novels, we don't learn the Op's real name, nor do we gain so much as a glimpse of insight into his personal life.

Hammett's Op brings to mind another well-known enigmatic character—Hawk, the no-nonsense regulator in the Spenser novels. Robert Parker's Spenser is in the same PI lineage as Marlowe and Archer (though unlike the latter PI, you can't imagine Spenser turning sideways and disappearing, as Archer's creator once said of him): they are all cynical, hard-bitten romantics in search of truths big and small, with their backgrounds fully fleshed out over time. But like the Op, Hawk's background and personal life are rarely revealed in the novels. His name, too, echoes the anonymity of the Op, as there are hints "Hawk" is merely a hardcore moniker—like a persona a gangsta rapper or mixed martial artist devises—adopted initially to take on the guise of being a hoodlum. But the name comes to stand for more over the ensuing years in the novels. It would be incorrect to state that either character, the Op or Hawk, is merely a cipher. They are instead defined by their actions, the often brutal methods they employ to resolve the thorny problems they've been hired to fix.

I don't know exactly what prompted Parker to introduce Hawk in the fourth Spenser novel, *Promised Land*, in 1976, though he did relate in an interview once that, "He is, racial pun intended, kind of Spenser's dark side. And he gives me an opportunity to do my small riff on race relations." Hawk is hired muscle working for gang lord King Powers (perhaps a character inspired by the infamous Whitey Bulger, then leader of the Winter Hill Gang in South Boston). When we first come upon him, he's wearing a powder blue leisure suit and a pink silk shirt with a fly collar unbuttoned to the waist, looking as if he'd been out the night before at the disco tossing the backgammon dice and checking out the honeys. While I cringe at Parker's choice for Hawk's vines—as the slang for clothes went then—I have to give him props for having him clean-headed, a la Isaac Hayes, years before brothers started sporting the look in the '90s.

Later in the same book, Hawk tells a client who needs Spenser to look for his runaway wife that, "I'll bet he can. He's a real firecracker for finding things. He'll find the ass off of a thing. Ain't that right, Spenser?" In these initial scenes, Hawk's taciturn persona is established via an economy of words that still manage to convey a lot of meaning.

It might be that at first Parker meant for Hawk to be a one-off. But in the next Spenser novel, *The Judas Goat*, Hawk is back, and enlisted to help track down the terrorists responsible for crippling a rich man and murdering his wife and children. The hunt takes Spenser to London and he enlists Hawk for his deadly combat skills. Now Hawk, like Spenser, has a code. But his is more of a Frank Castle, Punisher-like ethos: he's a man willing to cold-bloodedly take life if such is the demand of getting the job done. It's a matter of expediency to Hawk. As he tells Dr. Susan Silverman, Spenser's psychiatrist girlfriend, in *Promised Land*, "I get nothing out of hurting people. Sometimes just happens that way." He also suggests that he doesn't see that big a gulf between him and Spenser: "Maybe he aiming to help. But he also like the work. You know? I mean he could be a social worker if he just want to help . . . Just don't be so sure me and old Spenser are so damn different, Susan."

Even so, in the earlier novels in which Hawk appears, there are times when Spenser seems to be as clueless about Hawk's inner nature as we are. In *The Judas Goat*, Spenser ruminates:

In fact in the time I'd known Hawk, I'd never seen him show a sign of anything. He laughed easily and he was never off balance. But whatever went on inside stayed inside. Or maybe nothing went on inside. Hawk was as impassive and hard as an obsidian carving. Maybe that was what went on inside.

Based on this early description, Hawk is cool-headed to the point of being unfeeling. More than once, Parker draws our attention to Hawk's inscrutable nature. In *Hush Money*, Spenser makes this observation: "Hawk nodded and smiled. When he smiled he looked like a large black Mona Lisa, if Mona shaved her head . . . and had a nineteen-inch bicep . . . and a 29-inch waist . . . and very little conscience."

It's Hawk's contradictions that make the character come alive on the page. For the most part, Parker exercised deftness inserting Hawk into the Spenser stories. It wasn't just about upping the amount of mayhem and murder. It was about the consequences that arose from Hawk's actions and their effect on Spenser. With Spenser, Parker was consciously working in the Hammett tradition of ruggedness, tempered with shadings of Raymond Chandler and Ross Macdonald. Spenser is a Korean War vet, ex-cop, former boxer, and gourmet cook. Hawk is also an ex-boxer, a supposedly brutish machine who is given more nuance over time, as Parker subsequently reveals hints of the person under the armor.

Parker once stated that Hawk has a ferocious practicality, which invites us to assume, based on Hawk's street vet status and the warrior name he's adopted, that his history has prepared him for navigating a hostile universe. We only get fleeting glimpses of Hawk's backstory and have to read into him what we will. Some have dismissed the Hawk character as representing the stereotype of a big, bad, monosyllabic black man who lets his fists and gun do the talking. Had

Hawk been around for only one or two outings—and had his sartorial selections not improved—that charge might hold water. But gradually, over the course of the Spenser novels from *Promised Land* forward, Hawk becomes more than just a cut-out.

In some ways, it's cathartic to have a character who can act as the coldly efficient dispatcher of pain and life, seemingly untouched by it all. For once set in motion on a course of action, Hawk will do his best to achieve the designated outcome.

"I know Hawk. Something happens to you, he'll be a royal pain in the ass till he gets it straightened out," volunteers buttoned-down mob lieutenant Vinnie Morris to Spenser in *The Widening Gyre*.

Initially, I saw the Hawk character as a way for Parker to palm off the dicey work in a story, the ethically challenging shit that he couldn't have his hero Spenser do. Sure, to some extent Hawk took on that role, just as Robert Crais' Joe Pike did for Elvis Cole, Walter Mosley's ever-volatile Raymond "Mouse" Alexander did for Easy Rawlins, and Bubba Rugowski did as the muscle for Patrick Kenzie and Angie Gennaro in Dennis Lehane's detective stories. But these cats are no slouches as writers, and each broadened and deepened our understanding of who these badasses were, as well as their relationships to the conflicted main characters. The further honing of these writers' hard-bitten anti-heroes speaks to their skills, as well as to the demands of modern mystery readers, who respond to tough, but dimensional characters.

Spenser is an amalgam of the one-dimensionality of Mickey Spillane's Mike Hammer and Chandler's richer, more introspective Marlowe. Parker admitted early on that Chandler was probably too much of an influence on him. It's no mistake that Spenser was a man of violence, but understanding of alternative lifestyles and well read. He is a warrior-scholar called on to navigate the complexities of today's world of high-rises and high tech, but also someone who understands that, beneath all the gloss and shine, we're still animals who too often succumb to the reptilian parts of our brains.

Parker didn't shy away from addressing the darker side of human nature, whether of the individual or of society. His Spenser novels, many of which took place or began in segregated Boston, set the scene for him to confront, slyly, issues of race and racism, as he did various times with Hawk. Take for example in *Promised Land*, when Powers, Hawk's erstwhile employer, orders him to kill Spenser and Hawk refuses. Powers calls him the "N" word, and not affectionately as in, "Hawk, you my nigga."

Now and then, Parker would also contrast Hawk to other black characters, to show he was no "handkerchief head," but his own man in his own way. For instance, in *Crimson Joy*, a serial killer going by the sobriquet Red Rose is slaying African American women in their 40s. Tony Marcus, a black crime figure, invites Spenser and Hawk to lunch to pick their brains about what they might know about this psycho. Spenser and Hawk, in their terse, smart-ass way, discuss his possible motive.

> "Tony say he can help you with the Red Rose thing."
> "Why?"
> Hawk shrugged. "Don't like it that some guy's killing black women."
> "Tony's become an activist?"
> "Tony been making his living from black women all his life," Hawk said. "Maybe he don't like seeing the pool depleted."

At their lunch, Parker makes it clear that Hawk is not about posturing or posing.

> Hawk put his glass down and leaned slightly forward toward Marcus. "Tony," he said. "I ain't black, he ain't white, and you, probably, ain't human. You want to look good down around Grove Hall, that's your business. But don't waste a lot of time with the black brother bullshit."

Though Hawk often seems uninterested in racial politics, as he does here, he is decidedly not in the manner of the modest "good knee-grow," the humble credit-to-his-race type—like, say, John Ball's Virgil Tibbs, the black police detective introduced in the 1965 Edgar-winning mystery novel *In the Heat of the Night* (though it should be noted that both characters share a joy of reading off-topic. In that first book with Tibbs, we first come upon him reading a copy of James Conant's *On Understanding Science*, and Hawk has been known to read up on scientific topics such as genomes, occasionally even partaking of soft-boiled mystery fare as well). I imagine Parker must have caught some grief as a then middle-aged white man writing a younger black character with Ebonics-style speech, delivered laconically. But the more frequently Hawk was featured in the Spenser novels, the less he appeared to be a one-dimensional stick figure, and the more his character became developed and defined.

Another example of Hawk's development as a character can be found in *Double Deuce*. Hawk has been enlisted by a church group to find out who killed a teenaged girl and her child in a drive-by. He, in turn, recruits Spenser for backup. Much of the investigation takes place in the so-called Double Deuce housing project, where the two have run-ins with the local gang, the Hobart Raiders, and their leader, Major Johnson.

"I know what you're like," Erin Macklin, a former nun turned teacher and community activist, tells Hawk at one point:

> "I see young men who, were they stronger, or braver, or smarter, would grow up to be like you . . . Young men who have put away feelings. Who make a kind of Thoreauvian virtue of stripping their emotional lives to the necessities."

Macklin suggests that Hawk's duty is virtuous and admirable. Having seen the toll that gang violence has taken on her community, she lauds Hawk's emotional balance, stripped down, as she sees it, "to the necessities." Macklin's words may very well speak to the core of Hawk's character. Hawk isn't one-dimensional; he just works hard to keep whatever angst and conflicting emotions he carries around like the rest of us buried. Let the extraneous shit eat at you and that'll get in the way of your job, he might opine.

That mindset, and Hawk and Spenser's relationship, are adroitly captured by Parker in an early scene from *Double Deuce* where the two are parked in the housing complex in Hawk's Jaguar for all to see, including the gangbangers.

> Hawk nodded. He was slouched in the driver's seat, his eyes half shut, at rest. He was perfectly capable of staying still for hours, and feeling rested, and missing nothing.
> "Something will develop," Hawk said.
> "Because we're here." I said.
> "Un huh."
> "They won't be able to tolerate us sitting here," I said.
> Hawk grinned.

"We an affront to their dignity," he said.

"So they'll finally have to do something."

"Un huh."

"Sort of like bait," I said.

"Exactly," Hawk said.

"What a dandy plan!"

"You got a better idea?" Hawk said.

"No."

"Me either."

From the mean streets to the suites, another of Parker's mainstays was his riffs about his time in academia, and his send-ups of the self-important sort too often found within those hallowed halls. We get a taste of this, while also contrasting of Hawk against another pumped up character, in *Hush Money*. The plot involves a square African American English lit professor, Robinson Nevins, who comes to Hawk for help. He has been denied tenure over a rumored gay liaison with a graduate student who subsequently committed suicide. Nevins is the son of a man, Robert Nevins, who was something of a guiding force to a younger, greenhorn Hawk. As Hawk relates dryly to Spenser:

> "Bobby sees something he likes and he takes me on, and when he finds out I'm not living anywhere special he takes me in, and I learn to fight and maybe along the way to use a fork when I'm eating. Stuff like that."

The case brings Hawk and Spenser at one point to have a face-to-face with the self-important, would-be militant professor Dr. Amir Abdullah. This confrontation is foreshadowed when earlier in the book Hawk tells Spenser wryly, "Amir so down even I don't understand him when he talk."

At Abdullah's off-campus office, the interview deteriorates quickly when the prof tries to clown our man, insinuating he's a handkerchief head. Hawk's patience finally runs thin:

> He leaned across the desk and grabbed a handful of Abdullah's saffron robes. Abdullah screeched for help and several of the hard young men in dark suits came dashing down the corridor. Hawk slapped Abdullah across the face forehand and backhand, hard enough to rock his head back.

Hawk's outburst precipitates a dust-up with Abdullah's men, and he and Spenser must use their experienced fisticuffs against the others' dojo-learned kung fu. Afterward, Spenser questions Hawk's reaction to Abdullah.

> "You don't have feelings," I said. "I've heard blacks call you Tom, and whites call you nigger, and for all you cared they could have been singing 'Louie, Louie.'"
> "I know."
> "And all of a sudden you have a NO-BLACK-MAN-CALLS-ME-TOM fit and we're fighting four martial arts freaks."
> "I know. Done good too," he said. "Didn't we."
> "We're supposed to," I said.
> "What was all that wounded pride crap."
> Hawk grinned.
> "Scrawny fucker annoyed me," Hawk said.

Hawk being Hawk, there's more to his irritation with Abdullah, as Parker reveals later in the book. Years before, Abdullah had sexually propositioned a younger Hawk. It wasn't about the professor coming on to him, but about him trying to exert power over someone he perceived as power-less, Hawk explained.

Across the Spenser novels, Hawk emerges from being Spenser's darker reflection—the part to unleash when it's Hammer time—to exhibit a distinct and individual persona. Someone who makes sure he's not put in positions where he's powerless. Yet we learn about Hawk the individual without ever encountering the more personal aspects of his life. In none of the Spenser novels do we see Hawk's crib (though what with the leisure suit in his initial incarnation, it might then have been replete with black light posters, lava lamps, and bean bag chairs—well, not those, since if a man is shooting at you, they're hard to get out of in a hurry), or learn what part of town he lives in, or where he shops. When it comes to Spenser, we know these details all too well. Hawk, in contrast, often just appears, like an apparition, out-side Spenser's office, or at some bar and grill where the two occasionally meet. People know how to get hold of Hawk, but I imagine his number isn't listed. Whose name appears on his utility bills? But readers accept that a Spenser novel is not concerned with such banal details. Parker develops his characters—Hawk included—not by overdone exposition but by putting them into difficult situations and showing how they respond.

However, those situations are filtered through Spenser's first-person reflections and ruminations. We understand Spenser not just through his behavior, but through his thoughts. We come to know the PI internally and exter-nally, and we learn what drives him to make certain deci-sions that will have a psychological impact on him months and years later. Hawk we can only know externally. We know him from his actions, his dialogue—minimalist but generally to the point—and by what Spenser thinks of him. And while Parker sometimes portrays Hawk one way on the surface, through Spenser's observations, again it's the choices Hawk makes that define him. In *Hush Money*, we read about Hawk's inscrutable "Mona Lisa" reflection, but in *Cold Service*, we understand that Hawk, as Macklin observes in *Double Deuce*, feels duty-bound not only to ensure the safety of the remaining child of the man he failed to keep alive, but to rip off millions from the gangsters who shot him, not for personal gain, but to set funds up for the kid's welfare.

I don't know if there's an interview where Parker covered this, but given that 1976 was when *Promised Land* was published, I have to think Hawk coming into being and beginning the journey he'd take to become the Hawk we experience in *Cold Service* and *Hush Money*, was influenced to a degree by Ernest Tidyman's John Shaft, the tough black PI who first saw life on the page in 1971. Him and those stick-it-to-the-man filmic figures like Jim Brown as the relentless ex–Green Beret, Slaughter, in two Blaxploitation-era movies. Chester Himes' Harlem plainclothesmen, the circumspect Grave Digger Jones and the deformed, volatile Coffin Ed Johnson, with their don't-give-a-damn attitudes and fearsomeness, are crime fiction forbearers for Hawk as well.

In this passage from Himes' *All Shot Up*, published in 1960, it's as if Himes were describing the dual, dueling facets of Hawk's nature through the relationship between the two characters:

> Coffin Ed's hair was peppered with grey. He had a crescent-shaped scar on the right-side top of his skull, where Grave Digger had hit him with his pistol barrel, the time he had gone berserk after being blinded by acid thrown into his face.

Hawk's roots can also be found in the novels of Donald Goines and Roosevelt Mallory. Not particularly skilled as wordsmiths, these two are names probably not much known among today's mystery reading community. I'm betting sure money both writers were unknown to Parker, but we can nonetheless see a trajectory from their characters to Hawk.

I believe Mallory only wrote four novels, all of them about his merciless hitman, Joe Radcliff. We're told this, as with "Hawk," is not Radcliff's real name. What we do know is he's a Vietnam vet who not unlike fellow former servicemen the Punisher and Mack Bolan, the Executioner (star of some 600-plus paperback vigilante adventures), is on a mission to wipe out the mob—albeit with the motivation of profit and not revenge. Like Hawk, Radcliff is muscle for hire, as seen in this description of Radcliff from 1975's *Double Trouble*:

> It's Radcliff's deadly little game plan, a game he devised in the jungles of Vietnam where he calculated that he was knocking off VC for only fifty bucks a head. He figured the underworld would pay him more for knocking off their own kind than the good guys would pay him for doing so. And the end result was the same—except for the bread.
>
> And Radcliff's women and off-duty silky life called for lots of bread. For Joe Radcliff *bread* is the name of the game!

After those four novels, Mallory dropped off the pulp landscape. Much more is known about Donald Goines, who has been crowned the "Godfather of Ghetto Lit"—the term used to describe the hardboiled tales that arose in the late 1980s, initially self-published crime novels with a hip-hop flavor featuring men and women looking to get over—to live large, to attain a warped, funhouse mirror version of the American Dream—via drug slangin', thievery, killing, and other such unsavory pursuits. Goines' bio, like Parker's, includes a stint in military service in Korea as a military police officer. There the similarity ends. Goines was a dope fiend, petty thief, and minor pimp. While in the joint on a stolen goods beef, the Detroit native stumbled on the works of a former for-real pimp, Robert Beck, a.k.a. Iceberg Slim. Beck's fictionalized memoir, *Pimp*, inspired the convict to try his own hand at writing, given the fact that he and Beck shared the experience of being on the other side of the law.

Goines, Beck, and Mallory were first published in original paperbacks by the white-owned but "urban-themed" (as the euphemism goes) Holloway House, a now-defunct publishing enterprise in Los Angeles. Goines finished his first two books while still incarcerated. When he was released he got back on the needle and ground out fourteen more novels (five using the pseudonym Al Clark) between 1971 and 1975, until he and his girlfriend, Shirley Sailor, met their ends violently, shot to death in their apartment.

Daddy Cool, published in 1974, is arguably Goines' best effort. It's about a ruthless hitman, Larry Jackson, known as Daddy Cool, whose one saving grace is his attempts to keep his wild teenaged daughter from falling under the sway of a flesh peddler. Jackson, forgoing the *Father Knows Best*-style, speaks to his daughter in this fashion:

> "Hear this littl' bitch," he growled, and he didn't recognize his own voice. "If you ever try speakin' to me in that tone of voice again I'll kick your ass so hard, you won't be able to sit sideways in that goddamn Caddy, you understand?" Before she could shake her head one way or the other his hand moved in a blur. Twice he slapped her viciously across the face.

While we might imagine Hawk's character addressing a wayward child in a similarly blunt manner, Hawk doesn't resemble Daddy Cool nearly as much as another Goines character, Kenyatta, named for Kenyan revolutionary leader Jomo Kenyatta. Like the Russian insurrectionist V.I. Lenin, and presumably like Hawk, Kenyatta adopted his name as a nom de guerre. Kenyatta was a gang lord who became politicized and used violent means to rid the ghetto of crooked cops and dope peddlers alike, echoing Hawk's evolution from gang muscle to thinking man's enforcer.

Despite Hawk's growing complexity and the literary new wave of African American protagonists in the crime and PI genres starting in the late '70s, it appears Parker never seriously contemplated writing a solo Hawk novel, delving into his past as he'd done with Spenser throughout the series. I assume the subject must have come up when the television show *A Man Called Hawk* was spun off from *Spenser: For Hire*, with Avery Brooks embodying the muscle turned paladin, but it would have been hard to write a contemporaneously set Hawk novel in first person and still maintain the mystery of the character. Hawk's inscrutability was purposeful on Parker's part. He wasn't particularly forthcoming about Hawk in interviews, and I'm sure that's reflective, to a point, of his not wanting to explore or lay bare too much about the man. But he couldn't have written the number of Spenser novels he did and not have made notations, intended only for him, as to who Hawk was. Parker claimed he wrote in a straight-forward manner—no rewriting—but you can tell that, when he was hitting on all eight cylinders, he gave a lot of thought to word choice and phrasings.

I wonder if, in some safety deposit box on a street shaded by elms in a postcard-perfect Boston suburb, there isn't a secret history of Hawk. But, even if Parker had written such a file, and I somehow got a hold of the keys and the location of the bank, I wouldn't use them. I'd take a quick trip on the freeway from my house in Los Angeles to the beach and, standing at the edge of the ocean, toss those keys into the waves.

It's better not to know too much about Hawk. He's an elemental force who takes on the world in his own terms and that's plenty.

As Hawk might say, "It be like that."

WHO IS SILVERMAN, WHAT IS SHE?

I S.J. ROZAN I

AH, SUSAN SILVERMAN, the girlfriend we all love to hate.

Has ever a fictional character raised such ire, or caused such expressions of disdain and disgust—over and over?

As we do with real people who become our friends, when we come across a character we like in a book, our response is usually to stick with him. Or her. Thus, series. (And long-term friendships.) A character who gives readers a headache usually results in a book being prematurely donated to the library sale. Or, in a more robust reaction, thrown against the living room wall.

But Susan? No, it's not that way with Susan.

Readers—and they are but few—who don't like Spenser have no opinion on Susan. They're through with her when they're through with him; let's move on. But most readers love Spenser, even at his most wobbly. Love Spenser, love Hawk, okay. But for many readers that love does not extend to former guidance counselor, lately Harvard PhD psychotherapist Susan Silverman. Over the course of Parker's nearly forty-year career, readers hungrily snapped up each new Spenser book, gobbled down Spenser and Hawk—and spat Susan out. Most of the satellite and asteroid characters circling those two glowing suns—Paul Giacomin, Marty Quirk, Frank Belson, Rachel Wallace, even baddies like Joe Broz—met with reader approval. But not poor Susan Silverman. She's usually seen as the price the reader has to pay for admission to Spenser's world.

In 2003, Louis B. Park wrote in the *Houston Chronicle* that "Spenser readers are pretty much divided into two camps: those who love Susan Silverman and Spenser's dedication to her (not to mention constant mooning over her) and those who wish she would fall out a window."

With "constant mooning," Park makes his own position clear. Personally I've always been in the first camp (which doesn't make the weaker Spenser books—the books Parker wrote when he and his wife, Joan, were separated—any stronger for me). I read Parker when he first came out, so I knew Susan when. I met her when Spenser did. I think that matters.

Susan's introduction is intriguing, in view of what later becomes of her: "Susan Silverman wasn't beautiful, but there was a tangibility about her . . . It was hard to tell her age but there was a sense about her of intelligent maturity which put her on my side of thirty."

Tangibility, intelligent maturity, and a lack of beauty that's worth mentioning—Susan Silverman is an adult, a worthy partner for Spenser. This isn't the blonde bombshell whose legs go on forever, walking in the PI's open office door with a concocted hard-luck story he knows isn't the whole truth but goes along with anyway. In fact, when they meet it isn't because she needs him, it's because he needs her. As things go on, she doesn't fall into bed with him right away, and when she does, it's on her terms. A lot of their early relationship involves serious conversation; she tells him when she doesn't like something, and he tells her, too. They talk about The Code, Spenser's personal guide to how a man must live. It tends to be the case that readers, like me, who start with the early Spenser books think more highly of Susan than readers who come in later in the series. Early on, Susan shines with her own glow. By the middle of the series, Spenser's adoration glares so brightly that it obliterates her.

Which is what Susan thinks, too; it's why she leaves him. She needs to find herself, to know who she is without Spenser. This is a need in her that Spenser, as a modern man, tries very hard to understand, or at least to acknowledge as important; it also leads, in *A Catskill Eagle*, to one of the bloodiest drawn-out rampages in Spenserdom.

In this, one of Parker's longest books, violent killing sprees alternate with meditative stretches of helplessness as Spenser and Hawk search for Susan—even though it's not entirely clear that she wants to be found or will come away with them when they find her. At the beginning of the book, Spenser locks up some cops when he springs Hawk from jail, threatening all but hurting none. A little later he and Hawk kidnap some hookers to rob their pimp. Because they need money, that's why. To find Susan, you understand. So it's okay, right? He's a nasty piece of work, this pimp, and Spenser kills him and his bodyguard to protect the hookers from the pimp's wrath later on—wrath that would be occasioned not by anything the hookers did, but by what Spenser and Hawk are about to do. It's calculated and cold-blooded, but Spenser has the grace to throw up afterward. By the end of the book, sentries, bodyguards, and hired assassins scatter the landscape like blood-soaked autumn leaves. A group of illegal aliens is asked to create a diversion for Spenser and Hawk, though it's clear many of them might die.

> "What becomes of them," I said.
> Hawk shrugged.
> "What is becoming of them now," I said.
> Hawk shrugged again.
> I shook my head. "No, let's look straight at it. I don't care what happens to them if it gets Susan out."
> Hawk nodded.

Again, Spenser at least has the decency to admit he's not doing any of this to do these men a favor, although they sure could use a favor, and how it works out for them means nothing to him. Such, by now, in the series overall as well as in this particular book, is Spenser's love for Susan: all-consuming and unstoppable. Everything—including, around the frayed edges, Spenser's own Code—falls before it.

Susan Silverman, based on Robert B. Parker's wife Joan (Joan Parker denies it, but is there anyone who can't see it?), came into the series when it became clear to Parker that Spenser was an ongoing character: that there would be, in fact, a series. Parker wrote his first book, *The Godwulf Manuscript*, as a bid to quit teaching, which he claimed to hate. ("Hate" may be hyperbole; Parker was known to come out with pronouncements to make himself sound tougher and more curmudgeonly than he actually was. In my experience, though his ghost will scowl, he was a pretty sweet guy.) Parker's study as a literature PhD student was the private eye novel, so for his own first novel, he wrote what he loved. Spenser was Parker's own alter ego, which Parker, for his part, never denied. ("He's taller, though," was all he said.) Once Parker saw that Spenser would continue to live, he apparently didn't want to allow him to go through life without a great love. In the first books, Spenser has a girlfriend, Brenda Loring. We never get the idea she's the love of his life, but he's not shagging everything in a skirt, either. He meets Susan in *God Save the Child*; in *Mortal Stakes*, they make it into bed, and Brenda Loring becomes a thing of the past. Spenser strays a little—with Candy Sloan in *A Savage Place*—but that leads to her death, which creates a huge existential crisis for Spenser. And that, in turn, leads to the way he leans on Susan, which leads to her leaving him. In other words, Candy's death, Susan's defection, and all the carnage that attends Spenser's efforts to get her back are his fault: he lets the strength of the Susan-worshipping force field falter, and disaster results.

Reader reaction to Susan (and to Spenser's Susan-gazing) is an interesting phenomenon. Some readers, as I say, like her and enjoy her presence in the books, even at her most sketchy. That sketchiness would be the final dozen or so Spenser books Parker wrote, when Susan is reduced to a series of tics: the tiny bites, the clothes, the beauty (which seemed to grow as the series went on). By then, of course, Hawk is a series of tics, too—the sharp suits, the know-how with ever more exotic weaponry—but we like his better. Even so, precious few of those readers who like Susan all through are pro-Susan with the vehemence of the anti-Susan forces. Among those in the anti- camp, Susan Silverman doesn't just occasion shoulder shrugs or who-needs-her annoyance. She's actively disparaged and disliked, to the extent that in 2009 writer and blogger Mark R. Jones wrote a straightforward, Parkeresque piece, focusing on weapons, strategy, and tactics, about a hired hit man. It was entitled "Killing Susan Silverman."

> The psychologist worked out of her home and had clients scheduled all day. Her private investigator boyfriend and his sometimes business partner were working a surveillance case in Gloucester . . . The psychologist lived in Cambridge, on Linnaean Street, in a green Victorian which had a small fenced-in yard for the annoying dog she owned . . . [Note: the objection to Susan Silverman goes so far as to include poor Pearl, who never annoyed anyone.] As he showered Cash thought about the psychologist. As far as he could tell, the private eye boyfriend would be better off without her. During the two weeks of surveillance Cash had determined she was high maintenance and a very annoying woman. Other than her obvious overt physical good looks, there was very little to recommend her as a friend or a lover.

Leaving aside the thought that Mr. Jones may have had a little extra time on his hands in 2009, sixteen hundred words is a lot of trouble to go to for the dreamworld destruction of someone else's character.

But it's typical of the strong feelings readers have. When asked, the explanation often is, "She's so damn perfect!" Of course, she's not. She's messy, strewing her clothes everywhere; she's always late; she takes tiny, nibbly bites of food, but slaps Spenser's hand when he goes for her uneaten sandwich; she wears a lot of makeup and leaves that everywhere, too. Spenser is aware of all this. Consider the scene where Spenser takes up with Linda Thomas in *Valediction*, and they go to the movies in the rain.

The parking lot had been temporarily diminished by construction and it was crowded. I found a slot at the far end of the lot.

"Want me to drop you at the door before I park?" I said.

"No, I kind of like the rain," Linda said.

"Me, too." Susan would have wanted to be dropped.

Spenser likes the rain, but Susan wouldn't have walked in it with him. Then there's the aforementioned lack of beauty, though Spenser notices that less and less. No, Susan Silverman isn't perfect. But what if she were? Would that be a problem? Is anyone really bothered by perfection? Because there is one perfect person in the Spenser universe, and that's Hawk.

Hawk's unflappable. He's tireless. He's smart. He can use at the expert level any weapon known to man, including his own fists and feet. He has impeccable taste in wine. He's great looking, too, and a snappy dresser, and he puts all of his talents and his own moral code at Spenser's service without being in the least subservient, without any hint of a chip on his shoulder. Anyone got a problem with Hawk's perfection? Didn't think so.

But in any case, Susan's not perfect and Spenser never says she is. Which makes it all the more galling that he worships her.

Why?

For a couple of reasons.

Spenser—as any hero—has two kinds of fans: people who want to know him, and people who want to be him. (The fact that he's not real doesn't interfere with the desires of either group; in fact, it facilitates them. That's what fiction's for.)

Spenser himself isn't perfect either. The only reason we readers know this is because he narrates the books, so he lets us in on his doubts, his mistakes, and, importantly, how badly he feels about them. (If Hawk were narrating this series, Spenser would seem perfect, no?) He's not perfect, but the inside view only makes him more appealing. Who among us wouldn't want a guy with his skills, talents, brains, and resolve, plus his morality and essential tenderheartedness, willing to sacrifice anything for us?

But for us, not for Susan Silverman. Spenser's adoration of Susan is vast and total, but we don't see the reason for it. Even those of us who like her think Spenser's over the top about her. She's not so spectacular that we can understand the stratospheric level his worship reaches—nor can we see why she replaces us in his affection. A crime writer friend of mine, who says she's one of Parker's biggest fans and has read all of the books multiple times, told me she could never stand Susan and would expostulate at length on her reasons until her sister, also a big Parker fan, stopped her one day with, "You don't really hate Susan. You hate the fact that Spenser loves her better than he loves you."

Ain't it the truth?

This, by the way, was not a problem in the crime novel until Spenser. Some of the earlier PIs were married, and the literature includes some devoted detective couples. (Think about Nick and Nora Charles.) But none of the iconic detectives, the guys who slouch in trench coats under streetlights smoking cigarettes in the rain, were closely connected to anyone. Not even pals; they had friends, and lovers, and sometimes went to a great deal of dangerous trouble for them, but none was ever connected the way Spenser is to Susan. None was attached, none was tied down.

Which brings us to the second group, the readers who don't want to know Spenser, they want to be Spenser.

By which, I think, they don't really mean they want to be *Spenser*. They want to be the guy in the trench coat in the rain, but they want to be that guy with all of Spenser's erudition, with his truly smart (as opposed to merely facile) self-deprecating wit, his ability to cook as well as he fights, his sure self-knowledge and his Code.

But not his baggage. Which means Susan. There's also Hawk, yes, and Paul, but they're on their own. They come and go, and though Spenser worries about them if he thinks they need worrying about—and would, and has been known to, go to the ends of the earth to help them if they need help—their coming and going, their presence and absence, doesn't bother him much. Not so with Susan. When she's there, he worships her. When, in *Valediction*, she leaves him, it's the end of the world.

One of the attractions of the lone hero PI figure is his loneness. We're all encumbered, tied down by mundane obligations but also by our love for the people in our lives. We wouldn't want to be without them, really, but there's still that whispered, nagging question, sometimes rising to a scream depending on the circumstances: "What would life be like if I were free?"

We want to be Spenser in all his hero glory, but while we're being that, we also want to be free. When the blonde with the bogus story and the legs that go on forever walks into the office, we want to be able to follow that wherever it goes. We want to take whatever risks we dare with our own lives, without wondering whether the life insurance is paid up. At the end of the day, as the city darkens, we want to sit in our open-door office with our bottle of bourbon, feet up on the desk, watching the neon sign blinking on and off across the rain-slick street. Alone.

That's what Susan takes from us, and it's not Susan who does it. It's Spenser. Parker, humanitarian that he was, no matter what he said, will not let us take the easy way out. We may want escapism, a hero to wish we were, pretend we could be, for a few reading hours. But he won't let us have it. Of Spenser, Parker said, "What makes him interesting is the struggle for his autonomy; for Spenser, it is continuing struggle. Part of the reason he has to struggle is that he has allowed himself to be in love and to care. The struggle between care and commitment and autonomy lends tension to the form."

Robert B. Parker was a vast influence on the genre in many ways. Indeed, it's a commonplace that *The Godwulf Manuscript* lifted the PI novel from the grave. Parker did that, bestowing life on a corpse; but like anyone who's been through a near-death experience, the resurrected PI came back changed. Now, he is attached. Committed. Tied down. In other words, like us, he is human.

All fictional PIs after Spenser have had, in whatever ways they could, to deal with connection and commitment—at least the possibility of those things, if not their fulfillment. This is a sea change in the nature of this American hero. In forging a new shape for the PI novel as, revivified, it moves into the future, nothing else Parker did was as important as creating Susan Silverman.

A LOOK AT
SPENSER: FOR HIRE

| MAX ALLAN COLLINS |
AND
| MATTHEW CLEMENS |

IN 1973, WITH the publication of *The Godwulf Manuscript*, Spenser put himself up for hire for the first time. This classic Philip Marlowe–style detective was wrapped in modern trappings that quickly built a major following for Robert B. Parker and his appealing hero. Almost immediately fans began to speculate on what actor might best portray the Boston knight in a big-screen or television incarnation. Similar questions were raised about supporting players Hawk, Spenser's black sidekick (and id), and Susan Silverman, the detective's love interest (and conscience).

That question would finally be answered on September 20, 1985, when ABC first aired a TV series based on the novels, adding a new household phrase to Parker's already well-known detective—*Spenser: For Hire*. Though the show ran only three seasons, a modest success of sixty-five episodes, its impact was such that even some longtime readers of the series began to refer to Robert B. Parker's *Spenser: For Hire* novels.

• •

The show snagged a decent time slot—Tuesday night, following the network's up-and-coming spring replacement, *Moonlighting*, featuring Cybill Shepherd and somebody named Bruce Willis. Unfortunately, the Shepherd/Willis series was not yet a ratings juggernaut; though lead-in *Moonlighting* came in at number twenty-four in a year when *The Cosby Show* ruled the Nielsen ratings, *Spenser: For Hire* failed to crack the top thirty.

In season two, consigned to the no-man's land of Saturday night where *Star Trek* had once been sent to fail, the program played out its run. Though the series had a devoted following and won critical favor, making the coveted cover of *TV Guide* on July 19, 1986, *Spenser: For Hire* never reached the Nielson heights. Still, *Spenser* was enough of a hit to last three seasons and even spawn a short-lived Hawk spin-off.

Yet even as lesser-known shows of the 1980s have found their way to home video, *Spenser: For Hire* has not, despite the wide built-in audience of Robert B. Parker readers. (Jesse Stone, anyone?) Though it aired during the boom of home video, the show was never released on VHS tape. And, although assorted clips can be found on the Internet, the series has practically disappeared—nowhere to be seen in syndication, no boxed seasons on DVD.

Five years after the demise of the series, however, the popular character returned in four Spenser movies running between 1993 and 1995 on the Lifetime Network (at that time, not yet "the Network for Women"). These again featured Robert Urich as Spenser and Avery Brooks as Hawk, though other supporting players did not make the transition.

In 1999, the character returned in the first of three TV movies (with Joe Mantegna as Spenser) produced for A&E. This trio of Spenser adaptations has also virtually disappeared, leaving only the four mid-'90s films as readily available evidence of a television version of Parker's popular character.

Popular literary private eyes have often had a hard go of it in film and on TV for a reason tied to their source material: Robert B. Parker—like Raymond Chandler and Mickey Spillane before him—wrote in a distinctive first-person style that encouraged reader identification. These writers were fairly stingy with physical descriptions—yes, we know the private eye is a big guy who can handle himself (Spenser is a burly ex-boxer) but little else—and readers caught up in an effective first-person narrative create their own mental images of a protagonist.

Marlowe and Hammer went through a dizzying array of actors on the big screen. Hammer had two relatively successful runs with Darren McGavin and Stacy Keach TV incarnations in the '50s and '80s respectively, while Marlowe flopped in a 1950s network version starring B-movie actor Phillip Carey, with a more successful two-season cable run in the '80s featuring Powers Boothe. Detectives whose adventures were told in the third-person by their authors have tended to fare better on screen—Perry Mason, Hercule Poirot, Sherlock Holmes, Miss Marple, and especially secret agent James Bond.

As Parker himself said in a *TV Guide* article,

My novels are told in the first person. We see everything from Spenser's point of view. Television is, by definition, third person. We see everything through the camera. In my novels, we see Spenser from the inside. On television we see him, as we must, from the outside.

A reader's idea of a detective encountered in a first-person narrative can clash badly with the physical representation that an actor brings to bear. But while not every Robert B. Parker fan loved Robert Urich as Spenser, few would deny his appeal, and most would embrace him as a first-rate, even ideal, small-screen interpretation. A veteran of television and movies, the ruggedly handsome Urich earned stardom in a thirty-seven episode run of *S.W.A.T.* (1975–1976), then in sixty-nine episodes as private investigator Dan Tanna on Michael Mann's successful *Vega$* (1978–1981). To Spenser, Urich brought an easygoing charm and, due partially to his broad-shouldered physique, an understated menace. Though some thought him too affable for the role—he would, after all, later become captain of *The Love Boat: The Next Wave*—for many others, Urich *was* Spenser.

Like the detective he portrayed, Urich was capable, an adjective the actor himself once used to describe the character. Not merely able, "capable" meant that Spenser was a man to be reckoned with. Though plenty smart, he might not always be the brightest man in the room, or the biggest, or the strongest, but he was always the most capable. He could take it, dish it out, hold his own with fists or guns, and still find the time and summon the wit to crack wise as he did it. The part was perfect for Urich, and he proclaimed it the role he enjoyed most in his career.

Urich has an appeal in the intimate medium of series television that places him on that short list of casually charismatic actors who own the heroes they embody. It's a list that includes the likes of James Garner and David Janssen, and perhaps half a dozen others. In TV terms, Urich was a "great" actor, and his feel for Spenser—at least the small-screen variation thereof—was largely what made the series work.

The actor in particular knew just how to toss off a Spenser wisecrack in a manner that seemed neither obnoxious nor unlikely—there was a wink and a self-deprecating touch to the delivery of these signature lines. It's not hard to imagine readers picturing Urich as Spenser while reading the books and taking the smart-ass edge off many of Parker's lines. Whether that's a good thing or not is up to the individual reader . . . and viewer.

Displaying his own brand of smoldering charisma, Avery Brooks brought to life Hawk, Spenser's de facto partner and added muscle when needed. A respected acting teacher, Brooks had little television experience before *Spenser: For Hire*, but was so compelling and convincing in his role that he became a break-out star, leading to the 1989 spinoff series, *A Man Named Hawk*, which lasted thirteen episodes. (From 1993 to 1999, Brooks enjoyed even greater success on the series *Star Trek: Deep Space Nine*, appearing as Captain Sisko in all 173 episodes of its run.)

As Hawk, Brooks flirted with an over-the-top blaxploitation approach—Hawk really did seem at times to have wandered off the set of *Shaft's Big Score*—but his swagger had a tongue-in-cheek nature that sold it without, surprisingly, making the character seem any less menacing.

The only other cast member to appear in all sixty-five episodes of *Spenser: For Hire* was character actor Ron McLarty, who ably portrayed world-weary Boston police detective sergeant Frank Belson. Having begun acting in the early '70s, McLarty was a veteran of stage and television before *Spenser*. Since that show he has appeared in several films, worked on television, and become a popular reader of audio books by authors as varied as Stephen King, Louis L'Amour, and Clive Cussler.

In seasons one and three, Susan Silverman was portrayed by Barbara Stock. A school counselor, as in the books, Susan graduated from Harvard with her PhD and became a psychiatrist. After the 1985–86 season, producers decided Stock was out—suddenly Susan left for San Francisco to "find herself."

Actress Carolyn McCormick was brought in as Assistant District Attorney Rita Fiore to provide Spenser with a new love interest. The writers had found little for Stock to do and even less for McCormick in her single season. When producers wanted Stock back for season three, it took a personal plea from Urich himself to bring about her return. He would later say it was a mistake not to have fought for Stock when she was removed from the show in 1986. Stock, for her part, appreciated Urich's (somewhat belated) support.

The first two seasons also featured Academy Award nominee (*Sometimes a Great Notion*) Richard Jaeckel as Lieutenant Martin Quirk. Though credited through the third episode of the last season, Jaeckel disappeared from the show after that, for reasons never specified.

Of the show's sixty-five episodes, only one—the two-part pilot—was based on a Parker novel: the 1977 Edgar-winner *Promised Land*. After that, Spenser's cases came courtesy of top television writers, including producers John Wilder and William Robert Yates, and such pros as Lee Goldberg and William Rabkin.

In a *TV Guide* article, Parker said,

Some of the differences between their Spenser and my Spenser are dictated by the demands, real or imagined, of an enormous mass market . . . Thus, their Spenser is the spokesman for a Norman Rockwellesque version of apple-pie America, about which my Spenser would murmur, "Isn't it pretty to think so" . . . But these are mere policy changes. Their Spenser differs fundamentally from my Spenser because television differs from books . . .

And what of me? As I watch the somewhat different characters on television, am I influenced to change the books? Their Spenser, Robert Urich, is big, graceful, good-looking, and young (a runner-up in the Robert B. Parker look-alike contest). Will I change my Spenser to match? No. The books are mine. They were here before the series, they will be here when it's gone. *Spenser: For Hire* has no more effect on my writing than *Monday Night Football*.

In short, I like the show, and I like the novels. If I were you, I'd watch their Spenser and read mine and enjoy them both. A thing is, after all, what it is, and not something else.

The four mid-90s movies found Parker—initially—exerting more influence. Parker and his wife Joan wrote the first two scripts, and all four films were based on Spenser novels.

As noted, Urich and Brooks were back, but this time veteran Canadian TV actress Barbara Williams portrayed Susan Silverman in the first two films, *Ceremony* and *Pale Kings and Princes*, replaced by Wendy Crewson in *Judas Goat* and *A Savage Place*. All four movies are readily available on DVD from numerous sources, although a boxed set is out of print and pricy.

Ceremony is set in Boston's "Combat Zone," an area known for prostitution and its high crime rate. A student from Susan's school is missing, and Spenser sets out to find the girl. He and Hawk encounter numerous lowlifes, some in high places. A straight-ahead tough guy movie, the film stays fairly true to the plot of the ninth Spenser entry. One major plot point differs from the novel but actually adds to the suspense, lending the film a particularly nasty final twist.

The script, credited to Robert B. and Joan Parker, is somewhat talky in the way many screenplays by novelists sometimes are, but it is nonetheless effective and surprisingly unflinching in treating its brutal subject matter. The couple's son, Daniel, has a bit part (he appears in all four films in a rather typical TV-style humorous recurring character, a motor-mouth waiter). The version of the film available on DVD is apparently a variant cut intended for foreign release (perhaps theatrical) and includes nudity and a level of violence not seen in any other Spenser adaptation. Of the four, *Ceremony* feels the most like a real movie.

USA Today, in its review, said, "The movie script is better than the majority of the (*Spenser: For Hire*) TV episodes . . . crisp with classic Spenser one-liners that are such an integral part of the novels, but were often missing from the series. Robert Urich turns in his best Spenser effort yet."

Filmed in Canada, due to budgetary constraints, *Ceremony* was at least made to look like it had been filmed in Boston, with some limited second-unit filming in the actual setting. To a lesser extent, the same was true of *Pale Kings and Princes*.

In the first film, the Spenser and Hawk take-on-the-world variety of Parker's fiction is well-portrayed; in the second film, Spenser and Susan as Nick and Nora Charles is similarly well-portrayed, though the feel is more TV than film this time around, with the screenplay even talkier. Some of Parker's one-liners go flat, even with Urich's throwaway style (when a car explodes, Spenser's comment that "There should be marshmallows" is an eye-roller); but on the whole it's a tense, involving telefilm.

Spenser and Susan leave the city for the bedroom community of Wheaton, where they investigate the death of a reporter and the cocaine trade. Hawk helps, and together the group manages to save the life of a character who didn't survive the original novel, as well as (of course) solving the crime.

Based on the fourteenth book in the series, this script was also penned by Parker and his wife. Some fans rate it as the finest of the four Lifetime movies (the writers of this piece would give the nod to the first, which holds its own with many a theatrically released crime film of the period).

Discussing his hero in a 1985 interview in *Connecticut Post*, Parker said, "Spenser may expound philosophically on things from time to time, but he always chooses—and I will always choose—the individual rather than the group."

He added,

> I would not sacrifice you for the greater good. I think it was E.M. Forster who once said that if he had the choice between betraying his friend and betraying his country, he hoped he would have the courage to betray his country. I'll buy that. Someone else, I think it was Pound, said that if there were a fire in a museum filled with great works of art and there was also a cat in there, he'd try for the cat. I agree with that, too.

This second film reflects Parker's (and Spenser's) point of view well. In its original review of the novel *Pale Kings and Princes*, a *Newsweek* critic wrote, "Like Philip Marlowe, Spenser is an honorable man in a dishonorable world. When he says he will do something, it is done . . . But it is the moral element that sets them above most detective fiction."

Budgetary issues, including filming in Canada, became much more apparent after the second film. While the first two had at least attempted to reflect Boston and Massachusetts, the last two simply gave in to financial considerations, writing in Canada itself as the locale, no matter what the original novels had depicted. Also, the Parkers were no longer the sole screenwriters.

And, by the third film, *The Judas Goat*, Barbara Williams was out as Susan Silverman, replaced by fellow Canadian Wendy Crewson. Fresh from big-screen film roles in *Corrina, Corrina* and *The Santa Clause*, Crewson was likely seen as a bigger draw than Williams. As was the case with Barbara Stock in the original series, however, the writers found it difficult to find anything for her to do. Nonetheless, Crewson made a winning and intelligent Susan, and managed to do very well in a thankless role.

In the novels, Susan serves to draw out Spenser's true nature, both for the reader and the character himself. In later books, her Harvard education allows her to make insights into the behavior of characters that actually aid Spenser in his investigations. With the exception of *Pale Kings and Princes*, those aspects of their dynamic are missing from the movies.

No fewer than five writers have credits on the DVD jackets of *The Judas Goat*. The Parkers are "writers," while Nahum Tate and Carol Daley are credited with the teleplay. Monte Stettin receives credit under both headings.

The novel, the fifth in the series—and an especially strong entry—revolves around a wealthy businessman seeking justice against a terrorist group that killed his family, and involves a massive plot to disrupt the 1976 Olympic Games. Spenser and Hawk travel from Boston to London, Copenhagen, Amsterdam, and finally Montreal to root out the conspirators.

The film's budget could not manage this kind of travel. Instead, we have an African ruler facing assassination (not in the novel), we lose the Olympics, and globetrotting is reduced to Ottawa, Canada. The theme becomes one of greed run amok, a frequent topic of Parker's, and a nasty twist is added to the end.

While many avid readers of Spenser were frustrated by the significant reworking of the plot, the film, taken on its own terms, remains a strong, viable tale. As usual, Urich and Brooks shine while the supporting cast is able (if not "capable"), and Crewson does well with a role reduced to alternating between cheerleading and mere eye candy. It's a strong telefilm with a crisp script that may strike some as tighter than the banter-heavy, novelist's approach of the first two by the Parkers. *The Judas Goat* is perhaps more likely to appeal to *Spenser: For Hire* fans than readers of the novels.

The fourth of the mid-90s films, *A Savage Place*, once again alters the plot for the sake of finance, changing the novel's Los Angeles setting to Toronto.

In the novels, Spenser sometimes broods about lives he is unable to save. He feels responsible for someone involved in the case getting killed when he thinks he could have—and should have—prevented them from dying. Just as he was spared that pain in the adaptation of *Pale Kings and Princes*, he dodges the bullet again in *A Savage Place* when a main character murdered in the book manages to survive the film.

One can only guess at the motives for changing these events—in one film Parker himself co-wrote the script, and in the second, he did not. Another change in the plot has to do with the client: a stranger introduced to Spenser by a mutual acquaintance in the book, she is transformed into a former flame for the movie, probably an ill-advised, even inane, attempt to help put some meat on the bones of Susan's character.

Though this ploy should add tension to the story, it really doesn't; the two women only share one scene that resolves nothing. The plot has the former flame, a TV reporter, being threatened but not going to the police, and behaving in an illogical, even stupid, manner throughout. Spenser seems to have wandered onto the wrong film set.

As with *The Judas Goat*, a veritable laundry list of writers receive credit: the Parkers and Monte Stettin as writers, while Nahum Tate and Carol Daley get credit for the teleplay along with Donald Martin.

Not quite a fiasco, *A Savage Place* represents an ignoble end for the entertaining version of Parker's character and his world represented by *Spenser: For Hire*. That Urich retains his dignity—and Spenser's—is the best that can be said for this somewhat sorry finish.

In 1996, Urich, filming his eleventh TV series (*The Lazarus Man*), was diagnosed with synovial cell sarcoma, a rare disease that assaulted his joints and tendons. The fifty-year-old fought the illness head on, changing gears and working hard to raise both money and public awareness, taking his fight against cancer to a wider battlefield.

On *The Larry King Show*, Urich said,

I cannot spend a second of time going into a "woe is me." This is where I am and if this is going to happen to me, how can I find a way to make this a positive thing? Worrying is kind of a wasted energy, you know? It's okay to be afraid— let that in, it's part of the experience.

About his favorite television role, he said,

Spenser is an old-fashioned hero. He's a throwback to the days of chivalry, knights in shining armor, and super-heroes. He believes in old-fashioned values and the family unit, and he deals with its disintegration . . . He represents what we would like to be when push comes to shove. We'd like to be loyal, doggedly determined, never to give up, and see things through to the end. That's Spenser!

Urich succumbed to cancer on April 16, 2002.

Spenser's screen counterpart, minus Urich, made three more appearances. These TV movies were created for A&E, and once again Robert B. Parker was writing scripts based on his novels.

The first, 1999's *Small Vices*, was based on the twenty-fourth novel in the Spenser canon. Replacing Urich and Brooks were veteran actor Joe Mantegna and relative newcomer Shiek Mahmud-Bey.

Mantegna, whose professional career began in 1976, had appeared on many TV shows and in several films including *The Godfather III* and David Mamet's *House of Games*. Though still a smart-ass, the Mantegna Spenser was more world-weary than Urich's. Both actors brought interesting qualities to the character. It might be argued that Mantegna is a better actor than Urich ever was; it might also be argued that he was not the better Spenser.

The new Hawk, Shiek Mahmud-Bey, had just completed a nineteen-episode run on *Profiler* before *Small Vices*. Although he was a physical specimen, former Golden Gloves boxer Mahmud-Bey could not bring the gravitas to Hawk that Brooks so effortlessly had.

Marcia Gay Harden, already a Tony Award nominee, assayed the role of Susan Silverman. She had an easy chemistry with Mantegna, and the two seemed as close to the "at-home" Spenser/Susan dynamic as was ever achieved on screen. Within a year she would win the Best Supporting Actress Oscar for *Pollock* and in 2003 would collect another Academy Award nomination for her work in *Mystic River*.

In 2000, Mantegna and Harden returned for their second

Spenser film, *Thin Air*. Based on the twenty-second Spenser novel, this one found Spenser searching for the kidnapped wife of Frank Belson. This was the only Spenser film not to have an appearance by Hawk. Joined by respected actors Jon Seda (*Homicide: Life On The Streets*), Miguel Sandoval (*Clear & Present Danger*, *Medium*), and Luis Guzman (three-time Screen Actors Guild Award nominee for *Boogie Nights*, *Magnolia*, and *Traffic*), Mantegna and Harden slogged through a film most viewers considered merely average.

Still working backward, the third and final entry in the Mantegna/Spenser trilogy was *Walking Shadow*, based on the twenty-first Spenser novel. Investigating a murder in Port City, Spenser and Hawk—this time played by an unmenacing Ernie Hudson (*Ghostbusters)*—have to deal with the Chinese underworld as well as Police Chief DeSpain, played by Eric Roberts (*King of the Gypsies*).

Although there are fans of these movies—including Dean James and Elizabeth Foxwell in their fine *Robert B. Parker Companion*—the Mantegna tele-trio seems little more than a blip on the Spenser radar. Mantegna, it should be noted, is a much admired narrator on a number of Spenser audio books.

Maybe the best way to explain Spenser on screen is to recall the words Parker put in Spenser's mouth in *Promised Land*:

> I try to be honorable. I know that's embarrassing to hear. It's embarrassing to say. But I believe most of the nonsense that Thoreau was preaching. And I have spent a long time working on getting myself to where I could do it. Where I could live life largely on my own terms.

Parker and Spenser both had that going for them—they lived life on their own terms.

So did Robert Urich.

SPENSER ON TELEVISION

SPENSER: FOR HIRE

Promised Land
(1985, ABC)

TWO-HOUR PILOT FOR SERIES
BASED ON THE NOVEL BY ROBERT B. PARKER

Spenser: for Hire
(1985–88, ABC)

64 ONE-HOUR EPISODES
BASED ON CHARACTERS CREATED BY ROBERT B. PARKER

Writers: Daniel Freudenberger, Robert Hamilton, Stephen
Hattman, Robert B. and Joan H. Parker, John Wilder, William
Robert Yates, Lee Goldberg, William Rabkin, Howard Gordon,
Alex Gansa, David Carren, Steve Hattman, Michael Fisher,
Bob Bielak, Juanita Bartlett
Directors: Richard Colla, Harvey Hart, Winrich Kolbe, Virgil
Vogel, David M. Whorf, William Wiard, John Wilder
Developed for television by: John Wilder

Consultant: Robert B. Parker

Executive Producers: John Wilder, Juanita Bartlett, Stephen Hattman, William Robert Yates

Theme by: Steve Dorff & Friends

Starring: Robert Urich as Spenser and Avery Brooks as Hawk

Also starring: Barbara Stock, Ron McLarty, Richard Jaekel, Carolyn McCormick

Guest stars: Chuck Connors, Spaulding Gray, Lauren Holly, Jimmy Smits, D.B. Sweeney, Jay Thomas, Sal Viscuso

SEASON ONE

"Spenser: For Hire" (September 20, 1985)

"No Room at the Inn" (September 27, 1985)

"The Choice" (October 4, 1985)

"Discord in a Minor" (October 11, 1985)

"Original Sin" (October 18, 1985)

"Children of a Tempest Storm" (October 25, 1985)

"The Killer Within" (November 12, 1985)

"Autumn Thieves" (November 19, 1985)

"Blood Money" (November 26, 1985)

"Resurrection" (December 3, 1986)

"Internal Affairs" (December 17, 1985)

"Death by Design" (January 7, 1986)

"A Day's Wages" (January 14, 1986)

"A Madness Most Discreet" (January 21, 1986)

"Brother to Dragons" (February 4, 1986)

"When Silence Speaks" (February 11, 1986)

"In a Safe Place" (February 14, 1986)

"Angel of Desolation" (March 4, 1986)

"She Loves Me, She Loves Me Not" (March 11, 1986)

"At the River's Edge" (March 25, 1986)

"Rage" (April 1, 1986)

"Hell Hath No Fury" (April 8, 1986)

SEASON TWO

"An Eye for an Eye" (September 27, 1986)

"Widow's Walk" (October 4, 1986)

"White Knight" (October 18, 1986)
"Rockabye Baby" (October 25, 1986)
"And Give Up Show Biz?" (November 1, 1986)
"The Long Hunt" (November 8, 1986)
"Home is the Hero" (November 22, 1986)
"One if by Land, Two if by Sea" (November 29, 1986)
"Shadowsight" (December 13, 1986)
"The Hopes and Fears" (December 20, 1986)
"Among Friends" (January 10, 1987)
"I Confess" (January 17, 1987)
"Murder and Acquisitions" (January 24, 1987)
"Personal Demons" (February 7, 1987)
"Mary Hamilton" (February 14, 1987)
"Trial and Error" (February 21, 1987)
"One for My Daughter" (March 7, 1987)
"My Brother's Keeper" (March 14, 1987)
"The Road Back" (March 21, 1987)
"If You Knew Sammy" (April 4, 1987)
"The Man Who Wasn't There" (May 2, 1987)
"The Song of Orpheus" (May 9, 1987)

SEASON THREE
"The Homecoming" (September 27, 1987)
"My Enemy, My Friend" (October 4, 1987)
"Heart of the Matter" (October 11, 1987)
"On the Night He Was Betrayed" (November 1, 1987)
"Sleepless Dreams" (November 8, 1987)
"Consilum Abditum" (November 15, 1987)
"Thanksgiving" (November 29, 1987)
"Gone Fishin'" (December 6, 1987)
"Child's Play" (December 20, 1987)
"Skeletons in the Closet" (January 3, 1988)
"The Siege" (January 10, 1988)
"Arthur's Wake" (January 16, 1988)
"To the End of the Line" (January 23, 1988)
"Play It Again, Sammy" (January 30, 1988)
"The Big Fight" (February 6, 1988)

"Substantial Justice" (March 5, 1988)
"Company Man" (March 12, 1988)
"Water Colors" (March 19, 1988)
"Hawk's Eyes" (March 26, 1988)
"McAllister" (April 30, 1988)
"Haunting" (May 7, 1988)

MADE-FOR-TELEVISION MOVIES

Spenser: Ceremony
(1993, Lifetime)

Teleplay: Joan Parker and Robert B. Parker, based on his novel
   Ceremony
Director: Andrew Wild
   Creative Consultant: Joan Parker
Starring: Robert Urich as Spenser, with Avery Brooks as Hawk
   and Barbara Williams as Susan Silverman
Also starring: J. Winston Carroll, Dave Nichols, Tanya Allen,
   Jefferson Mappen, Lynne Cormack, Lili Francks, Alexa
   Gilmour, Janet Bailey

Spenser: Pale King and Prices
(1993, Lifetime)

BASED ON THE NOVEL BY ROBERT B. PARKER

Director: Vic Sarin
Screenplay: Robert P. Parker and Joan H. Parker
Starring: Robert Urich as Spenser, with Avery Brooks as Hawk
   and Barbara Williams as Susan Silverman
Also starring: Alex Carter, Matthew Ferguson

Spenser: The Judas Goat
(1994, Lifetime)

BASED ON THE NOVEL BY ROBERT B. PARKER

Director: Joseph L. Scanlan
Starring: Robert Urich as Spenser, with Avery Brooks as Hawk
and Wendy Crewson as Susan Silverman.

Spenser: A Savage Place
(1995, Lifetime)

BASED ON THE NOVEL BY ROBERT B. PARKER

Director: Joseph L. Scanlan
Starring: Robert Urich as Spenser, with Avery Brooks as Hawk,
Wendy Crewson as Susan Silverman, and Cynthia Dale as
Candy Sloane
Also starring: Tyrone Berskin, Neil Crone, Richard Fitzpatrick,
Jerry Levitan, Douglas Miller, Daniel Parker, Ross Pelty, Natalie
Radford, Michael Ricupero, David Spooner, Hayley Tyson

Small Vices
(July 18, 1999, A&E)

BASED ON THE NOVEL BY ROBERT B. PARKER

Teleplay: Robert B. Parker
Director: Robert Markowitz
Starring: Joe Mantegna as Spenser, with Shiek Mahmud-Bey as
Hawk and Marcia Gay Harden as Susan Silverman
Also starring: Eugene Lipinski
Cameo by: Robert B. Parker as CIA Agent Ives, and his son, Dan
Parker, as Lee Farrell

Thin Air
(September 2000, A&E)

BASED ON THE NOVEL BY ROBERT B. PARKER

Director: Robert Mandel
Starring: Joe Mantegna as Spenser and Marcia Gay Harden as Susan Silverman
Also starring: Eugene Lipinski, Jon Seda, Yancy Butler
Cameos by: Robert B. Parker as a sleeping cop; his son Dan Parker as a priest; and Joan Parker as a doctor.

Walking Shadow
(2001, A&E)

BASED ON THE NOVEL BY ROBERT B. PARKER

Teleplay: Robert B. Parker and Joan H. Parker
Director: Po-Chih Leong
Associate Producers: Joan Parker, John Albanis
Starring: Joe Mantegna as Spenser, Marcia Gay Harden as Susan Silverman, and Ernie Hudson as Hawk
Also starring: Eric Roberts, Christopher Lawford, Christina Moore, Tamlyn Tomita, Mackenzie Gray, Ronin Wong, Marcus Sim, Chang Tseng, Henry Mah

Thanks to Kevin Burton Smith of the Thrilling Detective website for sharing the above information.

GO EAST, YOUNG MAN

ROBERT B. PARKER, JESSE STONE, AND SPENSER

| REED FARREL COLEMAN |

No! I am not Prince Hamlet, nor was meant to be . . .
—T.S. Eliot, "The Love Song of J. Alfred Prufrock"

MUCH AS ELIOT'S Prufrock is not meant to be Hamlet, Robert B. Parker's Jesse Stone is not meant to be Spenser. In a 2005 interview, Mr. Parker stated, "I invented Jesse Stone so I could try my hand at third-person narration, and a guy who was nowhere near as evolved as Spenser. Jesse has problems with alcohol and his ex-wife, Spenser is complete. Jesse is a work in progress. I also liked writing about a cop and small-town police force."

Regardless of Parker's intentions, the question remains: Is Jesse Stone simply a thinly disguised and stripped-down incarnation of Spenser? Or, like Prufrock and Hamlet, who both suffer from an inability to make decisions—Prufrock: *Do I dare disturb the universe?* Hamlet: *To be or not to be*—do Stone and Spenser share certain common features that render them only superficially similar? And, in spite of those similarities—some obvious, some less so—do they maintain their own integrity as distinct characters or, at a distance, do they blur together?

As the preceding quote from the late Parker indicates, Jesse Stone was, at least in part, more invention than inspiration; a sort of literary test bed for Parker's experimentation with third-person narration. Aware of this, a reader might assume that Parker would not treat his writing of Stone with the same level of care and aplomb with which he approached his treasured Spenser, but Robert B. Parker was a consummate professional and a master craftsman. It is doubtful he would give less effort to any of his projects based on the inspiration versus invention quotient. The sharp, spare writing of the Stone series bears this out. Even an experienced mystery reader would be hard-pressed to divine from the Stone series that Parker was any less invested in Jesse Stone than he was in Spenser.

JESSE STONE

Convenient invention or not, Jesse Stone is an interesting construct because, although Parker specifically claimed to want to explore a cop, as opposed to a PI like Spenser, in the midst of Stone's development into a more fully formed person, like Spenser, Parker chose to give Stone a classic PI backstory. Stone, as the reader discovers early on in the originary Jesse Stone novel *Night Passage*, is a hotshot LAPD homicide detective fired due to a fondness for alcohol. A cop with a drinking problem! Go figure. This is such a popular convention in the genre that it borders on cliché. Well, no, it is cliché. And the apparent clichés don't stop there.

Stone is neither a zealous, wide-eyed rookie just out of the academy wanting to do good and to set the world right, nor a grizzled old veteran with one eye on the calendar counting down the days until he can retire to fish the rest of his life away on a lake in Idaho. Stone is thirty-ish, a ten-year man: on the job long enough to have learned all the tricks and to have seen all there is to see, a man with regrets, but not so embittered by his life or police work that they render him useless. Sounds like the perfect résumé for a hard-boiled PI.

Jesse Stone also suffers from a stage four case of that classic hardboiled illness, Bad Blonde Girl Disease. This is not at all surprising given that Parker was such a devotee of Raymond Chandler. A discussion of *Poodle Springs*, *Perchance to Dream*, or any of Parker's other Chandler-related works is for another time and place. Suffice it to say, however, that Raymond Chandler's famous line from *Farewell, My Lovely*—"It was a blonde. A blonde to make a bishop kick a hole in a stained-glass window."—does a neat job of describing Jesse Stone's wife, Jennifer. For about half of *Night Passage*, Jennifer, an aspiring actress, is in lockstep with the blonde from *Fare-well, My Lovely*: scheming, ambitious, unfaithful. To Parker's credit, however, he imbues Jennifer with some redemptive qualities, and not only does she exhibit the ability to grow, as the book progresses she actually becomes a steadying influence on her ex-husband.

Parker's Jesse Stone recipe also includes a healthy—or, depending on your perspective, unhealthy—dose of what I've come to think of as the Woe-Is-Me-I-Coulda-Been-A-Contender Syndrome. It seems Stone was a minor league baseball player, a shortstop in the L.A. Dodgers organization, with potential to have made the major leagues. Jesse Stone is often wont to raise a glass of scotch to a photo of Hall of Fame shortstop Ozzie Smith. If you read between the lines and listen very carefully, you can almost hear Jesse say, "Ozzie, I may never have been as good as you, but I coulda been a contender."

After all, you can't have a good old hardboiled detective setup without a protagonist who is haunted by something. That something, as in my Moe Prager series, can be a secret that, if exposed, can wreak havoc upon the detective and his family. Sometimes, as in Lawrence Block's Matt Scudder series, it can be as profound as the accidental death of an innocent victim. Quite often the haunting is the direct result of loss. That loss can be the loss of career, a spouse, or a loved one, or, as with Jesse Stone's baseball career, the loss of what could have been rather than what was. In many ways, the haunting of potential unfulfilled is more insidious than the loss of the tangible. Parker apparently concurred, as he used this same conceit twice in the Stone series. Jesse's friend and state police homicide commander, Captain Healy, is also a minor league baseball player who coulda been a contender.

Whatever the haunting, whatever the loss, the genre convention is that one loss leads to more loss and often to self-destructive behavior—usually drinking to excess. And Jesse Stone is the poster boy for all of the above. He feels his marriage slipping away, begins drinking heavily, and loses his shield in L.A. and his wife. His theme song might as well have been "I (Who Have Nothing)." And I think that's Parker's point here. He uses the time-tested hardboiled formula to isolate Jesse Stone. To totally drive him away from familiar territory, to remove him from his support system, whether that support system was functional or not. The momentum of loss and self-destruction is the engine that propels Stone's move from one coast to the other. First Mr. Parker isolates Stone, then Stone, doing a reverse Horace Greeley by taking a chief of police job in a tiny New England town, isolates himself.

It is Parker's willingness to use cliché, to tinker with it and to use convention in unconventional ways, that underscores his fine craftsmanship and depth of knowledge of the genre, but he doesn't stop there. Convention would have Stone landing the job as chief of the Paradise police because of his competence as a homicide detective. Convention would have him get the job in spite of his drinking. Here, Parker throws us another curve. Jesse Stone gets the job not in spite of his drinking, but precisely because of it. His new bosses assume drinking has made him weak and pliable, that whatever competence he once displayed has been drowned in a sea of Johnnie Walker Black on the rocks. And why wouldn't they believe it? Stone's record indicates he was fired for cause, and he shows up to his job interview blotto.

As I reread books from the series, Stone's troubles with the drink resonated with another book I'd read or movie I'd seen. I tried hard, thinking back to all the *noir*, hardboiled PI novels, police procedurals, and other crime novels I'd read, but the answer remained elusive. I searched movie databases to see if that could shake my memory loose. It was only after catching a few minutes of *The Ox-Bow Incident* on a classic movie channel that I realized I'd been looking in the wrong place. Jesse Stone may have come east, but I should have been looking west or, to be more exact, at Westerns. What I was remembering or mis-remembering was Robert Mitchum's portrayal of the drunken sheriff in *El Dorado*. Because of Parker's love of Westerns— books and movies—I wouldn't be at all surprised if that's what put the burr under his saddle to write Jesse Stone as a drunken lawman. That is pure speculation, but there is little doubt that the Western heavily influenced Parker's writing.

Readers of the crime genre are very familiar with the line of thought that holds that the modern PI/police novel is simply an iteration of the classic Western and that the Western novel is an iteration of the tales of medieval knights. All three traditions often feature lone men with strong personal codes of ethics—codes that are frequently in conflict with the social norm—who pursue their missions with a single-mindedness of purpose and zeal, not because it is personally advantageous to do so. In fact, it is usually quite the opposite: because it is just and it is right. Think Galahad's grail quest, *High Noon*, *The Long Goodbye*. In the aforementioned 2005 interview, Parker alludes to Spenser having "a knight-errant dimension about him." So, how did we get from Robert Mitchum's drunken lawman to Jesse Stone to Sir Galahad to Spenser and Marlowe?

In chapter seven of *Night Passage*, Parker throws in a few lines about Jesse Stone's taste in movies that might seem fairly insignificant to the casual reader but are very telling about both author and protagonist: "But he [Jesse] didn't pay much attention to movies. He thought they were boring except for westerns. Of which there weren't many new ones."

This establishes a link between Parker and Jesse Stone and a link between Jesse's situation as the new lawman in town and the classic Western, but what of Spenser? One need only search Robert B. Parker's official website to find the link, no pun intended. When you click on "The Spenser Series" under "Books," the next page starts with a clickable title: "Spenser's favorite restaurants, movies, and ball players." Here's where you cover your eyes and try to guess the five movies listed.

SPENSER'S TOP 5 MOVIES
Shane
Ulzana's Raid
The Magnificent Seven
The Searchers
She Wore a Yellow Ribbon

Okay, you can open your eyes now and look. Did you have any luck? As we're in the guessing mood—for those of you born after 1975—would you like to take a stab at what genre all of these movies fall into? That's right, Westerns. Classic Westerns. Four of these movies, *Ulzana's Raid* being the exception, are arguably among the top ten classic Westerns ever made. Parker may see Spenser in terms of a knight, not a sheriff, but he clearly sees a connection between the two.

These films also share a common thread that jibes with the earlier discussion of the knight-lawman-PI tradition. Each of the films features a protagonist who is given or elects to perform a thankless and dangerous task. (Although *The Magnificent Seven,* based on Akira Kurosawa's classic *Seven Samurai,* seems to have several protagonists, the character played by Yul Brynner is the leader of the seven and the one who initially commits to defending the peasants against marauding Mexican bandits.) And in spite of the fact that each of the protagonists is beset by conflicting moral dilemmas, they carry on with their duties, which often leads to dire consequences.

These five films are listed as Spenser's favorites, mind you, not Parker's, although one suspects Parker very well might have agreed with Spenser's big screen tastes. Now recall what the narrator of *Night Passage* tells us about Jesse Stone's taste in movies. As far as a person's values are reflected by his or her tastes, preferences, and choices, it would seem undeniable that Stone and Spenser share a very similar moral center. As an interesting side note, a heading on this webpage purports to list Spenser's five favorite movies that aren't Westerns—but no movies are listed, as if to underscore the importance of the classic Western to Spenser's value system.

You needn't rely solely on my interpretations or extrapolations concerning the classic Western as playing a central role in the moral compasses of both Jesse Stone and Spenser. Parker may no longer be with us, but Ace Atkins, the author entrusted to continue the Spenser franchise by Putnam and by the Parker estate, is. I wrote to Atkins and asked him to comment on the classic Western aspect of the commonality between Spenser and Stone and on the knight-Western-PI continuum.

"I find Stone is that bridge between gumshoe and gun-fighter," says Atkins,

> He's that link from the Western to the urban landscape. I find him much more in line with the Western hero—he did come east from California. But he's slow to speak and acts with great patience. He's the Wyatt Earp of the modern day. With a few things changed here and there, Paradise, Massachusetts, could be Tombstone. He's the sheriff hired to clean up the town.

Parker definitely tossed out those references to Westerns and knights of old in his books. I think what we continually read is men living by a code. Whether it's Spenser or Stone or Doc Holiday or Sir Gawain, they are men drawn to righting wrongs and restoring order. We could get into a larger discussion of someone like Sam Spade, who is immoral and realizes the world is without redemption. Spenser, Stone, and Marlowe do see the world for what it is—but they all have hope. Spade had little illusion of hope.

This classic Western tradition is not only an intellectual undercurrent in the novels, but has a direct impact on how the protagonists go about their business. In the very beginning of Parker's Virgil Cole/Everett Hitch novel *Appaloosa*, Virgil Cole, a small-town marshal, confronts a man called Bear on a dusty street outside a saloon. Bear, as described by Hitch, Cole's partner and the narrator of the novel, is "a big man, fat but strong-looking with a black beard and long hair," and is bleeding from the side of his head where Cole has struck him with his revolver. Cole is trying to arrest Bear, a buffalo skinner, who has threatened to gut a whore he claims hasn't given him his three dollars' worth. In spite of Cole's calm demeanor and repeated requests for Bear to go peaceably, Bear refuses—and not very politely. In the end, Cole shoots Bear and chases off his supporters.

Compare this with a scene from chapter fourteen of *Night Passage*, in which Jesse Stone confronts Jo Jo Genest at the residence of Genest's ex-wife. Genest, a weightlifter and steroid user whom Parker describes as "hulking," "a rhinoceros," "Tarzan," or "one of the apes," has assaulted his ex-wife as he has many times in the past with apparent impunity. When Stone tries to reason with Genest, Jo Jo basically laughs at him and says he can take his ex whenever he wants. She's his property. When Stone reminds Jo Jo that his ex-wife has an order of protection, Jo Jo again dismisses Stone and the power of law enforcement to restrain his activities. At this point, in front of Jo Jo's ex and a subordinate cop, Jesse Stone kicks Genest in the groin. He lectures the incapacitated Jo Jo, holds his .38 to the bridge of Jo Jo's nose, and threatens to shoot him if he comes anywhere near his ex-wife or their children.

Compare this to a confrontation Spenser has with a heavy machine operator named Eddie in chapter six of *Promised Land*. Spenser describes Eddie this way: "a big blond kid . . . He was a weightlifter: lots of tricep definition and overdeveloped pectoral muscles." Spenser goes on to say that, "I'd have been more impressed with him if he weren't carrying a twenty-pound roll around his middle." Spenser is in a Cape Cod bar trying to find information on a runaway housewife named Pam Shepard, whom Eddie is alleged to have slept with. After bragging about his sexual prowess and the ease with which he bedded Pam, Eddie becomes belligerent. Spenser, a former heavyweight boxer, tries to dissuade Eddie from this course of action. When Eddie persists, Spenser embarrasses the bully by smacking him around and then finally hits him hard in the gut.

In all three instances, Cole, Stone, and Spenser are calm and act only when pushed to do so. These three scenarios are so profoundly similar that with the exception of minor details they are nearly indistinguishable. This is true not only on a manifest level, but on a deeper, fundamental level. You have women—a whore, a divorcee, a housewife who sleeps around—who act or have acted in some questionable ways and made some terrible choices, but who Parker's protagonists defend with acts of reluctant violence. It is the nature of these scenarios that bears some analysis. Why are the dynamics of scenes like these so pivotal to Parker's novels? Also note that all three examples take place in the early sections of their respective books in order to establish the nature of the protagonists.

First, let's look at the players: the bad guy, the imperiled woman, and the hero. You can't have a hero without a bad guy, but bullies are a particular kind of bad guy and Parker's bullies are a particular breed of bully. They are all big men with big mouths who flaunt their disrespect for authority and the law. The accepted wisdom is that bullies are actually scared weaklings who pick only on those they are certain they can dominate.

So why bullies? They are convenient villains: easy to write, easy for the reader to root against, easy to hate. There are some sexy, loveable, charming, even sympathetic bad guys in the annals of fiction, but there's nary a bully among them.

Think of *Silence of the Lambs*. Who was the most detestable person in the movie? Hannibal Lecter? Buffalo Bill? No, it's Dr. Chilton. Why? Chilton is a petty, insecure bully who taunts Lecter and interferes with Starling's investigation. It's easier to love a serial killer than a bully.

Parker's bullies are also particular in their prey: women. In his choice of women to put in peril, Parker selects a specific kind of woman, a fallen woman. While it is clear the prostitute and the cheating wife fit into this category, it may not be obvious in the case of the divorcee, but through the course of *Night Passage* we find she never finished high school, isn't the most diligent mother, and isn't much motivated to change—so while she is not a fallen woman in the traditional sense, she's still morally ambiguous.

The motivation behind Parker's choices of women in peril is a little more complicated, however. I believe he chooses these fallen women because defending them and their honor says more about their defenders than it says about the women themselves. It's as if Parker is saying that any man would defend a beautiful virtuous woman, but that it takes a special breed of man—a man who lives by a strict code of right and wrong—to rise to the defense of these women. Can someone say Don Quixote?

PSYCHO EX MACHINA

Deus ex machina—god from the machine—is a term derived from the tradition of Greek tragedy in which the playwright resorts to using a trick to get himself out of a seemingly insolvable plot conflict. It refers both to the physical equipment—a crane or riser—used to deliver the actor playing the god to the stage and to the god him or herself. In short, the use of a *deus ex machina* is cheating the reader or the audience. It's the clue no one knew about or the character who swoops in at the last minute to resolve all the seemingly inexplicable plot conflicts.

Psycho ex machina is a phrase I coined several years ago to describe what I felt was a disturbing trend in the PI subgenre. I use it to refer to the sidekick who does the dirty work so that our protagonist can remain pure of heart and true to his code. I suppose this was an inevitable development as the PI novel evolved to reflect the society and culture at large. Would we find Easy Rawlins as likeable or as sympathetic a protagonist if he had to do the violence and murdering— some warranted, some not—that Walter Mosley has Mouse do? Would Matt Scudder be quite as appealing if there was no Mick Ballou, bloodied butcher's apron and all, for Scudder to turn to in a tough spot? If Sherlock Holmes were in a fix and needed certain crucial information to save a client's life, the current convention would have Dr. Watson torturing the person from whom Holmes needed the information. The most recent incarnation of the *psycho ex machina* is the genius computer hacker friend and ally that every modern PI seems to know. One might argue that Lisbeth Salander from Stieg Larson's Millennium series is Mikael Blomkvist's *psycho ex machina*.

Robert B. Parker's Spenser series features Hawk, perhaps the most famous of all *psychos ex machina*. Hawk, introduced in *Promised Land*, is an African-American leg-breaker for a local crime boss named King Powers. Hawk and Spenser have known each other for years and share a professional respect, but they are by no means friends. Only after Hawk is sent after Spenser by King, and Hawk refuses to kill him, do Hawk and Spenser form a lasting alliance. Although Parker has Spenser describe himself as "a professional thug," it is actually Hawk who is often given the dirty jobs to do. Both Hawk and Spenser live by their individual codes, but Hawk's code is grounded more heavily in street morality than the code of the knight-errant. Parker intended Hawk to be the yang to Spenser's yin, literally the black reflection of Spenser, and only a fool would argue that this wasn't a very fortunate choice. If writing is about making choices, this was one of Parker's best in terms of making the series a great success.

However, the underlying reasons for this yin/yang of Spenser and Hawk has probably less to do with sudden inspiration than with Parker's abiding attachment to the tradition of the Chandlerian detective adjusting to the graying moral standards in the latter stages of the twentieth century. In other words, it would be impossible for Spenser—a happier, more fulfilled, better-fed version of Philip Marlowe—to keep to his code of ethics intact when encountering the cases he was apt to take on during the times in which the series played out. I believe Parker made a calculated and practical choice with Spenser and Hawk, much in the same way he did when setting up his bad guy/imperiled woman/hero confrontations.

And though it is difficult to bicker with success, I would argue that while the use of the *psycho ex machina*, Hawk in this instance, insulates Spenser, the hero-protagonist, from heart-wrenching or even impossible moral choices and allows him to remain true to his ethical code, it, like a governor on a truck engine, robs some of the potential energy from the series. This may be a further contributing factor to the creation of Jesse Stone. While it's true that Spenser is a more "complete" person than Stone and is, unlike Stone, capable of carrying on a healthy long-term romance, and is quick to quote poetry or recommend a restaurant or good wine, I believe Stone is the type of man who would chafe at the prospect of a continuing relationship with a Hawk-like character. And, frankly, that makes Stone a more appealing character to me.

Stone and Spenser both may have started out as cops—Stone as an LAPD homicide detective and Spenser an investigator for the Suffolk County, Massachusetts, DA's office—but from there their career paths diverge. Spenser strikes out on his own, whereas Stone loses his way and his job. As discussed earlier, Stone lands the chief of police job in Paradise, Massachusetts. The nature of Stone's job would make a continuing relationship with a *psycho ex machina* very problematic but, beyond the constraints of his office, Stone is very much a man unto himself. I can't see Jesse Stone, for all of his relationship woes and problems with drink, in need of a dark reflection or a negative image for dramatic purposes. For one thing, his own dark side is very much on display for the world to see. He does, after all, work in a small town, and it's not like Stone's issues are buried very deep. At most, Stone might have a continuing relationship with someone like Hawk as an informant, though I couldn't see Hawk in that role.

None of this is to say that Stone wouldn't be tempted, depending upon the situation, to make an alliance with a Hawk-like character if it were in the service of justice. Nor is it to say that Parker did not introduce Hawk-like characters into the Stone series to shake up Jesse's world. In *Stranger in Paradise*, Jesse Stone is confronted by the Apache hit man Wilson "Crow" Cromartie. Cromartie was last seen in Paradise ten years earlier as a member of a robbery crew that had pulled off a huge heist at a wealthy island enclave. Not only has the statute of limitations expired on his crimes, but the women who were being held hostage during the commission of the robbery hail Crow as a hero, as the man who saved their lives while they were vulnerable and at risk.

Stranger in Paradise opens with Crow walking into Jesse Stone's office and announcing his presence in Paradise. This would seem an odd course of action even given that the statute of limitations had expired on Crow's alleged crimes, but of course there is a less obvious purpose for his coming to see Stone. Crow, who clearly respects Stone, is showing his respect by alerting him. He understands Stone has his job to do, but so does Crow. Crow is also indirectly asking Stone to help him do his job by staying out of his way. Interesting, given that Crow is basically a professional assassin, and Stone and his department try valiantly throughout the course of the novel to put together a case against Crow that will stand up in court.

Yet the respect between the two men is apparently mutual. Parker never wants us to lose sight of the fact that Crow and Stone share important qualities. Molly, one of Stone's cops, compares the two men:

> "He's [Crow] is a little like you, Jesse . . . You have the same silent center. Nothing will make you turn aside. Nothing will make you back up. It's . . . what do shrinks call it . . . ?"
>
> "Autonomy," Jesse said.
>
> "Yes. Both of you are, like, autonomous," Molly said. "Except maybe you have scruples."
>
> "Maybe he does, too," Jesse said.

Parker is very shrewd here in the way he peels away the onion skin for the reader. Notice that Molly, who through the course of the series is often Stone's truth-teller and sounding board, uses the word "maybe" when assessing Stone's moral compass. *Maybe* Jesse has scruples. That is a very telling statement. Jesse is so individualistic that his foibles are more evident to those who surround him than his values. Can you see the people surrounding Spenser having similar doubts about his scruples or lack thereof? And then to have Stone recognize a kindred spirit in Crow by using the same language to assess the killer is pretty amazing. Although Parker doesn't describe Stone's voice or his expression as he says, "Maybe he does, too," I cannot help but see and hear Stone as wistful. This is heady stuff and once again shows how fine a writer Parker was. He drops a bomb on the reader, but not by shining neon lights and announcing, "Here it comes!" Rather, he reveals his character's inner workings subtly, in a quiet moment of casual conversation. Wistful or not, kindred spirit or not, Jesse Stone is not destined to have a long-term relationship with Crow, at least not one in which Crow takes the tough moral choices out of Jesse's hands on a regular basis.

STONE VERSUS SPENSER

It is said that many authors rewrite the same book over and over again. While that is too broad and simplistic a statement, there is the ring of truth about it. I do think the nature of writing is the investigation of haunting questions. Different writers are haunted by different questions, and their works are often defined by how they ask those questions of themselves and how they choose to explore those questions through setting, plot, theme, and character. Very rarely do we find satisfactory answers by asking the question once, in a single form, and exploring it in only one way. It wouldn't be a very haunting question if it could be answered so easily.

Think here of Michael Crichton. It would not be hyperbole, I think, to say that Dr. Crichton was obsessed with the notion of humankind's insignificance in the face of nature and the belief that humankind's hubris and lack of respect in tinkering with the natural order of things leads inevitably to disastrous results. In other words, to quote an old TV commercial, "It's not nice to fool Mother Nature." Crichton explored this notion again and again in novel after novel.

The Andromeda Strain: A space probe sent to capture samples of alien life forms—possibly to be used as biological weapons—returns to Earth carrying a microbe that threatens to destroy all life on Earth.

The Terminal Man: A man given to violent fits due to a brain disorder receives surgery that implants a computer in his brain. The computer, meant to alleviate his violent symptoms, actually leads to him being more violent than before the surgery.

Jurassic Park: Scientists discover a way to reconstitute the DNA of long-extinct dinosaurs and bring them back to life. A wealthy man creates an amusement park populated with dinosaurs, including predatory ones, and all hell breaks loose.

While I would not say that Parker rewrote the same book over and over, I do believe that he also explored similar themes and looked at the same question from different angles in his books. To refer once again to the 2005 interview: in it, the interviewer suggests that Parker was fascinated by the concept of how to take care of people who could not look out for themselves. To facilitate this exploration, he imbued his protagonists' personalities with many common ingredients. So yes, on some level Spenser, Jesse Stone, and even Virgil Cole and Everett Hitch are all Hamlet, though they might not have been meant to be. They were created as protectors: as knights, Western lawmen, PIs, and cops. Any comprehensive reading of Parker's canon would bear this out. Yet I believe that the scope of Parker's works goes deeper than just his broad theme of caring for people who could not look out for themselves. He explored, almost reflexively, questions of loyalty to self, job, code, and friends, and the results of the conflict between these often competing loyalties. He explored the implications of love, of love fading, of love lost, and of love recaptured—not themes usually associated with crime writing.

One of the great joys in revisiting Robert B. Parker's writings in preparation for this piece was the discovery of so many things I'd missed the first time around, and it was a pleasure to read some of his novels that I hadn't read previously. His characters, for all of their faults, flaws, and blind spots, are alive and as real and memorable as any in literature, and Parker was masterful at spinning those foibles into gold. His place is secure as one of the masters of PI and crime fiction.

PARKER SADDLES UP

THE WESTERNS
OF ROBERT B. PARKER

| ED GORMAN |

AS THE REAL West was being settled, numerous writers back East were penning adventures about a mythic West that fascinated readers of every age. It was good versus evil, it was slap leather and draw, it was saving the schoolmarm's virtue and then marryin' her to produce a whole passel of young 'uns.

These cowboys, lawmen, and quick-draws were not much different from the knights of old. They were virtuous, clever, brave, and fearless. They were perfect for inspiring the daydreams of boys not only in America but around the world. Real Western figures were used to sell novels, too. Books supposedly written by Buffalo Bill became bestsellers of their day. That the derring-do the books described was fictional didn't matter. If Buffalo Bill said it was true, then, damn it, it was true.

At the end of the nineteenth century, the dime novels dealing with the West faced competition from a new kind of hero. With the industrialization of America that followed the Civil War, detective Nick Carter and other urban heroes came to the fore. Carter and his imitators were forerunners of the James Bondian protagonist. They used a variety of gizmos to help them solve their crimes and triumph in the name of all that was good and holy. Carter also introduced American boys and girls to the wider world. Carter villains represented some of the real-life forces that troubled our country. Urban crime was much more complex and in many ways more vicious than the crimes of the mythic West.

But soon enough the Western dominated popular culture once again. In 1903 there appeared a twelve-minute film called *The Great Train Robbery*, and silent films and America were never the same. Folks knew the film was authentic because it was filmed right out there in the Old West itself—Milltown, New Jersey.

It is impossible to guess how many Westerns were filmed in the century just past. From the A pictures with big stars, such as *Stagecoach* with John Wayne, *High Noon* with Gary Cooper, and *Unforgiven* with Clint Eastwood, to B pictures with rooster-like scrappers such as Bob Steele, to glitzy singing cowboys such as Roy Rogers and Gene Autry (though early on, Gene was a cowboy trapped in a terrible sci-fi serial called *The Phantom Empire*), lawmen, cowpokes, ranchers, farmers, and even preachers (Bible in one hand, six-gun in the other) took turns settling the mythic West.

The small screen had its turn at taming the Wild West as well; television was dominated by the genre in the '50s and into the middle '60s. There were some very good ones

(*Gunsmoke* and *Have Gun, Will Travel*) and some very bad ones (*Father Murphy* and *Here Come the Brides*). In general, though, TV Westerns weren't any better or any worse than the hundreds of motion pictures the studios had produced.

I mention all this to demonstrate that there's a straight line from the fanciful dime novels to the pulps and films we've come to see as "Westerns." Even John Ford, certainly the most celebrated of Western directors, chose the mythic West over the real West until late in his career. *The Man Who Shot Liberty Valence* is almost a repudiation of the themes Ford used in his earlier movies. In it he not only questions the veracity of legend and myth but is sardonic in the way he undermines it. James Stewart, a peace-loving man, must face down a very nasty Lee Marvin, who means to kill him. Somehow, against all odds, Stewart wins the gunfight and becomes a hero. Even Stewart believes he killed Marvin, but it is actually John Wayne hiding in the shadows behind Stewart who fires the fatal shot. I've never been a John Wayne fan, but the way Ford uses him here is unique, and powerful in Wayne's final scenes. Fifty years after the movie appeared, critics still argue about what the film means in light of Ford's earlier productions.

The Man Who Shot Liberty Valence was only one of the many movies and TV shows that chipped away at the mythic West. Earlier films, such as *The Ox-Bow Incident*, *The Gunfighter*, *The Naked Spur*, and numerous others, had already shown that the standard Hollywood depiction of frontier life was false. And only a few years after *Liberty Valence*, the first so-called Spaghetti Westerns began appearing in Italy and quickly throughout Europe. The Spaghetti Westerns demolished the Hollywood myth of the West but created one even more stylized and (in most cases) just as fraudulent. The Spaghettis created a West that was nothing more than drinking, whoring, killing, and dying, all rendered in grim close-ups and accompanied by music that was often more thrilling that the films themselves.

Meanwhile, television had been at its own revisionism. On radio, *Gunsmoke* had been the most intelligent and violent of all Westerns. It was toned down somewhat for TV, but its adult themes and Old Testament sense of justice brought many brutal truths into the living rooms of America. *Maverick* toyed with the myths using humor. Gambler James Garner had two interests—poker and beautiful women—and wasn't much for fighting or gunplay. In fact, in many episodes he ran from fights. *Have Gun, Will Travel* featured Richard Boone as a quite literate man of exquisite and expensive tastes who hired out to right wrongs. The liberal political beliefs of the show's writers and producers were often on display in the scripts; many of them dealt with racism, religion gone awry, and rich people who virtually enslaved those around them. The '50s and '60s were the boom decades for the TV Western, and many changes—at least a few of them ludicrous—were wrought on the standard formulas.

This was the state of the popular culture Robert B. Parker grew up in. I have no idea if he was a fan of Westerns, but based on his Spenser novels I suspect he was. It's not difficult to imagine many of the Spenser novels as Westerns. (The same can be said for Elmore Leonard's crime novels.) Both Spenser and his sidekick Hawk are larger than life, and their mission is to bring justice to situations that might otherwise favor the dark side. They ride into town and make everything right, while having a lot of adventures in the process. The difference here is that the Spenser novels are nuanced in ways few Westerns ever were. One of Parker's greatest strengths was his social eye. The Spenser novels offer a running commentary on the foibles and excesses of middle and upper class American life.

Still, for all the reality in the Spenser series, it's really about myth. For all his awareness and grumbly wisdom, Spenser is not much different from the private eyes in the pulps of the '30s and '40s. Much of what he does in the books would land him in jail for interfering with police investigations. The fights he gets into would result in lawsuits, if not arrests. And his ability to solve murders would make him a TV legend. Forget ESP; just give Spenser a gourmet meal, a glass of fine wine, and a night of blabber and sex with Susan Silverman, and the identity of the miscreant will be waiting for him in the morning.

This is by no means criticism. Parker just did what two centuries of American writers before him had done—created vivid romances involving derring-do and meting out justice. If it was good enough for Sir Walter Scott, it was good enough for Robert B. Parker.

Readers were surprised a few years ago when they heard Parker was publishing a Western. Why did this most urban of writers decide to ride the dusty trails of the traditional Western? Well, I would guess he liked the form and saw it as a challenge. Most importantly, he did with the Western what he'd done with the private eye novel: he reinvented it, made it completely his own. Yes, all the familiar elements of frontier tales were here—just as all the familiar elements of the private detective tale were in the Spenser novels—but with Parker's intelligence, his worldview, and his style, he made the genre completely his own. There are no other Westerns like the five he wrote. And, no surprise here, Parker's Westerns are very much like his Spenser novels, informed as they are by both violence and an entrenched melancholy.

Legend and myth had to have been on Robert B. Parker's mind when he sat down to write his Westerns. Even though his Wyatt and Virgil Earp in his first Western, *Gunman's Rhapsody*, were involved in the gunfight at O.K. Corral, neither was the folkloric figure popular in dime novels. Yes, Wyatt was a lawman, but he was also a businessman. He was attracted to boomtowns at least partly because of opportunities to make money while wearing a badge. He often bought and ran saloons and sometimes whorehouses. His older brother Virgil, who was the Tombstone city marshal at the time of the O.K. Corral gunfight, spent much of his early years as an efficient and effective peace officer until, later on in Tombstone, outlaws collected in the street and fired on him, shattering his left arm. Wyatt became the star of the family because of a largely fictional biography written during his lifetime. We do love our heroic stories. *Wyatt Earp: Frontier Marshal* by Stuart N. Lake became a long-running bestseller.

The Wyatt myths have led to innumerable books and films. In the '50s, Hugh O'Brien's *Wyatt* was in the top ten most popular TV shows. Even back then it was kind of goofy and dull, without any of the darker aspects I'd enjoyed even at twelve years old. On the other hand, the Earp story gave John Ford material for his excellent movie *My Darling Clementine*. Excellent, that is, as drama. As history, it was less than accurate—Ford and his writers based their script on the Stuart N. Lake book, which was filled with fictional derring-do.

Welcome to the fungible, fictional world of the legendary Earp brothers.

These are the raw facts and assorted pieces of hokum that Parker faced when creating his own version of the mythic West. Now, I have no idea if he ever watched the HBO series *Deadwood*, which came along in 2004. By then Parker's first Western was finished and he was well on his way to creating a successful and appealing new Western series with his own creations, Cole and Hitch. But *Deadwood* is important in any discussion of contemporary Western fiction because it redefined the entire genre, just as Parker himself did. *Deadwood* and Parker's Westerns are similar in many ways, in fact. They both depict the West as it was, a maelstrom of rich versus poor and politics as dirty as our own.

In *Deadwood*, the powerful families of the East paid surrogates to make them equally powerful—and rich—in the West. And as with any land that was being settled, Darwin's laws applied absolutely. The strong not only survived but prospered. Read any serious book about daily frontier life and you soon real realize how many families were impoverished. These themes had been touched on in various ways by traditional Western writers, but few had dealt with it in any depth. In short, *Deadwood* is about barbaric capitalism in the Old West. And it trashed just about every mythic Western cliché that publishing and Hollywood had ever created.

These days the conventional wisdom is that the dime novel Western heroes were the basis for the private eyes who began appearing in detective pulps. What needs to be added to this point is that the private eyes and assorted tough guys were also unlike the heroic and squeaky-clean cowboy heroes. For instance, Carroll John Daly's Race Williams bragged about the psychopathic pleasure he took in slaughtering dozens of bad guys. And the milieu of the pulp tough guys was different, too. Their authors allowed them to see and react to the poverty, the injustice, and the violence that was endemic in cities. The one thing pulp cowboys and pulp mystery protagonists had in common was that they faced the same kind of political forces that ruled their environments. In the Old West, robber barons and other wealthy miscreants were often the culprits; in the cities the culprits were many and varied, reaching from the privileged domain of businessmen to the brass-knuckled ruthlessness of mobsters and ward healers.

The heroic spirit of the cowboy stars was replaced by the tough guys' well-earned cynicism.

The characters in *Deadwood*, men and women alike, would have been much more at home in the pages of the crime pulp *Black Mask* than *Weekly Western Tales*. Once you see *Deadwood*, it's difficult to return to the conventional Western that is light on the true historical reality.

GUNMAN'S RHAPSODY

It was with all this as background that I picked up *Gunman's Rhapsody*, Parker's first Western, a few years after it appeared. I'd put off buying a copy because I really didn't want to read a Western by Robert B. Parker. I liked Parker's crime novels very much. In fact, I felt that I owed him a percentage of what I made on my first private eye novel. (He could've bought a pack of gum with it.) Without his presence in the market I doubt I would have been able to sell it.

In the '70s, private eyes were out of fashion. This continued into the early '80s. But as Parker's popularity grew, the private eye form became popular again. Parker did more than reinvigorate PI fiction—he reinvented it. These books were brand new, fresh, vivid, witty, abundantly violent, and very true (and wise) about the decades in which the novels were being produced.

I had no such hopes for Parker's attempt at Western fiction. I just assumed, incorrectly, that he needed a break from his various crime series and thought saddling up might be a lark. Thirty pages into *Gunman's Rhapsody* I knew better. It turned out to be an exciting and gripping novel.

The shootout at the O.K. Corral has been depicted numerous times in books and films. But Parker's take on

Tombstone, filled as it is with Wyatt Earp and the others associated with the event, works especially well because Parker uses a number of devices (news stories, bulletins, etc.) to lend the story real historical context.

The plot spins on Wyatt's unexpected love for the beautiful lady friend of Johnny Behan, a local politician whose sway in the town allows Parker room to give us a real sense of how towns like Tombstone were run.

Parker suggests the whole war between the Earps and the McLaurys and the Clantons was due to the woman Wyatt falls in love with, Josie Marcus. At the beginning of the novel, Wyatt is living with his "domestic partner," Mattie Blaylock. They live together, but it is an utterly loveless relationship.

> She'd been fun once. A good-natured whore with an easy temperament when he'd met her in Dodge. His brothers had women with them, and Mattie Blaylock was eager to accommodate the man who'd run Clay Allison. But the fun had been mostly saloon fun. At home ironing his shirts, Mattie had lost much of the brightness that had gleamed in the gaslit cheer of the Long Branch. In truth, he realized, much of the brightness and the good nature had come from alcohol, and, domesticated, she could no longer consume enough of it, even boosted with laudanum, to be much more than the petulant slattern that was probably who she really was. Still, she could cook and her sewing brought in some money. And he didn't have to spend much time with her.

This description sets the stage for the romance to come between Wyatt and Josie, a relationship as powerful and painful as the one that haunts Parker's Jesse Stone, and one that will lead to violence and despair.

Johnny Behan's relationship with Josie is similar to Wyatt and Mattie's—a loveless one. When Wyatt and Josie meet, there are sparks and a romance begins. As the relationship between Wyatt and Josie grows, Johnny Behan, who becomes sheriff, becomes more and more angry. Not because he is the jilted lover, but because he has political ambitions and Wyatt and Josie's relationship is known publicly; he is being made to look foolish in front of the whole town. This anger will drive Behan to bring hostility between the Earps and McLaurys and Clantons. This is a conversation between Wyatt and Josie as they discuss Behan:

"It's complicated being a man," Josie said.

"It's easy enough," Wyatt said, "knowing what to do. It's hard sometimes to do it."

"I don't think it's hard for you."

"Hard for everybody, Josie." He smiled and kissed her again. "Even us."

"I think even *knowing* what he should do was hard for Johnny."

"He sure as hell doesn't know what he shouldn't do," Wyatt said.

"I don't think Johnny is a bad man," Josie said. "He's more a bad combination of weak and ambitious, I think."

"Doesn't finally matter which it is," Wyatt said. "Comes to the same thing. It can get him killed."

Parker's crime novels often turn on matters of honor and integrity. To Josie's mind, Behan is not a "bad man" when you understand him on his own terms. He starts a war in which many die because he needs to avenge his honor, which Earp has destroyed by wooing Josie away from him. By that logic just about any kind of crime, including war, can be justified, but it's telling that Josie would think this way. She is used to justifying her own wrongdoing to anybody who will listen.

Gunman's Rhapsody is about people acting and reacting to the circumstances around them. We see a key driving factor between the Earps late in the novel. The O.K. Corral gunfight has taken place and Virgil Earp has been badly injured in a later bushwhacking. There are elegiac moments, laments for times past—for women, places, plans that went awry. Parker hints at fate in certain passages, how the Earps had seemed driven past reason, past common sense in some cases. But in an extended scene with Virgil we see the heroic notion of brothers who are lashed together by blood and tradition.

Virgil says to Wyatt:

> "You want Josie. I want Josie. Morg wants Josie. James and Warren want Josie. People don't like it, they don't like us. You do something. We do it with you. Brothers. The Earp brothers."
>
> "I know."
>
> "Don't never think anything else is true," Virgil said.
>
> "That's who we are. That's what we got. It's what we always had."

In these passages we have the heart of the book. No matter what grief comes to them, the Earps can always rely on each other—not only for back-up in gunfights, but even more importantly, for understanding and acceptance in a world that frequently spurns them. The Earps finds the same kind of support in each other that Spenser finds in Susan Silverman and Hawk.

APPALOOSA, RESOLUTION, BRIMSTONE, AND BLUE-EYED DEVIL

It is in the four Virgil Cole and Everett Hitch novels, the series of Westerns Parker wrote following *Gunman's Rhapsody*, that we really see the connection between Spenser and at least a version of Hawk in the Old West. Though *Gunman's Rhapsody* brought us the quick-take chapters and the pitch-perfect dialogue of the Spenser books, in *Appaloosa, Resolution, Brimstone*, and *Blue-Eyed Devil* we have not only the literary tactics of Parker's private eye novels, we also have the themes—a less-than-perfect protagonist meting out justice in a less-than-perfect world with a less-than-perfect woman always in his mind and heart. Hitch is not quite as tight-lipped as Cole, but his days as a buffalo hunter make him a sturdy and trustworthy deputy.

The set-up in *Appaloosa* is familiar, with a murderous ranch owner and his murderous crew doing as they please whenever they come to town. Killing lawmen is their specialty. They've also murdered a rancher and savagely raped and killed his wife. Parker redeems the familiarity immediately. Cole and Hitch sign on for good money to clean up the town, but only if the town council agrees to honor every single one of the laws Cole has written. No changes or he walks.

Parker did his homework in creating the social landscape of Appaloosa. He gives us a real glimpse into the daily lives of the important citizens and the politics of keeping a town safe. Louis L'Amour once argued that towns were rarely overrun because the local citizens just grabbed their shotguns and took care of the bad guys themselves. This implies that the idea of "town tamers" was exaggerated. I can't say for sure, but I think that somewhere in his numerous novels, which he always claimed were carefully researched, L'Amour used the trope of the "town tamer." And in authentic histories of the Old West there are references to such men, including the Earps and others.

Parker does well by Virgil Cole here, creating a believable and curiously melancholy figure who remains enigmatic to a fault. In the longstanding tradition of the traditional hero, generally Virgil lets his actions suffice for his words, though his conversations offer intriguing glimpses of his feelings. Hitch, who tells the story, is the open one, reporting what he's experienced with both his mind and heart. He's a likable character.

Parker's handling of the main female character, Allie French, is amusing and occasionally moving. A widow who has little or no money and is not sure what to do next is rescued by Cole's offer of getting her a job as piano player in the hotel. She has insisted that her background is musical—she emphasizes that she is not "common"—and so it may well be. But a good piano player she ain't. Cole doesn't laugh about this, but the reader certainly does.

One reviewer disliked Allie French enough to say that she is "manipulative" and implies that she is Susan Silverman redux. At the very least, like Spenser, Cole seems to enjoy women who make him work hard for his perch in their lives.

To his credit, Parker gives Allie a complexity that is sometimes maddening to Virgil. She is a woman who is never comfortable with herself or her circumstances. A prostitute, Katie, explains in a brief exchange with Everett Hitch how she understands Allie, at the same time giving us a glimpse of what it was like being a woman during those times and in those conditions. In these brief conversations, we see that many women back then were probably as strong as the men. Read any good history of frontier women and you'll find how difficult their work was, far more difficult in many ways than the men's.

"Most of us understand Allie French," Katie said.

"What do you all understand?"

"She ain't no different," Katie said, "from any of us working girls. She's willing to fuck who she got to fuck, so she can get what she needs to get."

"How 'bout love?" I said. "Love got anything to do with it?"

"Out here, love's pretty hard for a woman," Katie said. "Mostly it's the men worry about love. You know how many miners and cowboys told me they loved me just before they, ah, emptied their chamber?"

"Tell you the truth, Katie," I said, "I guess I don't want to know that."

"Men maybe can worry 'bout love," Katie said. "Most women out here got to think 'bout other things."

Appaloosa is as well written, as character-ripe and thrilling, as the finest Spenser or Jesse Stone novel. It is a magnificent piece of craft.

You don't have to read much of this novel to see why Hollywood was so eager to film it. (Ed Harris and Viggo Mortensen starred.) The book is packed with outsize, fascinating characters, and the pace builds perfectly to the inevitable but still provocative ending. *Appaloosa* became a memorable movie that the critics understandably loved.

The Cole-Hitch saga continued with *Resolution* and *Brimstone*. Private detective novels generally take place in a telescoped period of time. Ross Macdonald favored twenty-four hours, honoring the classical form of tragedy. In his Westerns, Parker breaks time frequently. Days, months, even years pass in the saga, lending the books a real sense of lives lived, lives subtly changed. The time frames for his Spenser and Jesse Stone novels are much more telescoped.

Resolution is largely Hitch's story. He's hired to watch over the Blackfoot Saloon, which is shorthand for "hell hole." After killing a man long overdue for death and making sure the prostitutes are treated better, Hitch becomes the point man for law and order in this small town. But widespread violence is inevitable. Then his friend Virgil Cole shows up, and the battle is really joined. What makes this novel work is the *Deadwood*-like squalor of the people and the setting. Parker shows us the lives of average citizens, and as I read I thought of how the gold and silver boomtowns operated: bad water, tainted food, filthy sanitary facilities.

There is an interesting exchange between Virgil Cole and Everett Hitch. Please note this is a spoiler alert. If you have not read *Appaloosa*, then this exchange will give away a key part of the ending of that novel. However, it explains where Virgil's mind is as *Resolution* starts. It also shows the bond and friendship between Cole and Hitch. And it sheds light on Hitch's behavior at the end of *Appaloosa*.

The two are sitting alone on the front porch of a hotel in Resolution, talking. Virgil Cole explains how he continued to be a lawman in Appaloosa after Everett Hitch had left town (after that novel ended). Virgil says he walked away from his job when Allie ran away with a "tinhorn" who promised to take her to his ranch in New Mexico. Of course, the tinhorn is lying; he has no ranch, he just says these things to "fuck her." Virgil explains how he leaves Appaloosa and chases them down and finds Allie left behind in a town called Little Springs with the tinhorn gone. He chases after the tinhorn and eventually catches up with him. He offers the tinhorn a chance to draw, but he refuses, so Cole draws and kills him in cold blood. Cole then reveals that Hitch shot Bragg because of Allie. Even though Allie is not seen in this novel, her presence is still looms large.

Brimstone also has some of the brooding qualities of the Jesse Stone books. Virgil Cole is still looking for Allie French. He is determined to find her, but when he does he almost wishes he hadn't. The very proper Allie has turned prostitute, and Virgil can't deal with that. This is the same way Jesse Stone's ex-wife haunts the Stone books.

Of all Parker's Westerns, *Appaloosa* is my favorite, but the following scene from *Brimstone* is the single most powerful moment in any of the Westerns. It occurs early in the novel.

The book begins with Cole and Hitch looking for Allie French. They have been searching for almost a year. They ride into a nothing town and find her working in a dump of a saloon as a whore, looking terrible. Cole and Hitch take her out, much to the displeasure of the owner and bartender. When the bouncer tries to stop them, Cole knocks him on his ass with the butt of his revolver. The next day, they get ready to leave town, and the boys from the whorehouse are waiting for them to get Allie back. The gunfight is Parker's masterstroke. The clipped prose and stark dialogue conveys Virgil's courage and Allie's terror.

> "I count six," Virgil said to me softly. "Anything develops, I'll take the first man. You take the last, and we'll work our way to the middle."
>
> I nodded. At this range, with the eight-gauge, I might get two at a time.
>
> "Virgil," Allie said. "What is it."
>
> "Nothing to worry about," Virgil said.
>
> Allie looked for the first time at the men across the street.
>
> "Oh my God, Virgil, it's Pig."
>
> "That his name?" Virgil said.
>
> "Don't let him take me back."
>
> "Nope," Virgil said.

"Everett . . ."

"We're fine, Allie," I said. "We're fine."

Pig was carrying a big old Navy Colt in a gun belt that sagged under his belly. There was dried blood on his shirt. It appeared that he hadn't changed it since Virgil hit him. The left side of Pig's face was swollen and dark, with a long scab where Virgil's front sight had dragged across the cheekbone. The five men with him were all carrying. I thumbed back both hammers on the eight-gauge.

We kept walking our parallel walk. Allie held tight to Virgil's left arm. At the end of the street was the Barbary Coast Café, and across the street from that the railroad station, and beyond that the river. And nothing else. It was obvious where we were going.

"I need you to let go of my arm now, Allie," Virgil said.

The gunfight itself, like many of the scenes in all of Parker's Westerns, is so cinematic a director could shoot the printed page and knock off for the day. The final Cole-Hitch book is *Blue-Eyed Devil.* The police chief of a small town invites Cole and Hitch to his office to introduce himself and to offer them jobs as part of his force. The problem is that Cole and Hitch have already figured out that Chief Amos Callico (great name) is a pig. Callico, of course, has political ambitions (governor) and won't abide these two standing in his way. *Blue-Eyed Devil* has a little bit of everything, including pissed-off Apaches and a mysterious stranger who Parker describes thusly:

He was wearing a beaded buckskin shirt, an ivory-handled Colt on his hip, and a derby hat tilted forward over the bridge of his nose. He looked like somebody from a wild west show, except, somehow, I knew he wasn't . . .

He had black-and-white striped pants tucked into high black boots, and his skin was smooth and kind of pale, like a woman's. He didn't look like he spent much time outside. His hands were pale, too, with long fingers.

In Western fiction lore there is always room for an eccentric killer.

The stranger's name is Chauncey Teagarden (another great name) and he is a gunman too, possibly sent to kill Virgil Cole. And Allie, in her sad yet infuriating way, shows she hasn't changed one bit as Cole finds her buttering up the gunman. Virgil and Everett watch, and this is the conversation between the two about Allie's nature:

> "And she knows that Chauncey is here sooner or later to kill me," Virgil said.
> I nodded.
> "And she knows that he might succeed."
> "Always possible," I said.
> "And so you know she's thinking ahead," Virgil said.
> I was quiet for a moment, looking across the street. Then I took in some air and blew it out slowly.
> "And lining up replacements," I said.

Once again a Parker protagonist must face the sorrow of love gone awry. Spenser and Stone have both faced this kind of grief.

There's more gunplay and dying here than in any of the previous books, and the pages turn even faster. An exciting and fitting conclusion to the Cole-Hitch saga.

The Westerns of Robert B. Parker work within the parameters of popular culture. In reviewing them we've dealt with crooked sheriffs, gunfights, women who can't be tamed, male bonding, and lawless towns. These are the mythic elements of a century and a half of Western genre fiction. And for the most part Parker presents them as they're usually depicted. Readers of traditional Westerns will not feel cheated by these books. Parker knows you have to give readers what they pay for. In this case, they want the myth.

But, again, as with his crime novels, he brings his worldview and his own sensibility into play, enriching the books for more demanding readers. While the trappings may be mythic, the characters are more realistic. There are many legends about the Earp brothers, but as we see with Virgil, the legends forgot to include the human element.

For all the action, for all the crossing and double-crossing, for all the colorful and clamorous history of the mythic West, finally it is the characters we will remember most about Parker's Westerns. The same way we recall the characters in the Spenser and Stone novels.

SPENSER

A PROFILE

| ROBERT B. PARKER |

SUSAN AND I sat at a table in the Charles Square courtyard having a drink in the late afternoon with Susan's friend Amy Trent. It was one of those days in late June. The temperature was about 78. There were maybe three white clouds in the sky. The quiet breeze that drifted in from the river smelled fresher than I knew it to be.

"I'm trying to write a book," Amy said. "The working title is *Men Who Dare*, a series of profiles of men who are strong and tough and do dangerous work. Mountain climbers, Navy Seals, policemen, firemen."

"Amy needs a sample profile to submit with her proposal, in hopes of getting a contract and an advance," Susan said. "I said you'd be perfect."

"Amy's looking for sexual splendor as well?" I said.

Amy smiled.

"Always," she said. "Will you talk with me?"

"Sure," I said.

"Okay, I have a bunch of questions written down," Amy said. "You can answer them, dismiss them, respond to a question I didn't ask, anything you want, I'm interested in what you're like. Okay?"

"Okay."

"Susan, feel free to jump in any time," Amy said. "You know him better than anyone. "

"Don't rat me out," I said, "about the sexual splendor."

"Our secret," Susan said.

Amy took a notebook out of her book bag and opened it. She was a professor at Harvard, and, faced with that limitation, not bad looking. If she had dressed better and done her hair better and improved on her makeup, and worn more stylish glasses, she might have been good looking . . . but then the faculty senate would probably have required her to wear a scarlet A on her dress.

She studied her notebook for a moment. I looked at Susan. She smiled. Zing went the strings of my heart. Then Amy took out a small tape recorder and put it on the table.

"Okay?" she said.

"Sure."

She turned the recorder on.

"Okay," Amy said. "Just to warm up a little. Why are you such a wise guy?"

"It's a gift," I said.

Susan frowned at me.

"If you're going to do this," Susan said, "you have to do it."

"You didn't tell me I had to be serious," I said.

"Well you do," she said.

Amy waited. She had a lot of kinetic intensity about her, but she knew how to keep it in check. I nodded.

"I seem to have an unavoidable capacity for seeing a thing and seeing beyond it at the same time."

"Would you say that you have a heightened sense of irony?" Amy said.

"I probably wouldn't say it, but it's probably true."

"It is also," Susan said, "a distancing technique. It keeps people and events from getting too close."

"Except you," I said.

She smiled again.

"Except me."

"Besides Susan, are there things that can get through that ironic barrier?" Amy said.

"I don't think so."

"Because?"

"Because if they did," I said, "I couldn't do what I do."

"But if you refuse to care . . ." Amy said.

"I don't refuse to care," I said. "I refuse to let it control me."

"How do you do that?" Amy said.

"It's a matter of perspective."

"Meaning?"

"There's a line from Auden," I said. "*The torturer's horse scratches its innocent behind on a tree.*"

"A poem," Amy said.

"*Musee des Beaux Arts.*"

"Life goes on," she said.

"Something like that," I said. "Though not for everyone."

"And you find that consoling?"

"I find it instructive," I said.

"Perspective," Amy said.

I nodded.

234 IN PURSUIT OF SPENSER

Amy wasn't reading her questions now. She seemed interested.

"In such a world," she said, "do you have any absolutes?"

I nodded at Susan.

"Her," I said.

"Love," Amy said.

I shook my head.

"Her," I said.

"Yes," she said. "I see."

One point for Harvard. The waitress came by and I had another beer, and Susan had another white wine. And Amy had more iced tea.

"So why do you do it?" she said.

"What I do? "

"Yes."

"Because I can," I said.

"That simple?"

"I'm pretty simple," I said.

Amy looked at Susan. Susan smiled.

"He is," she said. "And he isn't. That will show itself if you talk with him enough. But I warn you he is almost never one thing."

Amy nodded and braced herself with another slug of iced tea.

"So you do what you do because you can," Amy said. "You're good at it."

"Yes," I said.

"Do you like it?"

"Most of the time," I said. "It allows me to live life on my own terms."

"Aren't their other jobs?" Amy said. "That allow you to do that and don't require you to carry a gun?"

"Not that many," I said. "And almost none at which I'd be any good."

"You say you want to live life on your own terms, what are they?"

"The terms?"

"Yes."

I thought about it. As the afternoon moved along more people were coming in for a drink. Maybe several. It was a relatively glamorous crowd for Cambridge. Few if any ankle length skirts and sandals with socks. I looked at Susan.

"What are my terms," I said.

"He's being cute," Susan said to Amy. "He understands himself very well, but he wants me to say it."

"It's pretty hard for me not to be cute," I said.

Susan rolled her eyes slightly.

"He can learn; but he can't be taught," Susan said. "He can find his way; but he can't take direction. He will do very difficult and dangerous things; but he cannot be ordered to do them. Voluntarily, he is generous and compassionate and quite kind. But he cannot be compelled to it."

"Autonomous," Amy said.

"To a pathological extreme," Susan said.

Amy checked her tape recorder. It appeared to be doing what it was supposed to.

"Can you get him to do things he doesn't want to do?" Amy said.

"I'm doing this interview," I said.

Neither of them paid me any attention.

"Up to a point," Susan said.

"What is the point?" Amy said.

"I can't change him," Susan said. "I cannot make him cease to be who he is."

"Would you want to?"

"I would prefer he didn't risk his life," Susan said. "In a sense he's risking mine as well."

"Because?" Amy said.

"I cannot imagine a life without him in it."

"Do you try to change that?"

"No. It is part of what he is," Susan said. "He would not be him if he didn't do what he does. And it is the him he is that I cannot imagine life without."

"Wow," I said.

"The syntax is perhaps a little convoluted," Susan said. "But, so are you Ducky."

"You mean I'm not simple?" I said.

"You are and you aren't," Susan said.

"Oh," I said. "Yeah."

"I want to talk more about your relationship," Amy said. "Since it's come up. But I'm not sure I have yet gotten a solid handle on why you do what you do, which would be sort of the heart of my book, I think."

"There are a lot of problems which need to be solved," I said, "and their solution takes the kinds of skills I have. But because of my extreme pathology, I can't solve those problems in a structured context: police work, military, Harvard College. So I do it this way."

"And," Susan said, "you do it because it allows you to state who and what you are."

"So who and what is he?" Amy said.

Susan shook her head.

"It has something to do with honor," Susan said.

They both looked at me. I looked at Susan.

"I could not love thee half as much?" I said. "Loved I not honor more?"

She smiled again.

"Oh, shut up," she said.

"Which makes a nice segue," Amy said, "back to your relationship. Why have you never married?"

Susan and I looked at each other.

"I don't really like her that much," I said.

"Yes, you do," Amy said. "You have been together for years. You seem like the kind of people who would marry. Everyone says you are the two most connected people they've ever seen. Why not get married?"

I looked at Susan. She smiled and didn't speak. I was, at least for the moment, on my own.

"What we have," I said, "is a very . . . delicate . . . love affair. We are different at almost every level that doesn't matter. We are very, ah, committed to our own point of view . . . and what we have is amazingly good. I guess we don't want to mess with it."

"Have you ever lived together?"

"We tried it once," I said.

"And?"

"And all the differences that don't really matter, mattered, when they were contained in one space."

"You travel together?"

"Sure," I said. "And we spend nights together. But we don't live together."

Amy frowned.

"Do I hear you saying," she asked, "that what you have is too precious to risk compromising it by getting married?"

"Yes," I said.

Amy looked at Susan. Susan smiled and nodded. Amy looked back at me. I smiled.

"Well," Amy said. "Alrighty then. Let me ease onto simpler ground here. A little history."

"Okay," I said.

"You were born in Laramie, Wyoming."

"I was."

"And your mother bore you, as it were, posthumously."

"Yes," I said. "She died but they were able to save me."

"So you never had a mother."

"In any but a biological sense, no."

"And your father brought you up?"

"My father and my two uncles."

"Your father's brothers?"

"No," I said. "They were my mother's brothers."

"Really?"

"It's how my father met my mother. He was friends with her brothers."

"You all lived in the same house?"

"Yes."

"How was that?"

"Fine," I said. "It didn't seem unusual. It was just the way my family was."

"What did they do?"

"Carpenters, hunting guides, raised a few cattle, broke some horses, used to ride bucking horses in rodeos, used to box for prize money around Wyoming and Montana at carnivals and smokers."

"They sound like tough guys," Amy said.

"They were tough guys," I said.

"Were they tough with you?"

"No," I said.

"Did any of them marry?"

"They all went out with a lot of women," I said. "My father never remarried. Both my uncles married, but not while I was living there."

"So essentially you grew up in an all male household," Amy said.

"Yes."

"What was the effect of that do you think?"

"I suppose there must have been one," I said. "But I haven't got a glib answer for you. They made me feel valuable. They made me feel secure. They used to show up at every PTA meeting, all the time I was in school. All three of them, sitting in a row in the back. I'm told they made the teachers nervous."

"Anything else about them?"

"They made me feel equal. I was expected to share the work of the household, probably, which included the work of raising me. If I didn't want to do something they listened to me and sometimes I didn't have to, and sometimes I did. But they never were dismissive. I was always a participant. And they never were unkind."

I stopped and thought back about my family. It made me smile.

"Nobody much crossed them, though," I said.

"Is Susan the fulfillment of a long deprivation?" Amy said.

I drank some beer.

"Absolutely," I said. "But that would be true if I'd had a mother. The time I spent before I met her seems aimless."

"They teach you to box?" Amy said.

"Yes. My Uncle Nick, mostly. I fought some golden gloves and had some pro fights, and was looking like a comer. But I also got a football scholarship to Holy Cross, and so I went to play football for a couple of years."

"I don't know much about football, but what position were you?"

"Strong safety," I said. "And I ran back punts."

"Were you good?"

"Yeah, but I didn't like being coached, and college was boring, so I went back to boxing."

"Was it boring because it was Catholic?" Amy said.

"No," I said. "It was boring because it was college."

"You sound scornful of college," Amy said.

"I am."

"But you've read a lot of books, I'm told. You quote poetry."

"Self-educated," I said.

"Remember what I told you about him," Susan said.

"Were you a good boxer?"

"Not good enough," I said. "While I was still fighting, I took the police exam, and passed, and decided to do that."

"Were you good at that?"

"No, too many rules."

"So you quit," Amy said.

"I did," I said. "I may be unemployable."

"And became a private detective."

I nodded.

"You met Hawk while you were boxing?"

"You know about Hawk," I said.

"Susan introduced us," Amy said.

"Whaddya think?" I said.

"He terrified me, and . . . excited me, I guess."

"Me too," I said.

"I don't believe that for a minute," Amy said. "Hawk said you bailed him out of a difficult racial situation."

"We conspired on that," I said.

"Do you want to talk about Hawk?" Amy said.

"No. You'll need to talk with him direct. Hawk is what he is."

"Including your friend."

"Yes."

"Why are you so close?"

"We know the same things," I said.

"Like fighting?"

"Like . . . If I were black and Hawk were white then he'd be me, and I'd be him."

"Race makes the difference?"

"I grew up white in a white culture. Hawk grew up black in a white culture. When you are marginalized, you become very practical."

"Marginalized," Susan said.

I shrugged modestly.

"I'm with Harvard grads," I said. "I'm showing off a little."

"Talk a little more about the effect of marginalization," Amy said.

"You have less room to maneuver about what's right or wrong," I said. "Mostly what's right is what works. Your view becomes pretty up-close."

"It makes him immoral?"

"No, Hawk is moral," I said. "His word is good. He does nothing gratuitously. It's just that his morality is more result oriented. He does what needs to be done without agonizing over it before or after."

"You agonize?"

"Too strong," I said. "I probably think about it more than Hawk. And *right* may have a more abstract component for me."

"Is that a good thing?"

"I don't know," I said.

Amy sat for a moment contemplating the slowly turning tape in her recorder.

"Do you trust him?" she said.

"Absolutely."

Again Amy thought for awhile.

Finally she said, "I guess I don't entirely understand."

I shrugged.

"Best I can do," I said.

"Susan?" Amy said.

"He admires people who can do things," she smiled. "Hawk can do things."

Amy nodded. It was moving on toward supper time. I looked around at the now crowded and lively courtyard. Even though we were right in the heart of Cambridge, there was a heartening absence of Birkenstocks.

"Okay," Amy said. "Let's talk about you and Susan again."

"What is this?" I said. "Men and women who dare?"

Amy smiled.

"I think maybe I can't understand you without understanding you in her context," Amy said.

"Probably," I said.

"How did you meet?"

"I was working on a case, missing teenaged boy, up in Smithfield. She was the school guidance counselor. I questioned her about the boy, and she was immediately taken with me."

Susan rolled her eyes.

"What's your version?" Amy asked Susan.

"He was working on a case, missing teenaged boy, up in Smithfield," Susan said. "I was the school guidance counselor. He questioned me about the boy, and was immediately taken with me."

"There seems a disparity, here," Amy said.

"Just say we were taken with each other," Susan said.

"And you've been together ever since?"

"Except for when we weren't," I said.

"Can you talk about that?" Amy said.

"Nope."

Amy looked at Susan. Susan shook her head.

"We aren't who we were," Susan said. "We'd be talking about people who no longer exist."

I could see Amy thinking about how to go further with this. I could see her decide to give it up.

"You were married before," she said to Susan.

"Yes."

"And divorced."

"Yes."

"How do you feel about that?" Amy said to me.

"I don't," I said.

"Don't feel anything about it?"

"Correct."

"No jealousy, anything?" Amy said.

I shook my head.

"A famous shrink," I said, "once remarked, *we aren't who we were.*"

"You can put the past aside that easily?" Amy said.

I think she disapproved.

"Not easily," I said.

Susan said. "It is quite effortful."

"But you do it?"

Susan and I said "yes" at the same time.

"Earlier," Amy said to me, "you said something like *I don't refuse to care; I refuse to let it control me.* Now you say with effort you can put the past behind you. You, actually both of you, seem to place a premium on, what, will?"

"Yes," I said.

"First you need to understand why you do things that aren't in your best interest," Susan said. "Then, armed with that understanding, you have to stop doing them."

"And that would be a matter of will," Amy said.

"Yes. Given a reasonable level of acumen," Susan said.

"Most people can be brought to understanding their behavior. The hard thing is getting them to change it."

"But some people can change?" Amy said.

"Yes."

"And you changed?"

"Both of us," Susan said.

"Obviously," Amy said. "Susan, you've had psychotherapy."

"Of course," Susan said.

Amy looked at me.

"Have you ever had psychotherapy?" she said.

I looked at Susan.

"Every day," I said.

"Any formal therapy?" Amy said.

"No."

"What would be unacceptable behavior?" Amy said. "A, ah, deal-breaker, so to speak."

"An ongoing intimate relationship with someone else," I said.

"Susan?" Amy said.

"That," Susan said.

"What about a brief and casual dalliance?" Amy said.

"What did you have in mind?" I said.

I think she blushed, though it may have been the angle of the late afternoon sun. She studied her notebook for a moment, made a little mark in it, and put it down. Then she stopped the recorder, took out the tape, put in a new tape, and started it.

"How about hopes and dreams," Amy said.

"I'm in favor of them," I said.

Amy shook her head in a faint gesture of annoyance, as if she were shaking off a fly.

"Is there," she said, "anything you wanted to accomplish that you haven't?"

"No," I said. "I am everything I wanted to be. I've done everything I ever wanted to do."

"Nothing else left to do?" Amy said.

"Let no fates misunderstand me and snatch me away too soon," I said.

"Another poem," Amy said.

"Frost," I said. "More or less. I would be pleased to live this life and do what I do and be with her, forever. But I have no need to improve on it."

"My god," Amy said, "a happy man."

"Love and work," I said. "Love and work."

"Freud," Amy said, "Right?"

"I believe so," I said. "Though he didn't say it to me personally."

Amy looked at her notebook again and made another small mark. While she was doing that I managed to snag the waitress for another beer. Susan declined a refill, and I don't think Amy even noticed the opportunity. Probably just so much green tea you can drink.

Amy looked up from her notebook.

"What would you do if you couldn't do this?" Amy said, and smiled. "Whatever *this* might exactly be."

"I would think about international super star, or maybe retiring to stud," I said. "But if those answers didn't satisfy you, I guess I'd say I could be a carpenter. I like to make things. I know how to do it. I could be pretty much self-directed if I took the right job."

"And if you took the wrong job?" Amy said.

"I'd quit."

"Like you did the police?"

"Yes."

"Yet you have friends who are policemen."

"They're good at their work, and they probably don't have an extreme pathology," I said. "They can work in a context that I can't."

"A man needs to know his limitations," Amy said.

"He does."

The waitress brought me my beer and I asked her for the check.

"Oh, no," Amy said. "This is on me."

"Okay," I said. "Bring her the check."

The waitress produced it on the spot and put it face down on the table.

"I have a sense that the interview is winding down," Amy said.

"Me too," I said.

"Just indulge me one more subject," Amy said.

"Sure," I said.

Amy took out a credit card and put it on top of the check. Then she turned back to me.

"Does anything frighten you?" she said.

"Of course," I said.

"What?"

"Same things that frighten most people," I said. "Death, loss, pain, failure."

"And how do you overcome those fears?"

"Same way most people do."

"Will power?"

"I suppose."

"But you voluntarily chose to do things that involve the danger of death, pain, failure, and loss," Amy said.

"True," I said.

"What's up with that?" Amy said.

I smiled.

"I figure those are part of the deal," I said. "If I'm going to do what I do, I have to get around those fears."

Amy waited. I didn't have anything else to say. So I didn't say anything. After an appropriate wait, Amy looked at Susan.

"One of the things you have to keep in mind is that he doesn't expect to fail. And that diminishes the other dangers," Susan said. "He knows intellectually he could be killed. But I think, deep down, he doesn't think anyone can do it."

Amy looked at me, and raised her eyebrows.

"You're that confident?" she said.

"So far, so good," I said.

"So," Amy said. "Let's say you are facing a man with a gun. Do you feel fear?"

"Yes."

"What do you do about it?" Amy said.

"Ignore it."

"And you are able to?"

"Yes," I said. "Otherwise I couldn't do what I do."

"How much does confidence enable you to do that?"

"I don't know," I said. "I know I can shoot. I know I'm quick. And like anybody who used to fight, I'm pretty sure I can win one in the street."

"And that's what gives you confidence?"

"Some," I said.

"I think," Susan said, "that what gives him the most confidence is that he knows he can overcome his fear."

"He has confidence in his confidence, sort of," Amy said.

"He is convinced," Susan said, "that he can do what he has to do."

"And you believe that too about him?" Amy said.

Susan looked at me and smiled.

"So far, so good," Susan said.

A BIBLIOGRAPHY
of the WORKS of
ROBERT B. PARKER

SPENSER

1. *The Godwulf Manuscript* (Boston, Houghton Mifflin, 1974)
2. *God Save the Child* (Boston, Houghton Mifflin, 1974)
3. *Mortal Stakes* (Boston, Houghton Mifflin, 1975)
4. *Promised Land* (Boston, Houghton Mifflin, 1976)
5. *The Judas Goat* (Boston, Houghton Mifflin, 1978)
6. *Looking for Rachel Wallace* (New York, Delacorte, 1980)
7. *A Savage Place* (New York, Delacorte, 1981)
8. *Early Autumn* (New York, Delacorte, 1981)
9. *Ceremony* (New York, Delacorte, 1982)
10. *The Widening Gyre* (New York, Delacorte, 1983)
11. *Valediction* (New York, Delacorte, 1984)
12. *A Catskill Eagle* (New York, Delacorte, 1985)
13. *Taming a Sea-Horse* (New York, Delacorte, 1986)
14. *Pale Kings and Princes* (New York, Delacorte, 1987)
15. *Crimson Joy* (New York, Delacorte, 1988)
16. *Playmates* (New York, Putnam, 1989)
17. *Stardust* (New York, Putnam, 1990)
18. *Pastime* (New York, Putnam, 1991)
19. *Double Deuce* (New York, Putnam, 1992)
20. *Paper Doll* (New York, Putnam, 1993)

21. *Walking Shadow* (New York, Putnam, 1994)
22. *Thin Air* (New York, Putnam, 1995)
23. *Chance* (New York, Putnam, 1996)
24. *Small Vices* (New York, Putnam, 1997)
25. *Sudden Mischief* (New York, Putnam, 1998)
26. *Hush Money* (New York, Putnam, 1999)
27. *Hugger Mugger* (New York, Putnam, 2000)
28. *Potshot* (New York, Putnam, 2001)
29. *Widow's Walk* (New York, Putnam, 2002)
30. *Back Story* (New York, Putnam, 2003)
31. *Bad Business* (New York, Putnam, 2004)
32. *Cold Service* (New York, Putnam, 2005)
33. *School Days* (New York, Putnam, 2005)
34. *Hundred-Dollar Baby* (New York, Putnam, 2006)
35. *Now and Then* (New York, Putnam, 2007)
36. *Rough Weather* (New York, Putnam, 2008)
37. *The Professional* (New York, Putnam, 2009)
38. *Painted Ladies* (New York, Putnam, 2010)
39. *Sixkill* (New York, Putnam, 2011)

Also:

> *Surrogate* (Northridge, CA, Lord John Press, 1982; a short story)
> *Chasing the Bear: A Young Spenser Novel* (New York: Philomel/
> Penguin, 2009); a young adult novel.

JESSE STONE

1. *Night Passage* (New York, Putnam, 1997)
2. *Trouble in Paradise* (New York, Putnam, 1998)
3. *Death in Paradise* (New York, Putnam, 2001)
4. *Stone Cold* (New York, Putnam, 2003)
5. *Sea Change* (New York, Putnam, 2006)
6. *High Profile* (New York, Putnam, 2007)
7. *Stranger in Paradise* (New York, Putnam, 2008)
8. *Night and Day* (New York, Putnam, 2009)
9. *Split Image* (New York, Putnam, 2010)
10. *Killing the Blues* (New York, Putnam, 2011)

SUNNY RANDALL

1. *Family Honor* (New York, Putnam, 1999)
2. *Perish Twice* (New York, Putnam, 2000)
3. *Shrink Rap* (New York, Putnam, 2002)
4. *Melancholy Baby* (New York, Putnam, 2004)
5. *Blue Screen* (New York, Putnam, 2006)
6. *Spare Change* (New York, Putnam, 2007)

OTHER FICTION

1. *Wilderness* (New York, Delacorte, 1979)
2. *Love and Glory* (New York, Delacorte, 1983)
3. *Poodle Springs* (New York, Putnam, 1989); a completion of Raymond Chandler's final, unfinished Philip Marlowe novel
4. *Perchance to Dream* (New York, Putnam, 1991); a Philip Marlowe novel
5. *All Our Yesterdays* (New York, Putnam, 1994)
6. *Gunman's Rhapsody* (New York, Putnam, 2001); a Western
7. "Harlem Nocturne" (a short story in *Murderers' Row*, Beverly Hills, CA, New Millennium Press, 2001)
8. *Double Play* (New York, Putnam, 2004)
9. *Appaloosa* (New York, Putnam, 2005); a Western featuring Virgil Cole and Everett Hitch
10. "Galahad, Inc.," with Joan H. Parker (a short story in *Murder at the Foul Line*, New York, The Mysterious Press, 2006)
11. *Edenville Owls* (New York, Philomel/Penguin, 2007); a young adult novel
12. *The Boxer and the Spy* (New York, Philomel/Penguin, 2008); a young adult novel
13. *Resolution* (New York, Putnam, 2008); a Western featuring Virgil Cole and Everett Hitch
14. *Brimstone* (New York, Putnam, 2009); a Western featuring Virgil Cole and Everett Hitch
15. *Blue-Eyed Devil* (New York, Putnam, 2010); a Western featuring Virgil Cole and Everett Hitch

NON-FICTION

1. *Sports Illustrated Training with Weights* (with John R. Marsh; New York, Harper & Row, 1974)
2. *Three Weeks in Spring* (with Joan H. Parker; New York, Delacorte, 1982)
3. *A Year at the Races* (with Joan H. Parker and William Strode, photographer; New York, Viking/Studio, 1990)
4. *Spenser's Boston* (with photographer Kasho Kumagai; New York, Simon & Schuster/Otto Penzler Books, 1994. Previously published in Japanese; Tokyo, Hayakawa Publishing, 1989)

CONTRIBUTORS

ACE ATKINS was a crime reporter for the *Tampa Tribune*, receiving a Pulitzer Prize nomination for his examination of a 1950s murder that became the inspiration for his first novel, *Crossroad Blues*, which starred Nick Travers, who appeared in three additional novels. He turned to stand-alone novels, such as *Devil's Garden*, which featured Dashiell Hammett. After Robert B. Parker's death, he was selected to continue the Spenser series, which debuted with *The Ranger*.

LAWRENCE BLOCK is a winner of multiple Edgar Allan Poe Awards, including the Grand Master Award for lifetime achievement. A frequent *New York Times* bestseller, he has created several much-loved series characters, including those about the burglar Bernie Rhodenbarr, the spy Evan Tanner, the hitman Keller, and, perhaps his most enduring contribution to the mystery genre, Matthew Scudder, the former cop who functions as an unlicensed private detective.

MATTHEW CLEMENS has collaborated with Max Allan Collins on a number of projects, including the *CSI*, *Bones*, and *Criminal Minds* novels, as well as their forensics thrillers, *You Can't Stop Me* and *No One Will Hear You*.

REED FARREL COLEMAN is the author of twelve novels, including two under the pseudonym Tony Spinosa. Novels in his popular Mo Prager series have been nominated for two Edgar awards and have won three Shamus Awards for Best Novel of the Year from the Private Eye Writers of America. He also has won Barry, Macavity, and Anthony awards.

MAX ALLAN COLLINS wrote the graphic novel *Road to Perdition*, the basis of the Academy Award–winning Tom Hanks film. Among his other works are the award-winning Nathan Heller historical thrillers and his series about Nolan, a hitman. He also wrote the Dick Tracy comic strip for many years and completed several Mike Hammer manuscripts left behind at Mickey Spillane's death.

BRENDAN DUBOIS is the author of twelve novels and more than a hundred short stories, many of which have received such outstanding honors as two Shamus Awards, two Barry awards, and three nominations for Edgars. "The Dark Snow," originally published in *Playboy*, was selected for *The Best American Mystery Stories of the Century*; four of his stories have been selected for the prestigious *Best American Mystery Stories of the Year*.

LOREN D. ESTLEMAN is equally prolific in the Western and mystery genres. He has been nominated for a Pulitzer Prize, an Edgar Allan Poe Award, and a National Book Award, and has both won and been nominated for numerous Spur Awards from the Western Writers of America and Shamus Awards from the Private Eye Writers of America. His best-known series features private eye Amos Walker, who works in Detroit, the scene of many other of Estleman's crime novels.

LYNDSAY FAYE is a professional actress, singer, and gourmet cook. Her first book was *Dust and Shadow: An Account of the Ripper Killings by Dr. John H. Watson*, which earned her membership in the Baker Street Irregulars. Continuing with historical crime fiction, her second novel was *The Gods of Gotham*, about the origins of the New York City Police Department, which happened to coincide with the Irish potato famine.

ED GORMAN writes prolifically in several genres, winning a Spur Award from the Western Writers of America and being nominated twice for Bram Stoker awards from the Horror Writers Association, but he is mainly known for dozens of mystery novels written under his own name and numerous pseudonyms, most notably E.J. Gorman and Daniel Ransom. His award-winning suspense story, "The Poker Club," will soon be released as a motion picture with the same title.

PARNELL HALL has written thirty-four mystery novels, including seventeen about the inept and cowardly private eye Stanley Hastings; five courtroom dramas about Steve Winslow, written under the pseudonym J.P Hailey; and a dozen detective novels featuring "the puzzle lady," all of which contain crossword puzzles, on which he collaborated with Manny Nosowsky; later "puzzle lady" books featured sudoku puzzles, on which he collaborated with Will Shortz.

JEREMIAH HEALY graduated from Harvard Law School and taught law for eighteen years at the New England School of Law. He has written eighteen novels and more than sixty short stories, most of which are set in Boston. His twelve-novel series about private investigator John Francis Cuddy began with *Blunt Darts*. He also has written six legal thrillers about Mairead O'Clare under the pseudonym Terry Devane. He has won or been nominated for fifteen Shamus Awards.

DENNIS LEHANE was born and raised in Boston, where most of his fiction is set. His first novel, *A Drink Before the War*, introduced his private eyes Patrick Kenzie and Angela Gennaro and won the Shamus Award from the Private Eye Writers of America. The fourth in the series, *Gone Baby, Gone*, was filmed with Ben Affleck directing and Casey Affleck and Michelle Monaghan starring. Other films made from Lehane's works include *Mystic River* and *Shutter Island*.

ROBERT B. PARKER and his work are the subject of this book.

OTTO PENZLER is the founder of The Mysterious Press, a publishing house specializing in literary crime fiction since 1975, and The Mysterious Bookshop in downtown New York City. He has won two Edgar Allan Poe Awards, one for co-writing the *Encyclopedia of Mystery and Detection*, and one for editing *The Lineup*. He has edited nearly fifty anthologies, including the annual *Best American Mystery Stories of the Year*.

GARY PHILLIPS Gary Phillips is the creator of private eye Ivan Monk. On the occasion of the twentieth anniversary of the '92 L.A. riots, his debut mystery novel *Violent Spring*, set in the aftermath of that civil unrest, was reissued as an e-book by MysteriousPress.com. His most recent crime novel is *Warlord of Willow Ridge*; he also is the editor of and a contributor to *Scoundrels: Tales of Greed, Murder and Financial Crimes*, an all-original e-book anthology from downandoutbooks.com.

S.J. ROZAN has won and been nominated for countless mystery writing awards, mainly for the books in her series about the private investigator partners Lydia Chin, an American-born Chinese who remembers her roots, and Bill Smith, who is more fond of Lydia than she is of him. They more or less alternate in taking the lead role in the novels, one of which, *Winter and Night*, won the Edgar Allan Poe Award for Best Novel of the Year.

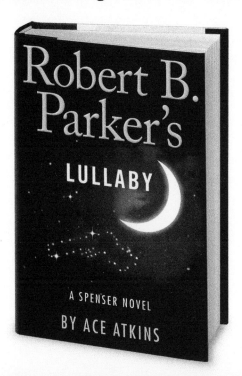